CW00853072

lumea
press

Lumea Press

Amelie Trott & The Mark of Triandor
Moyra Irving
Editor: Julian Middleton
Designer: Meryl Sabine Tihanyi
Cover Design: Barrie Eyden
First Edition: October 2023

Library of Congress Cataloging-in-Publication Data
Moyra Irving - 1st ed.
ISBN: 978-1-7395545-2-1

www.amelietrott.com

Amelie Trott & The Mark of Triandor

Moyra Irving

For Andrew, my beloved brother and friend

Acknowledgements

This second novel pays tribute to all brave young warriors who are manifesting their vision of a new and better world, and doing so through various acts of kindness, compassion, and social justice.
I have so many to thank for their involvement, including:

Julian Middleton, my eagle-eyed editor; Meryl Sabine Tihanyi for her excellent design skills and boundless enthusiasm; Barrie Eyden for another delightful cover design; and Jon Aldersea who has interpreted the story so beautifully in his promotional video. Also,

Tabitha Wilson, daughter of novelist Emma-Claire Wilson, my first ever reader and reviewer for *Amelie Trott & The Earth Watchers*. I promised her a part in the sequel. Get ready now to meet Tabitha!

Dot Maver, co-founder of *The Global Silent Minute* and a huge champion of Amelie Trott. Your love and support mean the world to me

Linda Williams who graciously allowed me access to her family archives while I was researching life and death at the Front during World War I

Alorah Parks for offering the initial idea of the *Mark of Triandor*, and Steve and Karen Alexander for generously allowing me to use one of their magnificent crop circle photographs to illustrate it

Alessandro Fanfano for kindly checking my Italian

Robin (Roby) Easton who allowed me to quote *Death will not kill you* from her book *Our Human Spirit: true stories*

Kerrie Frances whose alluring words (*Ah, yes, I've been looking for you*) are quoted in Chapter Twenty

And, not least: my darling son John-Patrick (Jeeps) for creating so many precious memories of Italy

Grazie a tutti.

Following their success in averting a major planetary disaster, our three Bright Hearts - Amelie, Tim, and Isla - are set to embark on another urgent mission for the Earth Watchers. With Hadleigh House now restored to its former glory, and Elias Dankstone safely dispatched to Daktron (the furthest planet from the sun), things are really looking up for the Trotts. Lucy's career as a portrait painter has finally taken off, Great-Grandfather Storm, now ninety-five, prepares for his first solar-powered flight, and best friend Isla Batty leaves Washington and returns to London for a while. Meanwhile, Amelie (now a best-selling author), delves into the secret life of wild-child Aunt Eggy.

But, as this unforgettable tale of danger, courage, and enduring love unfolds, further mysteries come to light and the past reveals a terrible crisis yet to come...

Chapter One

The Mark of Triandor

Friday 5th August 1910

From an upstairs balcony at Hadleigh House a crumpled scrap of paper drifts down on the breeze.

A lone figure emerges from the shadows, a rough-set man, short and stout. He reaches out a black-gloved hand and catches it deftly between his fingers.

'This is it then,' he leers, gazing at it in wonder. The *'Mark of Triandor*!'

A sharp-faced woman observes him from above. 'Hide it you fool, before you get caught…' She glances slyly over her shoulder then leans across the balustrade. 'And don't you dare mess with it, neither!' She retreats inside, closes the doors with enough force to rattle their panes and draws a heavy curtain across them.

Unable to resist, the man places his index finger on the paper and begins to count: *One-two-three-four*... and by seven is propelled off his feet by some unutterable force. Chalk-white with terror he rises, still clutching the little scrap of paper. Soon, he is soaring over rooftops and fields, an ungainly, spread-eagled figure, riding the air currents as he heads swiftly out to sea. There, he spirals down like a deflating balloon and plunges into the icy depths. The *Mark of Triandor* is, it seems, now lost for eternity.

❋

Well, my dear Reader, not quite. You see, the *Mark of Triandor* is recorded for ever and a day in the Cosmic Library of Life and, since I believe you are worthy of my trust, I've included a copy for you here. But first, a word of caution: it holds the Secret of Life itself and we've all seen what happens when that secret falls into the wrong hands. *Will you pledge to harness its power for the good of all?*

Do I hear you say yes?

Very well then, please take a deep breath… Now, turn over the page and there you will find it. Place your index finger firmly in its centre while slowly counting to seven. The Power of All Creation will soon begin to course through your hand.

O, *Child of Luga*,* you will never be the same again!

Are you ready?

**Luga* is the Earth Watchers' name for Planet Earth

Mark of Triandor

Chapter Two

The Rather Extraordinary Life of Eglantyne Trott

Sunday 1st September 2019

Footsteps sounded on the attic stairs and Amelie Trott came to with a start. *Am I ready? Of course I am!* Her eyes shone with surprise.

A book lay open on her lap, an old journal with a ragged tear where the *Mark of Triandor* had once been. There was only one thing for it then; she reached for a blank sheet of paper and with a steady hand began to draw. Two circles, a hexagon and…

'So, how's the new best-seller coming along?' Amelie's brother Tim poked his head around the door.

'Not bad,' she answered without looking up. 'I've just been studying Aunt Eglantyne's diaries and made an unusual discovery. You'll see what I mean in a moment.'

'Right you are then, Madam…' Tim drew close and placed a steaming mug of tea on her desk. 'I thought you could do with a brew.'

Amelie gazed at it fondly. It was one Isla had brought back from America - bright blue and inscribed with shiny red letters: *I may look like I'm listening but in my head I'm writing my next novel.* 'Cheers, Tim.' She squinted at him suspiciously. 'You're in an unusually good mood today. Have you put gel on your hair?'

Tim pretended not to hear. Instead, he glanced out of the attic window, hoping the rain would hold off. 'Me and Isla are training tonight.'

'Not *football* again?' Amelie sipped her tea and stared at the heap of rail tracks cluttering the attic floor. 'I thought you were building a high-speed railway…?'

'I am; I mean, I will,' he answered defensively. 'I'm just focusing on my football for a while.'

'Hmm, on Isla, you mean,' said Amelie, suppressing a smile.

'What?'

'Nothing.' The *Mark of Triandor* had become a little hazy now but Amelie continued to draw, tongue thrust between her teeth, anxious to capture every small detail before the memory faded completely. Satisfied at last, she laid down her pen and waved the drawing under his nose. 'Have you any idea what this is?'

Tim looked at it, baffled, and shrugged. 'I dunno, looks like something out of a geometry book…'

'No,' said Amelie, barely able to contain her excitement. 'It's the *Mark of Triandor*. It appeared while I was reading.'

'Jeez, she kept that secret safe for the whole of her life.'

Amelie's voice trembled a little. 'And it seems it's our secret now.'

'But this is the most powerful symbol in existence…' Tim threw her a worried glance. 'We mustn't ever let it fall into the wrong hands.'

'I know,' said Amelie, remembering the scene she had just witnessed. She fluttered her fingers playfully. 'But these aren't the wrong hands, are they, Tim? Watch me…' She placed her index finger on the paper and began to recite solemnly: '*Soon-the-Power-of-All-Creation-will-flow-through-my-hand. One-two-three-four…*'

'Hey, stop that, will you!' Tim reached out and grabbed her wrist. 'This really isn't something to mess with.'

Amelie rolled her eyes. 'I know perfectly well what I'm doing, thank you. Hold onto my feet if you're that bothered.' She took a deep breath and continued. '*…five-six-seven…*'

Moments passed and Tim watched her dubiously. 'Is that it then?'

Amelie stared down at her drawing, dismayed. 'No, I was meant to fly, wasn't I? Oh, why aren't they here when we need them? It's been almost a year since we saw them.'

Tim laid a brotherly hand on her shoulder. 'Earth Watchers never break promises. They said they'll be back so they will.'

'Mm, maybe you're right.' She traced her finger around the *Mark of Triandor*. 'I've a feeling we're going to need this soon, very soon. It wouldn't have turned up otherwise.' She gazed up at him earnestly. 'Tim, we really do have to make it work.'

'There's one easy way we can…' Tim reached into his jeans pocket and pulled out a small silver gadget which he clipped to one ear. 'Let's see what the *transonometer*[1] comes up with.' He closed his eyes and silently invited a response.

'Of course, why didn't I think of that?' Amelie stood behind him eagerly. But instead of an image, a message flashed onto the tiny screen: *Information currently inaccessible. User ID required.*

Tim scratched his head. 'Well, *that's* never happened before - looks like it's been locked for safety purposes. I suppose we could always try…' He stopped mid-sentence and tilted his head. 'Did you hear something then?'

A faint *tap-tap-tapping* echoed on the attic stairs.

'Oh, that,' Amelie said matter-of-factly. 'It's only Doris.'

They looked at each other and laughed. Doris, Aunt Eglantyne's old walking stick – the one she always used to get their attention!

'Strange, it's been silent all year,' Tim puzzled. 'She must have something fairly important to say…'

'Oh, she has,' Amelie announced. 'She wants me to hurry up and publish her book. Which is why,' she added artfully, 'I'll need a whole year off school to write it. It's called a *sattabical.*'

Tim snorted. 'No it's not, it's *sabbatical*[2], you dozy...' A muffled profanity escaped his lips.

'I heard that,' Amelie said smugly. 'Good, now you owe me another pound.' She rattled a tin labelled *Forbidden Words* under his nose. 'Thanks to you we'll soon have enough cash for our half-term trip to Italy.'

'You've totally cleaned me out now,' Tim grumbled, emptying out his pockets. He stuck his nose inside the tin. 'Blimey, there's a good fifty quid of mine in here already.' He glanced up to see his sister on her knees, rummaging through an old dressing-up box. 'And what's that ridiculous thing you've got on your head?'

'What do you think? It's Eglantyne's old hat, of course. It helps me get into character while I'm writing.'

Tim shook his head. 'Man, you're so weird.'

'Shut up, you haven't a clue…'

Hearing a car pull up outside they paused their squabbling and listened. A door slammed, followed by the toot of a horn. Soon, there were voices and laughter too, a thud of paws on the stairs, a loud clatter of heels. And there, in the doorway at last, stood Isla, flashing that radiant smile they all loved.

'Hey, y'all!' she greeted them excitedly. 'Look who came to meet me already – my gorgeous Lara!' She grasped hold of the young dog's collar and patted her head. 'Goldies are the sweetest dogs. Now, where's my cute little Freddie?' Her eyes roamed the attic until a small black cat appeared out of nowhere and wound his tail around her legs.

Amelie's face shone. Isla was the sister she'd never had - one who had quickly taken over from Great-Grandpa Storm as her BFF, her *very* best friend forever, though fortunately, he didn't seem to mind too much.

It hadn't taken Tim long to realise that one sister was more than enough, thank you, so Isla became his best buddy too; one who played football better than anyone else he knew, even though she was a girl.

'Oh, babe, just look at you!' Isla tilted her head and gazed at Amelie's battered old hat. 'You must be Aunt Eggy, right?'

Amelie rose to her feet and gave her a little twirl. 'Yes, actually, I'm writing her life-story.'

'Slaying, girl!' Isla planted a kiss on her cheek, and another on Tim's which he promptly wiped away with his sleeve.

Slaying? Amelie puzzled, wondering if this was a good thing or not. 'Shall I read you what I've written so far?'

Tim dived onto a giant red bean bag and patted it for Isla to join him. 'Don't forget our kick-about, will you?'

Isla glanced at Amelie. 'Would you mind too much? It's just that I promised Tim.'

'No, of course not,' Amelie said generously. 'It'll give me time to write another chapter.'

Isla hesitated, glancing from one friend to the other. 'Actually, there's plenty of time. Why don't you read me some now? You know I love a good story. And as for you, Timothy Trott, move over already! You've taken up the whole of this freaking beanbag.'

'Man, you're so annoying…'

Amelie warmed her hands on Isla's special mug and laughed at their silly bickering, just happy they were all back together at last. 'Okay,' she agreed, adjusting Eggy's old hat. 'Here goes. This is *The Rather Extraordinary Life of Eglantyne Trott…*'

Chapter Three

Let Me Call You Sweetheart

Thursday 4th August 1910

Hadleigh House

Thursday 4th August 1910

My dear Edgar,
Thank you for your most timely letter and offer of assistance. I shall duly inform Eglantyne of your kind invitation. She will, I know, benefit greatly...

Theodore Trott put down his pen and sighed. What more could he say of his troublesome daughter? That she had been recently expelled from school for riotous behaviour? He rubbed his chin thoughtfully. Or that she was, in his opinion, mentally deranged? No, least said the better.

'Enter!' Hearing a scuffle outside the door he looked up from his desk and glowered. A stern man with an impressive walrus moustache, he was accustomed to having his orders obeyed. 'I said *Enter*!'

The door swung open and a young girl with a mop of golden hair stood before him. 'You called, Sir?' She bobbed a mock curtsy and glanced around the cheerless room. 'What is it this time?'

Theodore thumped his fist on the desk and a cloud of dust filled the air.

'What in heaven's name do you think you're wearing?'

'Let me see...' She glanced down at her threadbare breeches. 'I think I'm wearing trousers. I'm asserting my right to dress as a boy.'

'Your mother would leap in her grave,' barked Theodore. 'You're a young woman, Miss Trott, not a blood… a blasted farmhand. Which reminds me, you're not to spend any more time with that loathsome boy - do you hear me? Take them off at once!'

'Certainly, Father…' She proceeded to unbutton her trousers.

'Not here, you stupid girl!' he blustered. 'Go! Just go! And get Ivy whatever-her-name-is to find you something decent to wear. Then return to me at once; I have a matter of utmost importance to discuss with you.'

Feared by many, Theodore provoked only amusement in his daughter. She dropped another curtsy and left, singing tunelessly.

'And kindly stop that ghastly music hall[3] gibberish,' growled Theodore, knowing that it would now be plaguing his mind all day. He signed his letter with a flourish. 'Thank God she'll soon be off my hands…'

❃

Jack Holland leaned against the fence at the far edge of the Trotts' estate and gazed over the fields. A lanky young man with arms browned by fourteen summers, he looked years older than his age. Tired of waiting, he yawned, ran a hand through his curly brown hair and made to go.

Eglantyne, known affectionately as Eggy or Eggs, climbed the scullery steps and glanced back at the lofty red-brick house. Despite her ill-tempered father it was good to be back. Three months at that awful school had been more than she could bear. She swung round and stood for a moment, shielding her eyes against the afternoon sun. Then, spotting Jack in the distance, she stuck two fingers between her lips and blew. A shrill whistle pierced the air and Jack winced, rather wishing he'd never taught her to do that.

'Wait!' She raced through the garden and over the little footbridge that crossed the stream, pausing only in the apple orchard to pocket a few windfalls.

'The Walrus kept me,' she panted, flinging herself down on the grass. 'He says I've got to change.'

'Some hope of that!' Jack said sourly. He glanced at an imaginary watch on his wrist and frowned. 'We've got less than an hour left now before milking. I've had these two saddled up all afternoon.' On the other side of the fence two young horses, one black, the other brown, had begun to circle impatiently.

'He means change into a *dress*,' Eggy giggled though his tone had cut her a little. 'I'm meant to ask Bumley to find me one. I shan't, of course.'

'Fourteen years old and you still need servants to dress you?' He noticed the pained look on her face and wished he hadn't said it, what with her having no mother and everything. 'I don't blame you though,' he added more kindly. 'Bottomley's an evil old witch...' He was interrupted by a shrill voice that made them both start.

'Eggletime Trott – you there? Yer farver wants you now!'

'Heavens, it's her!' whispered Eggy. 'She never could say my name.' They looked at each other and stifled their laughter. 'Quick, hide! She mustn't see me with you. If the old buffer finds out he'll send me away. He thinks you're loathsome, by the way.' Seeing Ivy Bottomley disappear into the house, Eggy heaved herself up and leaped over the fence. 'Actually, I loathe having servants. Apart from Loula, of course, but she's more like a mother than a housekeeper. She's the only family I have.'

'You've got Joe,' said Jack.

Eggy shrugged. 'I wouldn't know my brother if he walked through the door. Fell out with the old man years ago and hasn't been seen since. Spends all his holidays with a school friend in Dorset… Oh, darling, Starlight,' she crooned and began to pet the young brown horse. 'You're not cross with me too, are you? No, of course you're not.' She fed Starlight one of the windfalls and planted a kiss between her eyes. 'And here's one for you too, Arrow, you handsome beast…'

Watching her, Jack forgot how annoying she could sometimes be and put an arm round her shoulder. 'Come on then, Eggs. Let's make the most of whatever time we have left.'

'You've no idea how lucky you are!' Eggy cried, as they cantered across the sands. 'Not having school anymore.'

'Well, of course not, I'm fourteen, same as you.'

'You could easily pass for seventeen.'

Jack grinned, knowing it was true. 'I've got no choice anyway, not since Dad took ill. Education's important but there's only me here to run the farm.'

'I can teach you things if you like.'

'Yeah, and I'll show you how to skin a rabbit.'

'Not bloody likely!'

They rode on for a while, coming closer to the water's edge as the tide receded.

'I'm not ever letting him send me away again. It's not as if he cares a brass farthing about my education,' said Eggy, slowing down to a trot. 'He only wants me out of the way.'

'Why's that then?'

'He thinks I'm not right in the head.'

'He does have a point,' murmured Jack, as they came to a halt by the breakwater.

Eggy ignored him. 'I suppose it's my habit of wearing boys' clothes. I mean, why not? They're far more practical - especially since I spend half my life mucking out cowsheds.' She glanced down at her mud-caked nails and laughed. 'He's worried I'll never find a husband. Oh, and then there's my singing too.' She began to warble and they nearly fell off their horses laughing. 'Do you think I might have a future on the stage?' She deepened her voice a little: *'Good evening, ladies and gentlemen and welcome to the Royal Albert Hall where we're honoured to present Dame Eglantyne Marigold Trott with her performance of that great music hall favourite...'* and with that she launched into a tuneless rendering of: *'Let me call you sweetheart, I'm so in love with you-hoo!'*

'That settles it, you really are mad!' said Jack. 'And you've just ruined my favourite song. But as for not finding a husband, don't talk so daft. Almost everyone does; even hideous folk like Ivy Bottomley.'

'I can assure you, I won't.'

'Bet you a gold sovereign[4].' He was about to add that he didn't actually possess a gold sovereign when Arrow suddenly reared. 'Hey, what's that, Eggs? Look, up there…' He pointed to a bright metallic shape glinting in the distance. It seemed to hang there for a moment before it shot off, this way and that, and finally disappeared behind a cloud bank on the horizon.

'It's a glider,' said Eggy. 'I saw one in *The London Illustrated News*.' She gave a sly smile. 'I found it on the old man's desk while I was nosing through his letters. I wish I owned my own camera though. We could have taken a snap.'

'It's gone now anyway,' Jack said, still watching the skies.

'Any closer and it might have fallen on us. I've heard they can sometimes crash.'

'What a load of Tommy-rot!'

'Imagine though, being up that high…' Eggy let out a great sigh. 'What a glorious day it is! Do you remember when we first met? Right here it was, by the breakwater; I'd have drowned if you hadn't turned up when you did.' She shivered, remembering. 'And I thought swimming would be easy…'

He'd spotted her in the water that day, fully clothed and floundering; dived in at once and dragged her ashore. Her small body was limp and lifeless and he'd instinctively tipped her upside down and thumped her back until she began to choke. His heart had raced wildly until, thank God, she finally opened her eyes. 'Oh, it's you again,' she murmured, as though they'd somehow met already. Which they hadn't, of course, he reminded her. He taught her to swim after that.

'I so love it here,' breathed Eggy, feeling the salt spray on her skin. 'Although…'

'Although what?' It sounded to Jack like a very big although.

'Well, don't you ever wonder what else there is out there?' She raised her arms to encircle the view.

Jack nodded. 'I suppose I do.'

'I want to travel as far as it's humanly possible.' She turned to him, her face bright with excitement. 'Come with me. Just you and me in a year or so; anywhere you like. I'll have my mother's inheritance by then.'

His smile said yes. 'I've got a dream too, Eggs…' He gazed up at the summer sky, flecked with seabirds and wispy clouds. 'I want to fly one of those glider things. Can't see how I'll ever get the chance though,' he added bleakly. 'Not while I'm stuck here.'

'There'll be a way,' Eggy said confidently and for some reason she thought of her mother again. 'Life's far too short to waste.'

Jack put a hand on her shoulder. 'What was she like, Eggs?'

'Mother?' Eggy glanced up at him in surprise. 'I can hardly remember.'

They looked out to sea for a while, hoping the glider might reappear in the cloud breaks but seeing nothing, rode on in silence.

Chapter Four

The Young Suffragettes Society

'Sounds like I'm in trouble again,' Eggy observed, hearing an irate voice summon her. 'Is there any cake for tea, Lou? I'm ravenous.' She dipped her finger into an open pot of jam.

Loula Bellamy, the housekeeper, glanced up at her and frowned. A kettle had begun to boil and she had just scalded her wrist. 'Cake?' she repeated testily. She warmed a teapot and reached for a white linen dress hanging behind the door. Moving briskly from one task to another, she lifted a flat iron from the range, spat on it and seeing it sizzle, set to work on the dress. 'Never mind cake, you can have bread and pull it,' she declared, smoothing out the creases. This was Loula's usual response when asked what was for tea. *Bread and pull it*. It had remained quite a mystery until one day Jack explained what Loula meant.

'Pullet,' he said with authority. 'It's what we in the trade call a young bird that hasn't yet laid eggs.'

Feeding chickens was Eggy's favourite task at the farm and, since she now considered them to be her personal friends, it was unthinkable that she could ever eat one. A subject that caused endless arguments with Loula who feared she'd die of malnutrition.

'You'd better look sharp then, young lady,' Loula warned. 'You've kept him waiting long enough. Here, step into this.' She held up the freshly ironed dress. 'But as for that bloomin' hair, stand still a moment, will you?' She grabbed a brush and dragged it mercilessly through Eggy's tangled locks.

Eggy winced.

'There!' Loula's tired blue eyes brightened. 'You've not looked that pretty since you was this high.' She placed a hand level with her hip. 'You with those lovely curls all tied up in ribbons, trundling a hoop along the path. Proper little lady.'

Eggy wrinkled her nose in disgust. 'What a terrible thought.'

Loula concealed a smile. 'Whatever am I to do with you?' A fly hovered around the jam pot and she turned to trap it between her hands. 'And yes, there'll be a slice of cake for you later,' she promised.

But Eggy had already vanished and Loula waited, listening for the inevitable raised voices and clatter of feet in the hallway. Hearing nothing, she poured fresh tea into her cup and sank down in her favourite chair to browse the latest copy of Ladies Home Journal. Very soon she had nodded off, her mind full of corsets and the latest Butterick dress patterns from D.H. Evans.

She awoke suddenly to find Eggy staring at her accusingly, her eyes brimming with tears. 'You knew all along, didn't you?' She ripped off her dress and stepped back into her old corduroy trousers.

'Good heavens, whatever is it now, girl? Has he seen you out riding with Jack? Has he found you a new school?'

'No, but he's got me a new tutor, some hideous old aunt. And if that's not bad enough, I'm supposed to be some kind of companion for her and live there, in London of all places! What if she's deaf and senile and smells of old people?'

'Old aunt? I can't think for the life of me who you mean.'

'Uncle Edgar's wife, she'll be at least forty.'

Loula, who was almost forty herself, took Eggy's hand and cradled it in her own. 'London's not that far off, you know, and it's not like it'll be forever.'

'It's for four flaming years, until I'm eighteen! Hmm, don't worry. I'll be back long before then.'

Loula raised an eyebrow. 'Like when you was expelled for all that *sufferer jets* nonsense, I suppose. Here…' She handed her a clean lace handkerchief.

'My Young Suffragettes[5] Society?' Eggy blew her nose loudly. 'How can you possibly call fighting for equal rights nonsense?'

'Because it's a losing battle, that's why. Some things never change - it's just the way they are.'

'You'd like to bet on that?' Eggy recalled how they had tied themselves to the school gates, demanding *Mandatory Pocket Money for Girls and No More Needlework*. 'I ask you, what's the point of bloody needlework?' She saw Loula's horrified face and stifled a grin. 'Blame the old man, he says it all the time: *Bloody this, bloody that*. Anyway,' she added, 'I've heard you say far worse...'

Loula blinked dismissively. 'When I think of all that money wasted on your education…'

'Wasted on sewing handkerchiefs, you mean, and finding some daft husband!'

'Good Lord,' said Loula, 'you'll be lucky, my girl. Who's going to look at you dressed like a flaming scarecrow?'

'You think I want anyone looking at me?' Eggy scowled. 'And I always thought you had my best interests at heart.'

'But I do,' Loula said quietly. 'I just worry about you and what you might do with no husband to look after you and no little ones, and no nothing else to fill up your life with.'

'Doesn't seem to have bothered you too much, does it?' Eggy retorted and regretted it at once. 'Forgive me, Lou,' she said sheepishly, remembering poor Loula's ill fortune: married at nineteen, a widow at twenty - her husband killed in the Boer War.

What fleeting pleasures might have filled up Loula's life since then, she wondered? None that she could see…

But it appeared that Loula had already forgiven her for she was cutting into a large Victoria Sponge, oozing with strawberry jam and cream. She took two china plates from the dresser and placed a slice on each, along with a silver cake fork. 'Here, perhaps this will put you in a better mood.'

'I doubt it.' Eggy discarded her fork and lifted the cake to her mouth. 'Do you know how much I like working on the farm? It's about the only thing that makes me really happy. I'm good at it too.'

'A clever girl like you; ending up as a farmer's wife?'

'What! Heavens no, once I have Mother's money I'll be off, travelling the world.'

Loula pecked at her cake and gazed at her thoughtfully. 'You never know, my dear, you might even find you like her.'

'Aunt Adelaide?' Eggy looked at her askance.

'Well, I've heard she's an American.'

'Gosh!' Eggy mocked. 'In that case, I'll dislike her even more and make darned sure she does me too.' Eggy rather wished she hadn't said that. After all, she didn't actually know any Americans. Sometimes things escaped her mouth before she had time to stop them.

'If truth be told, I can't bear you to go neither.' A tear splashed onto Loula's plate.

'You mean you might miss me…?'

'Of course I shall, silly girl,' Loula replied, dabbing at her eyes. 'Same as I miss your dear mother, God rest her soul. Lillian was strong-willed like you.'

Eggy looked up at her, expectantly.

'My word,' Loula continued, 'she didn't half keep me on my toes with all them fancy luncheons and dinners and balls, not to mention beds to strip every weekend.' She gazed into the distance, remembering better, busier days. 'Lillian loved folk and they loved her - foreigners mostly, friends of your grandfather, Lord Hilton. A real gentleman he was, nicest man I ever met; served as a diplomat in the Far East.'

What a picture Loula painted: a household buzzing with excitement as Lillian's guests appeared: Indian gentry in bright turbans and saris, Tibetan ladies with fabulous headdresses and beads; and always, in the background, that strange babble of foreign tongues.

Sitting there in the steamy kitchen, listening to Loula's voice, Eggy toured the house in her mind. Bleak as it was with all those empty, unused rooms gathering dust, it was still her home and there was comfort in that. Just as there was comfort at Cloud Farm with Jack and the horses and chickens; and down by the endless sea with its lofty clifftops and quiet coves. How could she possibly say goodbye to all that? If only her mother were here to intervene.

Chapter Five

We Are Here!

'If only she could be with us now', said Loula, echoing Eggy's thoughts. 'The last Ball we had here was in 1898.'

'Two years after I was born,' said Eggy.

'Yes, your Joseph was only a baby and dear Lillian was carrying her third by then. Came too early though, poor lamb, and never survived…' (And neither did Lillian but it was best they didn't talk about that.)

'You won't catch me having babies.' Eggy grimaced and quickly pushed the thought aside. In its place came a stream of more pleasant memories - the scent of jasmine and rustle of taffeta as her mother stooped to embrace her; the warmth of the skirt as she buried her face in its folds.

'All dolled up in silver-grey taffeta she was that night. Or maybe it was blue…?'

It was blue, Eggy remembered, with panels of velvet. She closed her eyes and listened to Loula's voice, repeating the old familiar story, one she pretty much knew by heart now, except that Loula kept changing her mind about the dress. Chamber music played in the hall and feet clattered on the tiles as footmen hurried to the servants' lift. Somehow, Eggy had managed to sneak in behind one of them on his way to the Ballroom. She followed him right to the door, and there she hovered until suddenly, the room fell silent.

One hundred or more guests turned to witness a tiny barefooted girl gazing back at them. One by one, they rose to their feet - whooping and clapping – before a light-hearted Theodore sprinted across the room and scooped her into his arms.

‘Apple of his eye you was,’ Loula said, patting Eggy’s hand.

Hmm, Eggy wondered. Whatever happened to change him?

‘Grief,’ Loula replied, eavesdropping on Eggy’s thoughts.

‘Then we must have one again,’ Eggy said firmly, ‘a Grand Ball, and the grander the better. I can think of dozens of people to invite. After all, it’s not much to expect since I’m being so inconvenienced.’

Loula laughed. ‘Inconvenienced? Just listen to you, Miss Snooty!’

‘Well, I could be earning money now I’m fourteen, instead of having years more boring and useless lessons. And I’ve certainly got better things to do than look after some smelly old aunt. Who knows, a Ball might even cheer him up?’

‘I very much doubt it,’ said Loula, brushing cake crumbs into her hand. ‘You know how he hates folk disturbing his peace.’

‘That’s because he’s a selfish old fool.’ Eggy scraped back her chair, her face flushed with annoyance. ‘And it’s high time someone told him.’ She was on the point of doing so when something changed her mind. ‘I’m going out. Tell Jack when he calls with the milk, will you? But don’t say a word about London. I need to tell him that myself.’

Eggy strode down Cloud Hill, slowing down a little as she approached the church. There, bustling along the path was Mrs. Feathergill, the vicar’s wife, whose perennial smile masked a merciless nature. Eyes averted, she hurried on and finally came to a row of tiny stone cottages at the junction of Primrose Lane and the High Street where all the shops began. Here, she almost tripped over a young boy, huddled against the wall. She'd noticed him there once before and since then made certain to carry a few extra coins in her pocket, plus an apple or two from the orchard.

'Hello again,' she remarked, squatting down beside him. 'You look about as fed up as I am.'

The boy's face was swollen, one eye so badly bruised it had closed completely. He was also fearfully smelly but she held her breath and tried not to mind too much.

'What should I call you then?'

He regarded her with his one good eye and shrugged. Next to him lay an old cap, empty apart from a farthing or two and a couple of buttons, tossed in by some thoughtless joker.

'Blimey, that's quite a shiner you've got,' Eggy observed, tipping a pocketful of coins into his cap; enough shillings and sixpenny pieces to tide his family over till next week.

'Walter Smith,' he replied at last.

'So, where do you live then, Walter Smith?'

He didn't answer her at first, distracted by the sight of a white horse riding by. Finally, he jerked his head towards one of the cottages, a ramshackle one-up-one-down with broken windows and flaking paintwork. The front served as a depository for scrap iron and other assorted rubbish. A paradise for rats, thought Eggy, glad that Loula wasn't there.

'Gosh,' she gasped, wondering how anyone could survive more than two minutes in a hovel like that. 'I'm sorry.'

'Ain't your fault,' he said sourly.

'Well, it certainly isn't yours.' She looked at his hopeless young face and suddenly, the idea of living with old Aunt Adelaide faded into insignificance. 'Here, have this.' She handed him a shiny red apple. 'It's all I've got for you today, I'm afraid. But see, I've polished it for you. And I can bring you some cake tomorrow if you like.'

She left the town and followed a dusty track down to the beach. Halfway along she turned and looked back at the big red house on the hill. Sunlight glinted from its window panes, a welcome sight for fishermen who, on entering the bay, would know they were safely home. Lillian's Lighthouse it had once become known. A hint of jasmine drifted on the breeze.

She walked on until the track petered out and she found herself at a steep flight of steps leading down to the beach. At the bottom she slipped off her boots, treading carefully over the shingle until she arrived at the shoreline, stockinged feet slapping on the cool wet sand. She stood there for a while, puzzling over a set of six-foot letters engraved in the sand: ***WE ARE HERE!***

A distant thud of hooves caused her to turn. Coming towards her was a sleek white horse and, seated sideways upon it, a young woman dressed in full riding habit.

'Eglantyne!' said the girl, dismounting. 'I'm Tabitha.' She raised her right hand, placed it on her chest and bowed low.

Eggy looked at her in surprise. 'Do I know you?'

The girl called Tabitha smiled. Her eyes were as green as the sea. 'No, but you certainly will do. I noticed what you did for young Walter just now, and that's why I'm here.' Seeing the puzzled look on Eggy's face, she laughed. 'I've come to tell you about your future work…'

'What future work?' Eggy demanded irritably. 'And who the heck are you anyway?'

'Who am I? Now there's an interesting question. One I might well ask you too. Do you know who *you* are? Apart from being an extremely ill-mannered girl…'

Eggy watched her curiously. She was clearly not right in the head. 'You're not from round here then, I imagine.'

'No, I'm from Zalnea.'

'Oh, you mean Zennor - in Cornwall, on the road to Penzance…'

'Cornwall?' Tabitha looked uncertain. 'Let me just check.' With that she pulled out a small silver-coloured object which she held against her ear.

Eggy stooped to pick up her boots.

The girl signalled to her to stop and stared into the distance. 'Did you know we're being watched?'

Eggy glanced up and followed her gaze. There, on the cliff tops stood two dark-hooded figures, observing them both. A wave of nausea stirred in the pit of her stomach. There was something strangely familiar about them.

'Dark Hearts,' murmured Tabitha. She picked up a stick and drew a strange pattern in the sand. 'I don't think they'll see it from there. This is the *Mark of Triandor*. You must etch it into your mind at once. Be able to draw it at will should you ever find yourself in danger.' She looked up at the cliffs again. 'It holds the power of the universe. Watch this…' She bent down and placed her index finger on the sand and began to count to seven. Almost at once her feet lifted off the ground. 'Share this with your friend, if you will. I want you both to return tomorrow at five, here, by the breakwater.'

'Do you mean Jack?' Eggy gazed down at the shape in the sand. It looked like something out of her school geometry book. She searched around for a splinter of shell and finding one, began to scratch it onto the inside of her arm. When she looked up again both the girl and the horse had vanished.

She left the beach and hurried back to Cloud Hill, bumping into Jack on his way down.

'You're bleeding,' he said, peering at her arm. 'What have you been up to?'

'I'll tell you tomorrow,' she said, turning to go, 'but right now, there's something else I must do. I've just met a girl down by the shore. She seems a bit…' She tapped the side of her head.

'Do you mean mad?'

'Not exactly.' Eggy hesitated. 'But let's just say a bit odd. She wants to meet us both by the breakwater, tomorrow at five. You'll come, won't you?'

'Me?' asked Jack who wasn't at all keen on meeting new people, especially odd ones. 'Do I have to?'

'Yes, I think you do.'

Puzzled, Jack watched as she disappeared over the hill.

The Mark of Triandor! What could it possibly mean? Eggy raced up the stairs to her room. There, she tore a page from an old school notebook and made two copies, one for herself and the other for Jack, and tucked them away carefully at the back of her wardrobe.

Chapter Six

The Mark of Triandor Goes Missing

There was quite a racket going on downstairs the following morning. Maids running hither and thither, doors slammed, and even Theodore's demands for silence ignored.
It seemed like the whole household had gone berserk.

'Whatever is it?' Eggy enquired. 'Have we been burgled overnight?' Then, hearing Loula's screams, she rushed into the kitchen, just as a tiny grey creature scurried across the tiles.

'Rats!' Loula squealed, clutching Eggy's arm. 'They'll be the death of me!' She pointed to the larder. 'There'll be more of them evil beasts in there, you can bet. What we need is a cat.'

'Don't be ridiculous, it was only a mouse,' Eggy laughed, 'I saw it, a sweet little grey one. You can always tell by their ears. I'll ask Jack to save us a kitten, shall I? There's a new litter up at the farm - at least that's one tiny life spared from drowning.'

Rats! With all the commotion she had almost forgotten about poor Walter. 'Listen, I'll check inside the larder for you while you keep an eye on Ivy Bottomley. She's outside, wasting time with that awful man when they should both be working. Can you hear them?'

'Reginald Sligh?' muttered Loula, glad of an excuse to step outside. 'I've had enough of that lazy pair. Wait till I've finished with them.'

Eggy opened the larder door and fell to her knees, pretending to look for more mice. Inside, it was cool and inviting, laden with spice and buttery sweetness. There was plenty of cake in the tin, enough for a generous slice. Bread rolls too, left over from last night's dinner, and a big pot of dripping. She found an old wicker basket and hastily filled it with cheese and butter and jars of pickles and preserved plums. Anything she could lay hands on that wouldn't be too easily missed. Theodore Trott adhered to a very tight budget where everything was itemised, and stealing food was strictly forbidden.

'Right, Walter,' she murmured, swinging the basket over one arm, 'this lot should keep you happy for a while…'

Outside, a sulky Ivy Bottomley had been given carpets to clean. She had one draped over the washing line and stood poised, ready to inflict harm, with a wooden beater in her hand. Seeing Eggy pass by, she swung it back and began to thrash the life out of it, cursing as a cloud of dust filled her lungs. Eggy giggled, hearing words that even she was unfamiliar with and could only guess at their meaning.

When she reached the bottom of Cloud Hill there was no sign of Walter at all. Steeling herself, she marched up the little path to his cottage and knocked sharply on the door. Minutes passed and, getting no response, she left her picnic basket on the doorstep, praying someone might take it in before the rats discovered it.

The house was deserted when she returned. The larder floor had now been thoroughly scrubbed with carbolic soap, and steamed puddings simmered on the hob for lunch. She rolled up her sleeve and inspected her arm. To her surprise the strange pattern was still there and with no sign at all of it fading. She ran upstairs to find her two drawings, hidden safely at the back of her wardrobe. She took one out and seated herself at her desk. Even with the balcony windows open the day was uncomfortably hot. She turned the little drawing over and began to write: *Dear Jack, I shall explain later but this is yours. Keep it safe and if you ever need to use it just put your index finger in the middle and slowly count to seven...*

For some reason a wave of nausea hit her and she remembered the two figures on the cliff. A shadow had fallen across her desk.

'More love letters, Eggletime Trott? I'm taking this to the Master.' Ivy Bottomley reached out to snatch it. 'He says you're to go down at once.'

Love letters? For some reason Eggy couldn't stop the colour from rising up her neck. She clung stubbornly to her drawing. 'How long have you been standing there, Bumley?'

Ivy Bottomley smirked and plonked a jug on the wash stand. 'Long enough,' she said, and while Eggy's back was turned, spat into the water before retreating.

The lunch gong sounded and Eggy took an envelope from the drawer, slipped the *Mark of Triandor* inside and slid it under her blotter[6]. Noticing the water jug, she emptied it over the balcony, drenching Reginald Sligh the groundsman, who just happened to be passing by at the time. As Loula often remarked, they all needed eyes at the back of their heads where Ivy Bottomley was concerned.

She closed the door behind her. At the end of the landing she glanced around and, seeing no one was there, slid down every bannister till she reached the hallway below. There, she almost collided with Loula, on her way to collect the second post.

'Do be careful!' Loula exclaimed, patting her enormous chest. 'I've had enough shocks for one day.' She grasped hold of Eggy's sleeve. 'What on earth's that thing on your arm? Looks like it could turn nasty.'

Eggy froze and looked down at her captive arm. 'Oh, nothing, it's just a little scratch. I'm sorry, Lou, I have to go,' she insisted, pulling away, 'Father's on the war path and wants to see me at once.'

'But how can that be? He's in Littlehaven all day.'

'Are you sure?'

'Yes, he won't be back till late…'

'Oh, no…' Eggy felt the colour drain from her face; she turned to run upstairs, praying she wasn't already too late.

Luckily, the room was empty and there, under the blotter, was her envelope, exactly where she had left it. She sighed gratefully and tucked it into her pocket, ready to give to Jack later that day.

❀

Tabitha was sitting on a rock, gazing out to sea, when Eggy arrived at the breakwater. 'I'm glad you came,' she said without turning. 'Jack will be on his way; his father's just had another fall.'

Eggy spoke to the back of her head. 'You mean you've seen him?'

'Not exactly.' Tabitha turned to face her. 'Don't worry,' she teased, registering a trace of annoyance in Eggy's tone. 'I've no time for young men, not even one as handsome as yours.'

'But he's not…' Eggy flushed angrily. 'He's not my anything!'

Tabitha sprang to her feet and laughed. 'You're so easy to nettle, my dear. Ah, look, here he comes now…'

Eggy swung round to see Jack sprinting across the sands.

'Hey, how come you're so early?' he panted, gazing at his imaginary watch. 'It's not like you, Eggs.' He glanced briefly at Tabitha and tipped his cap. 'I'm sorry I'm late, Dad had another fall.'

'So I've heard.' Eggy gave him a withering look. 'But you didn't tell me you two knew each other.'

Jack took off his cap and squinted at Tabitha again. 'What are you on about?' He stared at Eggy, bemused 'We don't. And how did she know about Dad? It only happened as I was leaving…'

'*She* told me,' Eggy said frostily, indicating Tabitha.

'I've had my eye on you for a while, Jack Hilton,' Tabitha

declared. 'I must say you're doing an excellent job up there on the farm. Your father must be very proud of you.' A flock of gulls flew noisily overhead and she gazed up, shading her eyes. 'See there?' She pointed vaguely. 'That's where I'm originally from, though Luga's my home right now.'

'Luga?' Jack repeated. 'Is that far?'

'Don't be ridiculous, it's here.' Tabitha indicated the rock she had been sitting on and struck it with her foot. 'It's the real name for Planet Earth.'

Jack shifted uncomfortably, his boots making little ruts in the sand. The girl was pretty enough all right with those enormous green eyes but clearly not all there. He glanced furtively at Eggy, wondering why the heck she'd dragged him here.

'Because I told her to,' Tabitha answered, much to his surprise. 'Zalnea is my real home. It's a far more advanced planet than your own.'

'I'm sure you mean Zennor,' Eggy stated, folding her arms across her chest. 'We all know there's no life on other planets. Even I learned that much at school.'

'Which only goes to show how ignorant you are,' Tabitha replied coolly. 'Not surprising really since Luga is one of the most backward planets in our Galaxy.'

Jack and Eggy exchanged sideways glances and had a terrible urge to laugh.

Tabitha pretended not to notice. 'For one thing, we're able to fly. Oh, I don't mean those stupid little glider things you're so fond of. I'm talking about gigantic ships that ride the Waves of Space! It's how I escaped the apocalypse and ended up here.'

Hearing this, the two friends collapsed into whoops of laughter. If nothing else, the girl was a great storyteller.

Tabitha raised an eyebrow and waited for them to settle. 'You see,' she continued calmly, 'I am a refugee.'

There was something about her; something that suggested there might, just might, be a fragment of truth in what she had said. There was also the question of the *Mark of Triandor*. Perhaps, thought Eggy, she would tell them a little more. 'I almost forgot this,' she murmured, reaching into her pocket for the envelope. She passed it to Jack.

There was a small sheet of paper inside. Jack glanced at it and turned it over a couple of times. 'What is it?' he asked, promptly handing it back. 'There's nothing on it.'

Eggy stared at him in horror, and then at Tabitha who didn't look at all pleased. 'I'm so sorry, Tabitha. The *Mark of Triandor* - I think it's been stolen. What should I do now?'

'To start with you should learn to be more careful,' Tabitha replied. 'As you may have already guessed, the Dark Hearts have found it. Have you any idea what trouble this has caused?'

Eggy bowed her head and Jack, seeing her face crumple, put a comforting arm around her.

'I can't believe how stupid I've been...'

Tabitha's expression softened a little. 'Luckily, there's not been too much harm done this time, apart from a great tidal wave the other side of Littlehaven Bay.'

Jack frowned, annoyed that she had upset his friend. 'And what do you mean by that?'

'You will discover in time. The *Mark of Triandor* is the most powerful and dangerous symbol in creation. And you two…' She raised her hand and bowed to them both. 'You two have been entrusted with it.'

They glanced at each other and shrugged; then, somewhat self-consciously, gave a little bow in return.

Tabitha noticed and flashed them a smile. 'You see,' she said, 'once in the hands of the Dark Hearts it will cause untold chaos and destruction. It is out of their hands now, but always be certain to keep it hidden.'

'I do have another copy at home,' Eggy admitted. 'Jack can have that one instead. But what shall I do about this?' She rolled up her sleeve.

'Nothing,' said Tabitha. 'Just keep it covered and it will last you a lifetime. This will be your ultimate protection.'

'Are you really a refugee?' asked Jack.

Tabitha's face lit up. 'Yes, would you like me to tell you more?'

They both nodded.

'Sit down then.' She pointed to a little bench, fashioned out of driftwood.

'So,' she began, 'when we first landed on Luga, we settled in the North; a place in the Kebnekaise Mountains called Himmelbro.'

Eggy resolved to look up Himmelbro in the old atlas at home.

'It's actually the Swedish name for Havenbridge which, in case you don't know, means Heaven Bridge.' She paused and tilted her head. 'Now, you're probably both wondering why I am here…'

Chapter Seven

Dire Things Are About To Happen

A shiver ran down their spines. 'The *Earth Watchers* have sent you?' What a curious name that was.

'Yes' said Tabitha. 'And, as their name suggests, they have a particular interest in your planet. I'm simply a *kaíla*[7], a trainee Earth Watcher, one who has been sent to teach you the Mysteries…'

Jack, who had already heard enough mysteries for one day, listened warily. He liked things to be obvious and down to earth.

'Things no one likes to talk about, Jack. You know, like death.'

Jack really wished he hadn't bothered to come. Who in their right mind wanted to think about death?

'You see, the good news is this - *death will not kill you.*' Tabitha waited to let her words sink in. 'Yes, I thought I'd died once. It was during the apocalypse. But instead, I found myself here, on Luga. Look at me, Jack. Do I seem at all dead to you now?' She laughed helplessly as though it was the best joke in the world. 'Feel that?' She reached for his hand and squeezed it hard. 'I'm every bit as alive as you are. However, for me to become a fully-qualified Earth Watcher, I have to pass one final test. And this is where you two come in…'

'*But why us?*'

'Because you've been chosen to carry out my first mission...'

'I'm sorry,' Eggy said politely, 'I think there's been some kind of mistake.'

'Mistake?' Tabitha echoed. 'No, Earth Watchers *never* make mistakes.'

'Even if what you say is true, I don't see how we can help you. As you know, Jack's needed at Cloud Farm and I shan't be here for much longer.'

Jack stared at her, bewildered. Not here? What kind of excuse was that?

'It's true, I'm afraid,' said Eggy miserably. 'I'm being sent to London for four years.'

'But you can't, Eggs, you even said you wouldn't…'

Tabitha raised a hand to silence him. 'None of this is important, my friends. *Tuló*[8], my Commanding Officer, believes you are both perfect for the job.' She tilted her head and assessed them both. 'Yes, I suppose you'll do.'

Despite himself, Jack felt a sudden ripple of excitement.

'You Lugans really are a strange lot though, aren't you?' Tabitha said bluntly. 'I mean, letting people starve to death on your planet, even right here under your noses. Take young Walter and his family.' She fixed Eggy with her sea-green eyes. 'Therefore, Eglantyne, you really must start planning that Ball…'

Eggy caught her breath. 'How could you possibly know that? It was only a passing thought.'

Tabitha slapped her forehead playfully. 'No thought, however passing, is hidden from Earth Watchers.' She smiled, seeing the startled look on their faces. 'Relax, my friends, you've nothing to worry about. Despite what I said, Havenbridge is actually the most civilised town on your planet. The problem is you've got little sense of community.'

Jack thought for a moment and uttered the first thing that came into his head. 'We have got a Community Hall.'

'What I have in mind is something far grander!' Tabitha spread her arms like wings. '…Something that brings the whole town together in kindness and tolerance!' She placed a hand on her heart. 'After all, if little places like Havenbridge can't be kind and tolerant, what hope is there for your planet?' She took out the small silver gadget Eggy had noticed the previous day. 'See this?'

There on the screen were two hands enclosing a globe. 'If my plan succeeds I'll finally earn this, my Earth Watchers' badge!' Her voice dropped to a mere whisper. 'Eglantyne, those dark figures we saw on the clifftops…'

Eggy nodded. 'Yes, I know who they are.'

'I'm afraid there are thousands more like them. They're a sign of dire things to come.'

Jack glanced at Tabitha dubiously. Dire things didn't really happen in Havenbridge.

Tabitha's eyes flashed. 'But I'm afraid they do elsewhere on your planet, Jack. And, because of this, a team of Earth Watchers will arrive in force; in four years' time to be exact...'

That's 1914, thought Eggy. The year I'll finally be free. 'Why then?' she asked curiously.

Tabitha placed a finger on her lips. 'Meet me here on Friday the 26th of August at five and we'll speak of it more. Meanwhile, I'll leave you to organise your Grand Community Ball. It's vital that you Lugans learn to come together as friends.' She lifted her hand and pointed to the far horizon. 'See that?'

They glanced up and there emerging from the clouds was another bright metallic shape.

'Oh, good, it's that glider again,' said Jack.

'No,' laughed Tabitha, 'but it is another sign.'

He was about to reply when he realised there was no one there. 'Crikey, what happened just then?' he asked, scratching the back of his head. 'Did I just imagine it?'

Eggy shivered. 'No, you absolutely didn't. Come on,' she sighed, 'let me tell you the rest of my news.'

Chapter Eight

A Curious Story Emerges

'Four years?' Jack repeated, crestfallen. 'I'll still see you in the holidays though, won't I?'

Eggy nodded. 'Don't worry - she'll kick me out long before then. I have a plan.' They had reached the entrance to Hadleigh House. 'Why don't you come in? The old man's in Littlehaven till late. Anyway, since I'm going away, I've nothing to lose.'

'The *Mark of Triandor…*' Jack looked at her, bemused. 'So it actually caused a tidal wave?'

'Hmm, so she said. I've made you a small copy but you must keep it safe.'

'I will,' Jack said solemnly, though he still wasn't sure he believed her. 'What the heck has she got us into now, Eggs?'

'A Community Ball apparently…'

They walked up the gravel drive towards the house. 'Be extra careful around Ivy,' Jack warned. 'That name Dark Heart definitely suits her.'

'Bumley? Don't worry, I shall.'

Jack shook his head and grinned. 'If anyone heard us they'd think we were mad.'

'Yes, another good reason to keep it a secret. Come on, let's have a word with Lou and see if we can persuade her to help.'

Loula's eyes filled with tears when she saw them. 'It was him,' she gasped, pointing to some invisible entity behind her. And for some odd reason she then began to laugh. Without knowing quite why, Eggy and Jack joined in. Loula's sudden fit of merriment made it impossible not to, and they tittered and howled and clutched their sides, until finally all their laughter was spent. It was only then that a curious story emerged.

Loula let out a great shuddering sigh and wiped the tears from her eyes. 'It was old Billy Birch – he turned up late with the groceries, looking proper peaky he did. So, of course,I poured him a tot of brandy. *You'll need one yourself,* Mrs B, he told me. *Once you've heard this...'*

Jack glanced at the almost empty bottle of brandy on the table.

'He'd just come out of the Hearts of Oak,' Loula continued, 'when, all of a sudden a lad ran out of Devil's Gulley. Nearly sent him flying, in a right state he was, blabbering and pointing up at the sky. And there,' she whispered, 'a good thirty feet up in the air, they saw a...'

'Was it a glider?'

'No, Jack,' Loula croaked, 'it was a man, flapping and squawking like a bloomin' seagull. Someone said he'd fell in the sea. Well, I didn't believe that for a minute...'

But Eggy did and she clapped a hand to her mouth. 'Do you think Billy was drunk?'

'That's what Mrs. Birch said when she threw his dinner at him.'

'Blimey!' said Jack, wondering if life would ever return to normal again. 'What a waste of a good dinner.'

'Gravy stains all down his shirt...' Loula's voice began to waver again. 'And just as he'd finished telling me, who the dickens do you think walked in next?'

Jack knew. It was all to do with that tidal wave. 'Go on,' he said.

'Why, Reggie Sligh, dripping with seaweed and smelling

like a stagnant fish pond! Said he'd slipped and fell off a rock near Littlehaven Bay…' Loula shook her head in disbelief. 'Though what the heck was he doing over there? Yes, very odd, and that Ivy's behaving all shifty again.'

Eggy gave Jack a sideways glance. Perhaps it was time to change the subject. 'Lou, do you know how many people live in this town?'

'In Havenbridge? How the devil should I know that?'

'We need to,' said Eggy. 'Remember what we discussed yesterday? A Grand Ball will be something special for us all.'

'Now don't start all that again. You know your father won't have any of it.'

'Jack thinks it's a good idea, don't you?'

'Yes,' Jack replied staunchly, hoping he wouldn't be expected to go. 'It'll be a nice send-off for Eggs. Come on, Mrs. Bellamy, be fair now. I'm sure Mother will help you. I can ask her tonight.'

Loula recoiled, remembering the state of Nellie Holland's kitchen. Filthy, dog hair all over and Lord knows what else besides. But she liked what he'd said about a send-off. The house would be desolate without her. 'Right…' She picked up a pencil and moistened the tip with her tongue. 'I suppose I'd better make a list then. Though I don't know who's going to fund all this palaver. Your father won't, that's for sure.'

'Of course he won't,' said Eggy. 'Jack says when Theodore Trott drops a penny it lands on the back of his neck.'

Jack blushed, wishing he'd never said it but, as it was, Loula nodded in agreement.

'And there's all that money Mother left me,' Eggy reminded her.

Loula sucked her pencil thoughtfully. Oh, dear, that was a secret only she and Eggy had shared. Now Jack knew too. 'Very well then,' she relented, 'but you'd better have a word with him first.' She cast a warning glance at Jack. 'He'll be back in a while, young man.'

'Right then,' said Jack, promptly pulling on his old jacket and cap. 'I'll be off now, Mrs. Bellamy. Thanks for the chat. Same time tomorrow, Eggs?'

'Yes, but you can't go till I've fetched you my drawing. I'll walk with you as far as the fields…'

Loula tipped the remains of the brandy into her glass, her eyes already glazed with drink. It had been twelve years since Lillian had summoned her. She'd handed her a package; hurriedly wrapped and tied up with ribbons. Take this, she had whispered, as though she already knew there was no time to waste. Uncanny really since a week later she was dead.

Loula had stared at it, speechless; then opened it enough to see what lay inside. '*Oh, Madam, I can't take this! There's what, thousands in here…*'

'*Yes, you can, Lou. I don't want my little girl growing up without something of her own. But Theo must never know. Promise me you'll keep it safe until she's eighteen, and should she ever need anything before, well, it's there to be used. I've left the same for Joseph but that's already in Theo's keeping. You'll notice I've put a small gift in there for you too. Spend it as you please.*'

But Loula never did spend a penny of it. Small gift! It was twenty pounds! Fearful of being caught with more money than she'd ever seen in her life, she stitched it into her mattress and for all those years it had lain there, untouched. Maybe now was the time to put some of it to good use.

'What did you say?' Theodore bellowed, 'Community Ball? Don't be so ridiculous, Eglantyne, Mrs. Bellamy has more than enough to do. Kindly finish your dinner.'

'She's very keen on it, Father,' Eggy persisted, 'I thought we might invite the vicar…'

'Feathergill?' Theodore grimaced. 'Can't stand the man, nor his shrew of a wife…'

'The Earl of Littlehaven seems quite jolly.'

'The man's a bloody idiot, quite insane.'

'Oh, come on, Father, you must at least like Lord and Lady Havenbridge, everyone does. I'm told they're selling the Hall. They could probably do with some expert advice.'

'Really?' Theodore's interest was piqued a little, she could see. *Theodore Trott Solicitors* was losing money fast, according to the gossip in town. He badly needed an assistant but apparently, no one cared to work for him. 'Very well,' Theodore conceded, 'as long as any expenditure exceeds no more than five shillings.'

Loula was meanwhile making plans of her own. The idea had begun to grow on her. She climbed the stairs to Lillian's old room. It had not been lived in for twelve years yet she still placed flowers in the window every other week, plumped up pillows and smoothed the counterpane. She liked to think that, wherever Lillian was now, she might appreciate those same small comforts. With that wistful thought, she opened the mahogany wardrobe and brought out a pretty taffeta ball gown which she laid on the bed. All it needed was a little nipping in at the waist.

Chapter Nine

A New Life for Walter

‘Well then, said Mrs. Feathergill, squinting at her through a gap in the Vicarage door. ‘I suppose you’d better come in.’

Eggy hesitated, unsure if her Community Ball was such a good idea after all. It was hard to feel kind and tolerant with Mrs. Feathergill around. Bracing herself, she stepped inside the hallway. At once, a cranky old clock chimed as though irritated by her presence, even though it was only six minutes to the hour. The whole house reeked of dogs and over-cooked cabbage. Unsure where to go next, she followed the sound of snoring and found the vicar slumped at his desk. He looked up and let out a great toothless yawn.

‘Hello, Vicar,’ Eggy announced, displaying a pile of silver-edged cards. ‘I have some news that may interest you.’ She and Jack had spent hours at the old farmhouse table writing them out. Unfortunately, Jack’s scrawl was mostly indecipherable so she had secretly discarded his attempts, apart from the odd one or two in case they ran out.

Your company is requested at a
Grand Community Ball at
Hadleigh House on Saturday 20th August 1910
at 7pm.
Please join us for a delectable supper,
with music and dancing.
ALL ARE WELCOME.
RSVP to Miss Eglantyne Marigold Trott

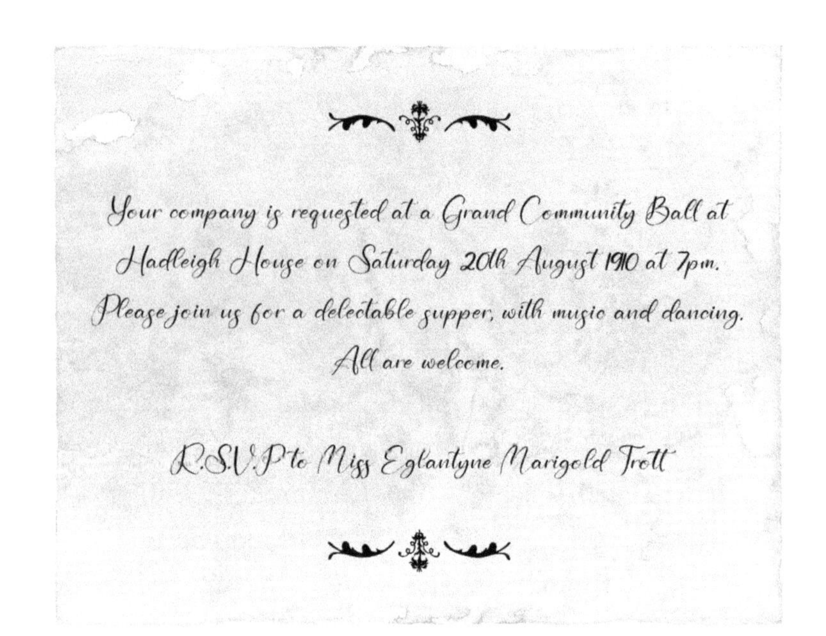

Your company is requested at a Grand Community Ball at Hadleigh House on Saturday 20th August 1910 at 7pm. Please join us for a delectable supper, with music and dancing. All are welcome.

R.S.V.P to Miss Eglantyne Marigold Trott

She pulled one of Jack's spidery endeavours from the bottom of the pile. 'This is one for you and Mrs. Feathergill. And these…' She placed two of the neater ones on his desk. 'These are for the Earl of Newhaven and Lord and Lady Havenbridge. Since you know them a lot better than I do, would you mind passing them on?'

'Good Heavens,' the vicar cried, sensing an opportunity for scandal. 'Those poor Havenbridges…' He threw up his hands in mock despair. 'Sit down, sit down.' He pointed to a chair, already occupied by a mangy old dog. 'It appears they've fallen on hard times. No surprise, of course. Lord H has a shocking addiction to gambling. And as for his wife, well…' He lowered his voice a little. 'Between you and me, she's been seen with young Mr. Threpstone, the cellist, handsome fellow, engaged to Miss Crabbitt …' He waited for a response but since there was none, he continued regardless. 'No, young lady, you must come along and present them yourself.

Tomorrow morning at Mattins, eleven o'clock sharp… And by the by,' he added, clasping his stubby little hands. 'Did you hear about Reginald Sligh's recent shenanigans? Not that I believe a word of it, of course… and young Miss Tribble's liaison with Mr. Lean at the Picture House…?' He tut-tutted in disapproval. 'Outrageous, I know…'

It was late Sunday afternoon when Eggy arrived at the farmhouse door, carrying a new batch of invitations. All the others had disappeared that morning such was the interest in church. She stooped to stroke a small black kitten who had brushed against her legs, begging to be allowed inside. 'Are you much good at catching rats, my little friend?' she asked. 'Loula will love you if you are. May I call you Emmeline, even if you're a boy? It's my favourite name.'

'Door's open,' called Nellie, needlessly since no one ever bothered to lock it. Seeing that it was Eggy, she beamed, red-faced from toasting bread at the open fire. 'Well, what a surprise to see you at church today, my dear!'

'I had no choice, did I?' Eggy replied. 'Though it did have its lighter moments, I admit. Isadora Havenbridge reading *Lady Audley's Secret* under her shawl and the Earl of Littlehaven conducting a heated conversation with himself. Seriously though, I don't know how you do it every week.' She settled down at the big pine table and stole a slice of buttered toast from Jack's plate.

'Only chance I get for a sit-down, that's why,' said Nellie and turned to shout up the stairs: 'Jack, tea's ready and you've got a visitor. You'd best come down now before everything's gone.' She loaded her toasting fork with another slice of bread and turned to admire Eggy, still wearing her Sunday best. 'Just look at you, all dressed up like a dog's dinner[9]…'

Eggy glanced down at her grey linen suit with distaste. 'I haven't even had a moment to change. Too busy writing these.' She placed the new bundle of invitations on the table. 'These are for you and Jack to give out if you don't mind.'

'You certainly had them all intrigued. There's been nothing like this at Hadleigh for years.' She looked up, hearing Jack on the stairs. 'Ah, there you are, son…'

'Reckon many will turn up then, Eggs?' Jack said, slumping down on a shabby old sofa.

'Out of curiosity if nothing else,' said Nellie, watching as the last slice of bread turned to golden brown.

'Nosey parkers the lot of them,' Jack sniffed. 'No one's been invited up there for as long as I remember.'

Nellie nodded. 'Just what I told her.'

'I think Lady Havenbridge might,' said Eggy. 'She even stopped reading her novel to squint at me through her lorgnette. And do you know who turned up at the end? No, don't tell him, Nellie. You haven't already, have you?'

'No,' Nellie lied.

'I don't know,' said Jack, rubbing his chin and pretending to guess. 'Reggie Sligh?'

'No, you idiot, it was that young Walter I told you about! I've been worried about him.'

'After the collection money, was he?'

'Don't, Jack!' cried Nellie, jumping to Walter's defence. 'Poor little soul, he only came in for a bit of a sit down like me, and that snooty bitch of a vicar's wife, pardon my language, only tried to shoo him away, the heartless devil.'

'That's until I stopped her,' said Eggy, 'and explained he was my personal assistant. He wasn't then of course but he will be now.'

Jack laughed. 'That was both kind and clever of you, Eggs.'

'I've given him a great pile of invitations to deliver. Let me think: S.J. Lutterworth and Sons, Booksellers; Tinkerwells' Hardware Store; Miss Edith Tribble's Haberdashery[10]; Joseph Lean, Esquire, Funeral Director; oh, and Leonard Crabbitt at the Fishing Tackle shop. I also told him he mustn't forget the Gypsies on the other side of the bay. Then I got him to say the whole lot back to me.'

'You mean he can read?'

'Not really, but he soon will, starting from tomorrow. I also told him we'll need him there on the day; which means we'll have to get him spruced up a bit.'

'Shoes, jacket, and a decent pair of trousers,' replied Nellie, addressing Jack. 'You'll have something, won't you, son? Go and see if that water's boiled for our tea, will you? And take your dad a cup while you're at it…'

'Doubt if any of my old stuff will fit him,' Jack said, scooping tea leaves into the pot.

'Lou's already found a few things she'd put by for our Joseph,' said Eggy. 'Seeing as he's never coming back.'

'Shocking business that,' Nellie said ruefully. 'Your poor brother, but thank God he's got a decent family looking after him now.'

Eggy nodded absently. 'I suppose I could always get Walter kitted out at Hutton's outfitters in town.'

'There, you two.' Nellie placed a fresh rack of toast on the table. 'Eat this while it's hot.'

'Thank you, Nellie,' said Eggy. 'You will come to it, won't you?'

'What me, miss a night out at a Ball? Try stopping me!'

'What about you, Jack?'

'Do I have a choice?'

'No,' said Eggy, 'you blooming well don't.'

❀

The following day, Nellie had to visit her cousin in Littlehaven so Eggy spent a few hours helping out on the farm. 'I've filled the troughs in the hen house,' she said, tucking a stray lock of hair behind her ear, 'but I also found these while I was there.' She held out an enamel bowl containing three large brown eggs.

'Let Walter have them,' Jack said at once. 'We've collected more than enough eggs today.'

'I hoped you might say that.' Eggy ran towards him and planted a kiss on his cheek. 'We had our first English lesson today. I took him to the Harbour Tea Rooms.'

'So, when are you taking me then?' asked Jack. 'You're always telling me I can't write.'

'I will if you're as good a student as he is,' she teased. 'I promised him we'd order anything he could read. Very silly idea…'

It had turned out to be far more than either of them had imagined: potted shrimps and fish cakes for starters, mashed potatoes with mutton stew, followed by gooseberry pie, custard, and a huge slice of marble cake.

Eggy blew out her cheeks. 'He took most of it home so hopefully, there'll be no black eyes for him tonight. Tomorrow though, I'm moving him on to this.' She delved into her old school bag and produced a dog-eared book.

'*A Terrible Tomboy* by Angela Brazil?' read Jack. 'Are you crazy? He'll never read that, it's for girls!'

'Don't be so negative. It's not girlish at all or I wouldn't have read it. Jack, you will carry on with his lessons while I'm away, won't you - reading and a bit of adding up?'

'Me?' Jack stared at her in horror. 'What time will I get for all that?'

'The time you'd have spent with me, of course,' she replied

sensibly. 'Seriously, there's something quite special about that boy.'

Grudgingly Jack agreed, but only on condition that Walter helped him with the horses.

'Well, that's perfect,' said Eggy, 'and then you can teach him to ride as well. I'm sure Starlight will be happy to oblige.'

Chapter Ten

A Resounding Success

'Right you are, this lot can go in the lift,' said Loula, heaving a mountain of neatly folded tablecloths onto the trolley. 'Now, dear, have you decided what you're wearing? You can't turn up in those smelly old rags.'

'I hadn't given it a thought,' replied Eggy, eyeing the array of desserts in the larder. 'I dare say you have though. These trifles look nice. Will there be enough, do you think?'

'I should jolly well hope so because I'm not making any more. And you can keep those grubby fingers away from my trifles…' Loula grasped Eggy's hand and led her towards the door. 'Go and have a nice hot bath, young lady; you stink like a flaming farm yard.'

'Did you know we set up a bathhouse at the farm? For Walter and his brothers and sisters, all eleven of them…'

'You never did! Oh my, eleven kiddies, imagine that…' Loula threw up her hands in horror. 'Their poor, dear mother…'

'We lured them there with the promise of a hearty breakfast - porridge and buttered eggs - and then took them off to the milking shed to visit the cows.'

Nellie was already waiting there with a big tin bath full of steaming water. She dunked them in, one by one and fully clothed, then doused their heads in salt and vinegar (Nellie's famous cure for nits). They were then duly dispatched to the scullery to dry off by the range. Not only did they survive their ordeal but asked gleefully when they might do it again.

'Must have stunk like a blooming chip chop!' said Loula, wrinkling her nose.

'They did but at least they were clean.'

'Poor little mites.'

'We packed them off with some nice new clothes too; well, not new exactly…'

It was a curious assortment of garments, hastily assembled by Mrs. Fairweather, the doctor's wife, who kept an emergency supply for the poor and destitute: mostly moth-eaten cardigans and patched woollen breeches but there were a few outgrown party frocks too, plus a brand new sailor's suit (never worn since the poor child it was intended for died of tuberculosis before he got the chance).

Loula stepped back and admired the results of her labours: neat rows of white linen napkins; silver cutlery, gleaming after years of neglect; and dozens of garden flowers arranged in miniature vases. The Grand Community Ball was giving them all a bit of a boost. Even the maids had risen to the occasion, with the exception of Ivy Bottomley, of course. Now, with Eggy safely out of her way, there was just one more detail to attend to: Lillian's ball gown.

Theodore was outraged when the whole population of Havenbridge began to troop up his drive. And what a bizarre assembly it was: Lord and Lady Havenbridge in their sleek, chauffeur-driven Daimler, succeeded by the extraordinary Earl of Littlehaven on an old Penny Farthing, wearing knickerbockers[11] and a straw boater.

'Silly old fool,' Loula scoffed. 'Dangerous things, they are!'

'Knickerbockers?' Eggy said absently, keeping her eye on shy Mr. Threpstone. Despite the vicar's misgivings, he appeared to be perfectly devoted to little Ada Crabbitt, while Mr. Lean and Miss

Tribble sat at opposite ends of the table with not so much as a glance passing between them.

To Eggy's astonishment, the whole town had come bearing gifts. Even the poorest contrived to bring some small thing: a hand-carved cigar box retrieved from the Rag and Bone cart, a battered tin whistle, a bag of pretty shells gathered from the beach. One charming little Gypsy girl arrived with a bunch of overblown roses, wrapped in old newspaper, which irate Mrs. Feathergill recognised as purloined from the Vicarage garden. Six bottles of stout appeared, thoughtfully pilfered from the Heart of Oak by Walter's father who was known to be light-fingered, along with a tin of chocolate biscuits from Billy Birch's shop.

Somehow, the whole of Havenbridge managed to cram itself around two trestle tables that ran the length of the Ballroom. And after a few bottles of cider and homemade wine, plus a crate of champagne from the Havenbridges' cellars, they all confessed to being rather fond of the wild-haired ragamuffin who dressed like a boy; especially since she lived with a miserable wretch who hadn't even the grace to speak civilly to anyone.

Only two people were notably absent: Reginald Sligh, still smarting from his humiliating aerial experience and Ivy Bottomley who had emptied dirty dishwater into the custard and prayed they'd all die of food poisoning. 'Here, you…' She placed an elaborate swirl of rancid cream atop the final tureen of soup, Ɛ, and promptly grabbed Millie Pickles, the youngest maid. 'I done this special for Miss Eglantyne. Make sure she gets it or I'll poke yer bleedin' eyes down yer throat.' Millie was so nervous that she tripped as she entered the servants' lift and tipped the whole lot on the floor.

Meanwhile, Jack sat awkwardly at the end of the table, surveying the room. He had never been more bored in his life. The Ballroom was swarming with guests, all shouting animatedly above the sound of the

Gypsy fiddles.

'I'll miss Eggy once she's gone, same as your Jack will, no doubt,' Loula remarked to Nellie as though he weren't sitting there.

'Never forgotten that day she lost old Bobbie,' Nellie mused. 'Lovely dog he was. Our Jack did his best to comfort her, didn't you, love? Even got her a new one, only to find it caught in a rabbit trap next day. How he lost his finger, poor lad, trying to save it. Just hope she was grateful. Jack - elbows off the table, please!' Nellie yelled.

Jack fidgeted, uncomfortable in his borrowed suit and tie, wishing he was back at home, having his tea at the old pine table where he didn't have to mind his manners. It was only the mention of his name and the occasional growl of his stomach that reminded him how hungry he was. The tables were filling up now with soup tureens and miniature sandwiches, lattice topped pies, fruit salads and trifles, together with enormous iced cakes and jugs of cream.

'He's a credit to you that boy, Nell,' Loula said, nibbling on a bread roll. 'Young Eggy never grieved for her mother, God rest her soul, but once that little puppy went, it hit her like a tidal wave in winter.'

Jack cringed, wishing they would stop discussing his friend so openly for all to hear. But soon, his wish was granted and there was a moment of silence, followed by a great stamping of feet as the whole room began to clap and cheer.

'Look, Lou!' Nellie exclaimed and Loula swung round to see what all the commotion was about. There was Eggy, poised at the Ballroom door, no longer the scruffy tomboy but a dazzling beauty in midnight blue taffeta, her hair dotted with flowers. Lady Havenbridge rose to her feet, tapped her glass with a spoon and declared the Grand Community Ball officially about to begin.

'My, what a picture she looks in that dress,' Loula murmured proudly. 'Just like a star!'

'Mary Pickford, that's who,' said Nellie who had watched every film at the Picture House[12] in Littlehaven.

'Can we eat now?' said Jack, trying not to stare as Eggy made a tour of the tables. His mother was right. He'd seen a picture of Mary Pickford once in the Daily Mirror. 'Best not sit here,' he warned, as she plonked herself down next to him. 'Your old man won't like it.'

'Too bad!' Eggy laughed. 'I'm staying.'

'You look rather…' Jack fumbled for the right word and blushed. 'You should do it more often.'

Eggy shrugged. 'Well, maybe I shall.'

Just then, poor Millie Pickles crept in with the empty soup tureen. 'I'm ever so sorry, Miss Eglantyne. It was made special for you but I spilled it all. Ivy Bottomley said she'd kill me…'

'Oh, Millie, please don't cry! We shan't tell her,' Eggy promised, taking her hand. 'Anyway, you've probably saved my life! I'll bet it was disgusting - full of dead flies and toenail clippings and maybe even worse…'

Later, the guests would all reflect on the evening and conclude they had just witnessed something quite extraordinary:

The bewitching sounds of the Gypsy folk from the other side of the bay, and Mrs. Fairweather's charming string quartet; the juggling and unending hilarity, courtesy of the Earl of Littlehaven who had raised a few sniggers that night with his bawdy jokes and limericks.

They'd all been shocked into silence by a humbled Mrs. Feathergill who wept when Walter Smith's mother curtseyed to her and offered her the last piece of chocolate cake; and not least by the miraculous transformation of Walter himself. A perfect young gentleman in his butler's outfit, he had brought a look of remorseful pride to his drunken father's face.

But what they would remember forever was the unexpected sense of community they now shared; strangers had become firm friends, regardless of their status. Indeed, a new spirit of kindness enveloped the little town; spoiled only by Theodore who hovered at the door, hoping they'd all hurry off home. Perhaps the presence of Lady Havenbridge persuaded him that maybe it hadn't been such a bad idea after all. It was, she declared, a resounding success and should now become an annual event.

While Jack was crossing the fields that night something made him glance up. There, high up on the cliffs, were two dark-hooded figures staring down at him, just as Eggy had described. He walked on briskly, hoping his mother hadn't noticed, thinking how very strange life had suddenly become.

Chapter Eleven

The Power in Me Greets the Power in You

'Tabitha was right, wasn't she?' Eggy reflected. 'Things really are beginning to change. Take Ada Feathergill, she gave sweet Mrs. Smith a bouquet of flowers from her garden today.'

'Is that Walter's mother?'

'Yes, she said it must be like having a birthday even though she'd never had one before. Can you imagine that? The poor woman didn't even know the day she'd been born!'

'I heard Walter's dad got her a box of chocolates.'

'You mean, actually paid for them?'

Jack nodded. 'It's since he's been working for the Havenbridges. He's even stopped knocking her and the kids about.'

'Yes, I've heard things aren't disappearing from Billy Birch's shop anymore. Isn't that incredible? Though poor Constable Turnbull could soon be out of a job…'

'Eggs, have you forgotten?' Jack's face became serious. 'It's Friday the twenty-sixth; nine days before you leave for London…'

'Don't remind me,' Eggy said. 'I'd rather live in the cowshed than with Adelaide Trott.'

'But it's also the day we agreed to meet Tabitha. And, before I forget…' Jack reached into an old kitbag and pulled out a pair of corduroy trousers. 'These are no good to me now and they're far too big for Walter.' He grinned. 'Mum was about to give them to Mrs.

Fairweather but I stopped her.'

Eggy's face lit up. 'They'll be perfect!' she cried and held them against her face. They smelled delicious, of sea breezes and farmyards, and all she loved most. Mostly though, they would ensure her swift return.

Summer had almost ended and a chill mist moved in from the sea.

'So, you remembered,' Tabitha said, dismounting her white horse. Her face looked unusually troubled. '*Tuló* insists I apologise. I made a grave mistake.'

Eggy was unable to hide her smile. 'I thought Earth Watchers didn't make mistakes.'

'I know,' Tabitha admitted gloomily. 'I described Luga as backward, which it is, of course. But I also forgot to add that it offers the harshest lessons in the Cosmos and only the most courageous of souls dare to live here. It's known everywhere as the Planet of Suffering. Not an easy place to survive on. Which means you two should be commended for your bravery.'

'Well, in that case,' Jack said evenly, 'it was pretty brave of you too.'

'Ah, but I had no choice. I was a fugitive - from flooding and plagues, and the most terrible wars you can imagine.' She stared at them pensively. 'I'm afraid we Zalneans brought it all on ourselves.' With that, she raised a hand, placed it on her heart and bowed deeply. '*The Power in Me Greets the Power in You.* You've done a spectacular job here already. We've been watching and your Community Ball has been an enormous success.'

She indicated a pile of rocks close to the sea wall. 'Come and sit with me out of the wind.' She tethered her horse and squatted beside them. 'I'm afraid we're approaching a time of great turmoil. You two must stand together as a unified force.' She moved closer and took their hands in her own. 'Remember that whatever happens, you'll always be together, wherever in the world you happen to be…'

Eggy looked startled. 'I'm only going to London, you know.'

Tabitha smiled; a kindly smile that suggested she hadn't quite understood. She tapped Eggy's arm. 'It's vital you keep this safe.'

'Yes, of course,' they answered in unison.

'Excellent. And don't try to use it unless you absolutely need to. It'll get you out of danger in a flash.' She eyed Jack solemnly. 'Only those capable of love are entrusted with its power. As you now know, in the wrong hands it creates havoc.'

Jack shook his head. 'Sligh's tidal wave, you mean?'

Tabitha nodded. 'Two fishing boats nearly sank.' She glanced warily over her shoulder. 'Today, I have a small gift to cheer you; it's known as a *Stone of Power*.' She opened her hand and there in her palm lay two very small pieces of crystal. They flashed with blue and gold sparks. 'These are healing stones and will quickly eradicate pain. They do have an additional benefit too: you can focus on them should you ever need to become invisible. But again, do this only in an emergency. Like the *Mark of Triandor*, these are not playthings. Keep them as close to your hearts as you keep each other. Goodbye, my friends, *together or not, you are never apart!*' And with that, Tabitha and her white horse disappeared into the mist. They closed their fists around the little stones, wondering if they would ever see her again.

'I wish she wouldn't keep doing that,' Jack said, 'here one minute, gone the next.' He staggered to his feet and on a sudden whim, laid a hand on his chest and bowed low. '*The Power in Me Greets the Power in You.*'

'You're sounding like a real Earth Watcher now,' Eggy said, clambering onto Starlight's back. 'Look after her for me, won't you?' Tears stung her eyes and she looked away quickly.

Jack nodded. 'Walter and me both. Life won't be the same without you, Eggs. But I'll get to visit you somehow,' he added, knowing it would be impossible.

Eggy fingered the little stone in her pocket. 'It's going to be very tempting to try this out. Imagine being able to disappear at will, like she does!'

'What do you think she meant?' Jack said with a frown. 'A time of great turmoil…'

Eggy shivered. 'I don't know, but let's remember one thing: *together or not we'll never be apart…*' She nudged Starlight with her thighs and they both rode back to Cloud Hill.

When Sunday came, Eggy assembled a bag of small treasures and stashed them behind a panel at the back of her wardrobe: some old diaries and a collection of seashells, a cat's whisker for luck, an invitation to the Grand Ball, several spidery letters Jack had sent her while she was away at school. They would be safe there, away from certain prying eyes. The house wrapped itself around her like a great mother. 'I'll be back very soon,' she promised and slid down the bannisters one last time.

Emmeline, the little black kitten from the farm, yawned and greeted her with a silent miaow. She was, in Loula's opinion, a complete waste of time since she had no hunting skills whatsoever and spent most of her time reclining on a silk cushion by the morning room fire.

Warily, Jack sneaked in through the scullery door and crept into the parlour. He gazed around him in awe. It was the sort of place you only read about in books: shadowy and mysterious with creaking floorboards, and always the sense of some unseen presence. There was a photograph on the piano by the window; one of Eggs, set in a tiny silver frame. She was wearing a big hat spiked with feathers and such an innocent smile that no one would guess what mischief lay behind it.

He picked it up, held it for a moment and on impulse pocketed it, not wishing to be caught with it in his hand. It was, he thought guiltily, the first thing he'd ever stolen but it would certainly be the last.

Chapter Twelve

An Excellent Review

September 2019

Amelie searched their faces for a response. 'So, what do you think?'

'No!' said Isla, horrified. 'Please don't stop, I'm longing to know more. It's an awesome story, isn't it, Tim?'

Tim shrugged. 'Yeah, if you like that kind of stuff.' He saw Amelie's dismay and let out a howl of laughter. 'It's like she said, you dork. I can hardly believe you've written it.'

'Well, I have,' said Amelie, 'with Eggy's help, of course.'

'I loved Jack stealing that photo, it's so cute,' Isla said dreamily, 'and how cool about Tabitha. Wasn't she a refugee or something...?'

'Yes, because of the *aclopylips*,' added Amelie and Tim hadn't the heart to correct her.

'Seriously, mate. It's ace.'

Amelie's eyes glowed with pleasure. She liked it when Tim called her mate; it made her feel slightly less like an annoying little sister. 'I'd like to have been Eggy,' she said wistfully.

'Really?' said Isla. 'What, even losing your mom and living with that awful old aunt?'

'No, of course not - it's more the idea of being in London…'

'Then why not come visit us in our new apartment? I can take you sight-seeing.'

'Including Madame Tussaud's?' Amelie asked eagerly. 'I've always wanted to go there.'

'And the London Eye!' said Tim. 'The views are incredible.'

'Sure, so how about next weekend? I'll have to check with Mom first but I'm sure she'll say yes. What do you say, Tim?'

Tim was already consulting his transonometer. 'Yeah, there's a train every hour from Havenbridge. That means we can catch the four-thirty straight after school.' He stopped suddenly as Mrs. Lambe, the housekeeper, sounded the gong for dinner. 'C'mon then, let's ask her now…' He jumped up and pulled Isla to her feet.

'I've missed Havenbridge more than you can know,' Isla sighed, linking Amelie's arm. 'Everyone in this little town is so nice.' They stood at the top of the long staircase, surveying the floor below.

'Does that include old Curtain Twitcher?' Tim laughed. 'She's busier than ever since she bought Storm's old RAF binoculars.'

'You know, at our Grand Ballroom Sale last year,' prompted Amelie.

'Ah, you mean Miss Sowerbutts, the Neighborhood Watch lady!'

'Yeah, with her gossipy old mate from the Post Office, Mrs. Duff…' Tim sat astride the banister and prepared to make his descent which immediately made Amelie think of Eglantyne.

'They're nowhere near as bad as they were,' she insisted. 'Not since our Ballroom Sale.'

'You're so right!' Isla exclaimed. 'We brought the whole of Havenbridge together in kindness and tolerance, just like Eggy did in 1910!'

'What about old Pettifer? He hasn't changed much,' said Tim, landing spread-eagled at their feet. 'He's still the meanest man in town. Drops a penny and it lands on the back of his neck….'

'Ah yes, like Theodore!' Isla flashed him another beautiful smile. She ran her hand along the newly painted woodwork. 'Promise me you'll keep Hadleigh a little bit shabby, will you? It's part of its charm.'

'Hmm,' said Amelie. 'I don't think Mrs. Lambe would agree.'

Libby Lambe equated 'shabby' with slovenliness. She liked things to be 'pristine' and smelling of Dettol. It was her mission to keep the house that way, as she constantly reminded them.

'Mum's the only one allowed to be untidy now,' observed Amelie. 'She sat Libby down one day and explained that all artists need a certain amount of disorder and chaos to create. I wish she'd told her that writers do too. Either way, I don't think Libby understands.'

Libby wasn't having any of that nonsense in *her* kitchen. Pans shone, windows gleamed; the cooker no longer spewed forth black smoke when anyone opened its door.

Yet despite their housekeeper's obsession with orderliness, the sitting room remained a haven for old treasures and trinkets though these were not much to her liking either. 'Takes me hours to dust this flaming lot,' she frequently carped.

'Then please don't bother, my dear,' Lucy would tease her. 'A little bit of dust never hurt anyone.' Libby sometimes wondered what planet Lucy was from, certainly not this one, she concluded, and often said as much.

For Isla the best surprise of all was the elevator! The ancient servants' lift had now been repaired which meant that old Storm could travel to the attic without any effort at all. 'Can we visit the playhouse?' she asked wistfully. 'We made so many beautiful memories there last year, not to mention miracles.'

'It's hard to believe we stopped a planetary catastrophe,' Amelie agreed.

'Looks like it'll have to be next time now,' said Tim as Libby banged the dinner gong a second time. 'And that goes for our football practice too...' Oddly enough, he didn't seem to mind in the least. Amelie's story had got him thinking and, like Isla, he was secretly longing for more.

'Isla,' Amelie ventured suddenly, 'before you leave, we've got something important to tell you.'

Isla looked from one to the other, unsure whether the news was to be good or not. 'Nothing bad, I hope.'

Amelie smiled. 'No, not at all. You remember that missing page in Aunt Eggy's old journal?'

Isla's eyes widened. 'The tattoo thing on her arm?'

Amelie nodded. 'Well, I kind of found it.' She passed her drawing to Isla. 'The trouble is it doesn't seem to work.'

'Ah,' Isla said thoughtfully. 'Maybe it's not meant to right now. Have you shown Grandpa Storm already?'

'Not yet, but I will.'

At nine o'clock a taxi arrived and the whole family gathered on the steps to say their goodbyes to Isla and Bettina. Lucy sighed, Lara whimpered, Freddie jumped on the bonnet and had to be shooed away. Storm waved Doris, Eggy's old stick, Tim stared at his feet, and Mrs. Lambe dabbed her eyes with the corner of her apron. She had grown fond of the young American, albeit in such a short time.

'Bye Isla, 'bye Bettina!' Amelie shouted above the hubbub. 'You will text when you're back, won't you?'

Isla raised her thumb and climbed into the taxi beside her mother. She rolled down the window just as the taxi pulled away. 'And don't forget to bring the rest of your book...'

'I won't,' promised Amelie, waving them off.

Tim stuck his hands in his jeans and turned away. 'London's only four days away if we don't count Friday.'

Chapter Thirteen

The House of Endless Possibilities

The summer holidays ended abruptly and September ushered in a week of blue skies and sunshine. 'Thank heavens it's Friday!' Tim dumped his school bag on the table. 'No one can work in this heat.' He debated whether to wear jeans or jogging bottoms and still undecided, shoved both into his rucksack. He glanced at his watch and panicked. 'Yeah, we'd better get moving. I'll get changed on the train.'

Amelie was actually ready for once, dressed in her best white tee-shirt and shorts, with a new pair of sunglasses perched on her head. 'I bought these for our trip to Italy. It's a bit like we're going on holiday, isn't it?' She was beginning to feel quite excited and could tell that Tim was too. 'I bet we won't want to come back.'

Tim's school tie still hung loosely about his neck but once on the train he slipped it over his head and stuffed it into his backpack. 'With a bit of luck we'll miss the worst of the rush hour,' he remarked, and proceeded to unzip his grey uniform trousers, not caring who might be watching.

Amelie cringed. She imagined herself stranded at London Bridge while the railway police marched him off, and arrested him for indecent behaviour.

'Pass me my jeans, will you, Amelie? Thanks.' He sat down again and checked his reflection in the window, feeling at least two years older than the schoolboy who had boarded the train a moment ago.

The carriage was relatively quiet that day so they weren't prepared for the busy throng of commuters that greeted them when they stepped onto the platform at London Bridge. Amelie caught hold of Tim's arm but, distracted by the bustle and noise, let go for a moment and was instantly thrown off course. A businessman wielding a rolled umbrella cut across her path and soon, she found herself heading towards an exit. Tim, still battling his way through the crowds, noticed she was no longer attached to his sleeve. He turned and waved with both arms, hoping she might somehow spot him. Then, before he had time to worry too much his phone rang.

'I'm here!' It was Amelie, sounding triumphant. 'I'm at the far end of the concourse, with Isla!'

It was much too warm for the Tube that day, Isla remarked. 'Let's walk and I'll show you some sights on the way.'

The sun hadn't quite dropped behind the office buildings yet and the streets were flooded with light. Late Friday shoppers queued for buses, and office workers ran for their trains, while Amelie and Tim strolled across the bridge behind Isla, feeling like tourists in a foreign land. They all stood still for a moment, gazing into the distance. There, ahead of them, rose the magnificent dome of St. Paul's. It dominated the skyline and it was all they could do not to gasp. Isla saw their faces and nodded. 'I know. It gets me every time.'

Soon, they left the busy streets behind them and turned into a quiet tree-lined square. Each russet-coloured house flaunted bright window boxes and a pair of potted bay trees each side of the door.

'I knew I'd love it here!' Amelie exclaimed. As she walked, her hand trailed a line of black iron railings, tipped with gold. 'It's almost like I've come home at last.'

They arrived at a glossy red door, newly painted with a brass lion's head knocker. Isla paused to find her key. 'We're so lucky to have gotten this apartment. The house is being done up to sell but we're able to rent the top floor for a while. Come in…'

'You'd never think this was the middle of London,' said Tim, gazing back at the empty street. 'It's amazingly quiet.'

'Yes,' said Isla, closing the door behind them. 'It's great having no one living next door. Hey Tim, you take your bags up, will you? Top floor, two rooms at the front. Mom's working late so I'll fix us dinner. Pasta okay for you?'

'Ace.'

'Mom's made us a pumpkin pie for dessert.'

'Pumpkin?' Tim was unimpressed. 'That's a vegetable, isn't it?'

'Soo, you like carrot cake, don't you? You'll love it, I promise.'

'Tim wants more pie but daren't ask.' Amelie grinned, carrying their empty dishes into the kitchen.

'I knew he would,' laughed Isla, cutting another slice. 'More for you too?'

Amelie blew out her cheeks. 'I've eaten far too much already. Anyway, shouldn't we save some for Bettina? What's she up to now, or is it top secret?'

'Not at all,' said Isla, filling the kettle. 'She's in charge of finding accommodation for the Refugee Council. You know, people escaping from war and persecution and so on. She'll be back soon so you can ask her yourself.'

'Refugees? Wow, that's exactly what Eggy was involved in too.'

'How cool is that? Especially since Tabitha was a kind of refugee too.'

Just then, they were interrupted by Tim. 'Hey, Isla!' he called, 'are you sure it's empty next door? I definitely heard some voices just now.'

'Must be from outside then,' said Isla, placing Tim's pie and three coffee mugs onto a tray. 'There's been no one here for years. Let's have our coffee and I'll show you around.'

❀

'It's feels a bit like an abandoned hotel,' Amelie observed, following Isla downstairs. 'I could easily get lost here. What's that door over there?'

Isla turned to look. 'Oh, that… it's where the decorators keep their stuff.'

'Looks like this was once a lift,' said Tim, patting the polished walnut door. 'It's a bit like ours at Hadleigh.' Next to it were two small buttons that looked rather like light switches. He pressed one and waited. 'Nah, dead…' But as he spoke the lift came to life with a lot of loud clanking and whirring until finally the door creaked open.

Amelie peered inside. Sure enough, it was just a little cabin full of old paint tins and rolls of wallpaper. She stepped inside. 'Get in,' she laughed. 'I think there's just enough room for us all. Going up?'

The clanking and whirring started up again and a great jolt threw them all backwards. Finally, it came to a halt and a panel at the back of the cabin slid open. Cautiously, they stepped out onto a plush, carpeted landing.

'We must be next door, I think,' whispered Isla just as the lift door closed behind them. 'I think we'd better go back.' She attempted to wrench it open again. 'Jeez, this won't budge at all and now we're trespassing on private property…'

'Let me have a go,' said Tim, endeavouring to prise it open with his fingers.

Amelie had never seen Isla so worried. Not even when Storm nearly died the year before. 'It's a good job there's no one living here then.'

'Cool,' said Tim, relishing the prospect of exploring an empty old house. 'If we sneak out through the front door no one will ever know.'

'This is a House of Endless Possibilities,' murmured Amelie and Isla gave her a baffled look.

'What do you mean?'

Amelie shrugged. 'No idea, it just popped into my head.'

'Come over here!' called Tim. Beyond the landing lay a vast network of corridors.

There were rooms, large, empty rooms, each with a comfortable lived-in appearance as though its occupants had been suddenly called away. Fires burned in grates, coats lay flung over chair backs, and here and there were further signs of life such as an open book or a letter half-written.

'So where can everyone be?' Isla wondered, her sense of adventure returning. 'It's like being in a dream.'

'Isla!' Amelie sounded relieved and beckoned to them. 'Here's a staircase at last!'

They followed it down and found themselves in a large hallway. Here, the air was steeped with warm spices and roasting food. Further on they came to an enormous dining room where napkins lay discarded and chairs overturned.

'Still no sign of a front door, I'm afraid. Wait here for me while I find a loo.' Amelie disappeared behind a small door. Soon she returned. 'It was one of those old-fashioned ones with a chain to pull. There's plenty of hot water in there though,' she said, drying her hands on her jeans.

An old brass carriage clock struck eight and Isla looked alarmed. 'Eight already! Mom'll be wondering where we are and I've left my cellphone next door. She'll think we're wandering about outside.'

'There's no signal in here anyway,' said Tim and on impulse

took out his transonometer. 'But hey, look at that, I've got a Sat Nav!'

Turn-right-after-ten-metres. Continue-to-the-end-of-the-corridor-and-take-the-stairs-up-to-the-next-level. Past-three-doors-on-your-left-and-turn-left. Up-two-flights-of-stairs-and-carry-on-till-you reach-a-pair-of-double-doors. Straight-on-and-bear-right. Your destination-is-on-your-left.

And before they knew it, they found themselves back at the lift where the door was open again. They had recognised the voice at once. It was their old Earth Watcher friend, Dorin.

Well-done-Bright-Hearts, he continued. *Let's-meet-again-soon!*

They clutched one another other in delight. 'You know what this means…'

'Yes,' said Amelie. 'They're back at last!'

'Why don't we spend tomorrow during regular touristy things?' said Isla once they returned from the far from regular *House of Endless Possibilities*. 'Like visiting the London Eye and taking selfies at Madame Tussaud's. Then we could have lunch at Camden Market. I've heard there's an awesome vegan café there with live music.'

Somehow they managed to do all this and a lot more besides: Tower Bridge and Covent Garden, and even St. Paul's again, which meant that the following morning they slept till gone ten. Bettina woke them with a special Sunday treat: fresh coffee and orange juice and warm croissants from the little French patisserie around the corner.

'Can't you stay for a while?' Amelie said, patting the end of her bed. 'I'd like to hear about your new job.'

'Oh my, Amelie,' Bettina laughed and kissed the top of her head. 'What a sweetie you are. I might have guessed you'd be interested. Yes, perhaps I will.' She smoothed the duvet cover and sat down gladly. 'I could talk to you all day but we can't have you missing your train.'

'Grandpa Storm's aunt devoted her life to refugees,' said Amelie. 'And I'm writing her biography.'

'So Isla's been telling me. I can't wait to read it! She'll have been especially busy during the wars. Unfortunately, the situation is even worse today, what with increasing climate disasters and political conflicts. We've literally millions of displaced people… ' Amelie saw the worried look on her face. 'And now, because of the recent floods in Asia we're expecting another huge influx. I'm really not sure how we'll cope. We're desperately short of accommodation...'

'We could probably take a few at Hadleigh.'

'Not nearly enough though, Amelie, I'm afraid. However…' Bettina had an amused smile on her face. 'Maybe you could have a word with your Friends in High Places?'

'We shall,' replied Amelie, thinking of their encounter next door. 'I'm sure we'll be seeing them soon.'

'Oh, dear…' Bettina glanced anxiously at her watch. 'We'd better get a move on already. Otherwise, there's no train till tomorrow.'

In the end, she decided to call a taxi. 'Isla, honey - go wait outside with Tim and Amelie while I grab my coat. It'll be here any minute.'

'What a perfect house this is,' Amelie breathed, gazing up at the glossy red door. 'It feels like a second home.' She stopped suddenly and tugged at Tim's sleeve. 'No, surely not? It can't possibly be!'

'Can't be what?' asked Tim.

'Number Sixty-One Dorlington Gardens! This was Aunt Adelaide's house.'

❃

Yes, the weekend had passed far too quickly, they all agreed. There hadn't even been time for Eglantyne's story.

‘No, how did we miss out on that?’ Isla said sadly, ‘especially as she actually lived here!’

‘And oddly enough,’ Amelie added, ‘that’s the very next part of the story.’

‘Send it, already!’ Isla shouted, waving as they boarded the train. ‘You’ve got my e-mail address.’

‘Yes, I promise!’

‘Hey, I’ve had an idea,’ said Tim, as the train pulled out of the station. ‘Why not do Isla a recording instead? You can send it on WhatsApp or something.’

Amelie’s face lit up. ‘Would you like one too?’

‘Of course I would!’

‘Wasn’t it great to hear from Dorin at last? I can’t wait to tell Storm. And you were so right about those voices next door. Do you think they were from the past maybe?’

‘Past, future, whoever knows?’ Tim rubbed her shoulder affectionately and they both fell asleep until the carriage jerked and they found themselves drawing in to Havenbridge Junction.

Chapter Fourteen

Sixty One Dorlington Gardens

5th September 1910

Lady Isadora Havenbridge took up her lorgnette and gazed curiously at the young girl beside her. 'You're not, are you?' she asked bluntly, eyeing her up and down.

'Not what, Isadora?' Eggy watched sullenly as open countryside gave way to drab, overcrowded streets. Not trusting his daughter to board the train alone (and far too mean to pay for a cab), Theodore had somehow persuaded the Havenbridges' chauffeur to drive her all the way to London. Isadora had agreed readily since it gave her the perfect excuse for a night at the Savoy.

'Why, *enceinte*[13], as the French would say,' Isadora replied. 'A little bird told me you were expecting… is that why you're being sent away?'

Eggy stared at her in horror. It was as though their wonderful Community Ball had never happened. 'Expecting? Is that the vicar's bloody nonsense?'

Isadora's eyes twinkled.

'Yes, I thought so. Well, you do know,' Eggy added slyly, 'he suspects you're up to no good with Stanley Threpstone.'

Isadora threw back her head and chuckled. 'What a sordid imagination that silly old fool has. Bad enough to hear we've fallen on hard times! Shall I instruct your father to take him to court? Sue him for defamation of character! Oh, bliss, darling girl! Just look, there's Russell Square already…' She clutched Eggy's hand. 'That means we're almost there…'

Deposited at the steps of Number Sixty-One Dorlington Gardens, Eggy lifted the heavy brass lion's head and knocked as boldly as she dared. Footsteps sounded in the hall and a maid appeared and, following behind her, a pale, nervous-looking woman who offered Eggy her hand. 'I'm Adelaide and you must be Eglantyne. Please come through to the drawing room and I'll find someone to take your trunk…'

Eggy stared at her in surprise. She was nothing like she had expected. Nor was the drawing room which was bright and welcoming. Arrangements of lilies and roses adorned every available surface. There were lamps like flower heads, lit even though it was still broad daylight; family photographs sat on polished mahogany tables with china bowls that looked like they might ring out like bells when tapped. Everything in this lovely room was totally at odds with Aunt Adelaide who wore a permanently anguished expression. It seemed to Eggy that every scrap of joy the woman had once known had emptied itself into this beautiful room. But, despite Adelaide's rather dull appearance, her voice was light. She spoke with a pleasant American accent that lingered even after twenty years in England. 'I'm afraid your uncle is away on business till next week, so there will only be you and me here for now.'

She led Eggy upstairs to inspect her bedroom. 'You don't like it, do you?' A long silence followed as Adelaide clasped and unclasped her hands. 'I guess after Hadleigh this must all seem a bit of a dump…'

'Like it?' Eggy exclaimed. 'Crikey!'

A look of relief transformed Adelaide's mournful face. 'You'll find it very quiet here since there's no one living next door. But wait…' She swept out of the room. 'Let me show you our schoolroom. Perhaps before we begin our classes, you may like a few days to settle in, maybe take some walks in Hyde Park. As you'll find, there's so much here to see…'

And there was, and it was all becoming rather confusing. London wasn't quite so bad after all. And nor was Aunt Adelaide who turned out to be neither old nor hideous and, to top it all, was a passionate supporter of women's rights. Eggy gazed at her while she wasn't looking. She was even rather beautiful in her own unusual way.

It seemed that nothing Eggy did could anger them; not even when Uncle Edgar returned and noticed her wearing Jack's old corduroy trousers, designed to turn them against her. What on earth was the matter with them both?

'Adelaide,' he declared, glancing up from his morning paper. 'Who pray is this delightful fellow?'

'Oh my, Eglantyne!' laughed Adelaide, joining him at the table. 'What a charming outfit you're wearing today! Come and sit here…' She patted a chair next to Uncle Edgar. 'I've saved you some scrambled eggs and there's fresh coffee in the pot. How do you fancy a visit to Parliament Square? I've heard whispers of a suffragette gathering today.'

A huge crowd had assembled in the Square, women waving Votes for Women banners and wearing their now familiar purple, white and green scarves.

'I'm sure that's Emmeline Pankhurst over there,' gasped an awe-struck Eggy. 'Gosh, I never thought I'd see her in the flesh.'

'Yes, she was jailed three times last year. Not that it's deterred her in the least.'

They were totally fearless, Eggy observed, watching as a slight young woman was wrestled to the ground and carried off by two hefty officers.

'Brave ladies indeed,' agreed Adelaide. 'I can understand how angry you modern girls must be, deprived of things our menfolk take for granted - like having the right to vote…'

'And having a say in creating our laws - it's outrageous!' Eggy declared, liking the word.

'Unconscionable!' Adelaide agreed and Eggy liked that one even more.

'I'm surprised to see so many men here, all the same,' she remarked.

Adelaide looked at her and smiled. 'Your Uncle Eddie would have come too had he not been called into the office.'

'People are always telling me not to bother with things I can't change.'

'People?' Adelaide raised an eyebrow.

Eggy frowned. She couldn't tell Adelaide that people meant Loula. It felt disloyal somehow and she didn't want anyone thinking badly of her. It was just that Loula couldn't understand. 'Is it true that men get paid twice as much as women?' she said instead.

'Far more in many cases,' said Adelaide. 'I met a young woman from Cheapside recently who told me she'd left school at twelve. Careful, my dear! Watch out for that horse and cart.' She took Eggy's arm and guided her across the busy street. 'Yes, twelve, can you believe that? A mere child yet forced to work in a boot-lace factory, poor lamb - and for just tuppence an hour in wages. Me next job was even worse, the girl told me: Packin' fags… (Adelaide had a perfect Cockney accent.) We gels never 'ad no time off for our dinners, an' those who did 'ad to eat 'em in the bloody lav…Nah, not like the bloomin' men o' course...'

Eggy laughed even though it was so awful. 'It's pretty rubbish being a woman,' she admitted, and found herself disliking Adelaide a little less with each day.

'Do you mean you'd rather be a boy?'

'Well, only because I'm more comfortable in boys' clothes...' Eggy glanced down at Jack's old trousers. 'But Loula has other ideas...'

'Like what?'

'She says: think of all those poor men who lose their lives down the mine, or in pointless wars, dying for King and Country...'

'Well, she's right,' said Adelaide, 'except it's never the women who start wars.'

'No, but women have other battles to fight; like having babies. My mother died having her third. No, you won't catch me doing that.'

Eggy, too caught up in her own story, didn't notice the look of distress on Adelaide's face.

The next day, Edgar summoned her into his study. He drew a chair a little closer to his and beckoned her to be seated. 'It seems you know how to work miracles, young lady.' With that he took a gold sovereign from his waistcoat pocket and handed it to her. 'So, this is for you. I hear you're making exceptional progress. Yes,' he nodded, 'keep this up and I'll write to your father at the end of the month. I imagine it's a bit dull for you here after being at school with other girls. We thought you might like to invite a friend to stay...'

❀

Dear Jack, Eggy wrote later.
I'm so excited – Uncle Edgar tells me I can have a friend to stay! I expect he means a girl but I don't think he'll mind. I got full marks for my first essay. It was on Women's Rights, following our visit to Parliament Square. Aunt Adelaide wrote: 'Eglantyne already shews[14] great talent as a writer.' She's not half

as bad as I thought and it's certainly better than sewing hankies. The worst thing though is not sleeping. Like now; it's two in the morning and they're off again, the bloody voices next door. Yet the house is meant to be empty. Tomorrow's Saturday so after morning lessons I'll have a good look round and see what's going on...

❀

And there it was; the old servants' lift which, according to Adelaide, had been out of commission for years. Dreadful story, she explained. One of the maids had fallen down the shaft some years ago and was killed outright.

The lift had highly polished walnut doors and two small buttons to operate it. *Up* and *Down*. Maybe she could get it to work again.

Uncle Edgar was still busy in his office while Adelaide was taking her afternoon nap. She glanced warily over her shoulder and pressed the *Up* button. She waited a while and tried a few more times but since nothing happened she pushed the *Down* button instead. Almost at once the doors swung open and revealed a little wrought iron cage, just big enough for her to step into. And then something really dreadful happened. The lights went out and the cage began to shake. Remembering the po or maid, a wave of terror overcame her. It was then she did the only thing she could think of. The *Mark of Triandor*! She rolled up her sleeve and was about to place her finger on it when quite suddenly, the lift came to a halt. A panel opened before her and she stepped out onto a spacious carpeted landing.

'Why, Miss Trott, you've found me at last!'

Eggy swung round to see Tabitha waiting with a huge grin on her face. 'You?'

Tabitha bowed elaborately. 'Welcome to the House of Endless Possibilities. There is someone here I want you to meet. This is Zolos…'

A man was lurking behind her, his hat pulled right down to shield his face. Tabitha nudged him and he raised it a little. There, right in the centre of his forehead, was a single eye. Eggy did her best not to stare.

'Zolos is an esteemed Cosmic Guide from Planet Trankon. When you're as wise as he is, you'll develop the All-Seeing Eye too.'

Zolos raised his hand in salute and Eggy, remembering her manners, raised hers in return. 'I've been hearing voices for nights,' she said.

'Follow!' Tabitha beckoned. 'You'll soon understand why…' She and Zolos led her swiftly past a kitchen with signs of recent activity - a loaf sliced and buttered, a pan of vegetables, and bottles of wine, uncorked. Further along, there were unmade beds, as though abandoned in a hurry; a desk where a letter lay unfinished, its ink barely dry.

'What you heard were voices from the future,' Zolos explained. 'Past, present, and future: it's all the same in the end.'

Eggy looked at him, askance. 'But that's impossible.'

'Only to a Lugan,' Tabitha replied. 'You all live by clocks.'

'I don't,' said Eggy, 'which is why I'm usually late.'

A clock struck next door at Number Sixty-One.

'How very *timely…*' Tabitha commented wryly. 'It seems you'd better go back. And, remember, you're to tell no one about our meeting for now.'

'Not even Jack?'

'Tell Jack, of course. After all, you two work as one.'

Hearing this, a sudden bolt of energy hit Eggy and she smiled. She would write to him at once. 'Tell me though, who does this house actually belong to?

'To all who need it,' said Tabitha, guiding her back to the lift.

'It was created for all who seek refuge. And since I was once a refugee myself, it's a place very close to my heart.'

'We were about to call you, my dear,' said Uncle Edgar when she arrived half an hour late for dinner. 'Your aunt went up to your room and found you soundly asleep. She didn't like to disturb you.'

Chapter Fifteen

Two Gold Sovereigns

It was late September and a cold wind blew in from the east. One night it tore the roof off the Hollands' barn and Nellie's cousin Frank had to be summoned. 'If you can spare us a couple of days you'd be company for our Jack too.' Nellie breathed a long sigh of relief when he agreed.

'What's up with your lad then, Nell?' said Frank once the roof was safely restored. 'Miserable as sin. If you ask me he needs a day or two off.'

'Like a lost soul since she went off to live in London,' Nellie said ruefully.

'That posh lass what dresses like a boy?'

Nellie nodded. 'Eggs he calls her. Like one of the family she was. I miss her too.'

'Well, there's a train from Havenbridge Junction, you know. I've got a mate who works on the Southern Belle. Twelve shillings a ticket…'

'Blimey, Frank, who can afford prices like that?'

'Don't you worry.' Frank winked. 'Stan owes me a favour or two. He'll stow him away somewhere, I'm sure.'

'Wouldn't mind going myself in that case,' Nellie laughed. 'I suppose he could always wear Fred's old suit. A bit short in the leg, mind.'

Two days later, Frank slipped a gold sovereign into Jack's pocket. 'There you are, my lad. I've been saving this for years. I think you've earned it.'

Jack gazed at it in wonder, remembering his recent bet with Eggy. 'Why, thanks a lot, Frank. I've never seen one of these before. Never been up to London either.'

'Mind those pickpockets though,' warned Frank, patting Jack's shoulder. 'You keep that money safe.'

And so it came to pass that Jack stepped off the luxurious Southern Belle one morning, carrying a bunch of weary roses and a small leather case filled with sandwiches and a bottle of ginger beer. Grimly clutching his Stone of Power (to ward off thieves), he set off in search of Dorlington Gardens. He crossed London, stopping every few minutes to ask the way, discarded the drooping roses and bought fresh ones from a flower girl in Russell Square. Finally, he turned a corner and climbed the steps to Number Sixty-One Dorlington Gardens. Here he stood, tugging nervously at his borrowed suit trousers to gain extra length, and lifted the heavy brass lion's head and waited.

As it happened, he had arrived just in time for a foreign trade luncheon Edgar and Adelaide were hosting.

'Marvellous, Eglantyne!' cried Edgar. 'Your young friend has arrived.' Meanwhile, he took Adelaide quietly aside. 'Though not quite the one we'd expected!'

'Not a word to that brother of yours, darling,' whispered Adelaide. 'Jack is her only friend, apart from the housekeeper.'

Edgar nodded and marched Jack off to find him another suit, one of his own, and a crisp white shirt to match: 'These should fit you a little better, Sir! I think we're about the same height.'

'What a handsome pair you two make!' Adelaide exclaimed when Jack returned, transformed. Eggy felt a wave of pride pass over her.

'We must have a portrait of you both,' Adelaide continued. 'Eddie, call the photographer over once he's finished taking snaps of Gyatso…'

Gyatso was just one of many fascinating visitors they met that day. His father had been a painter of mandalas at one of Tibet's most ancient monasteries.

'Greetings, please accept *thangkas*[15]…' Gyatso bowed and offered Adelaide two colourful silk paintings of Buddhist deities.

He told them of his early life in the Himalayas and the Holy Ones who lived high up in the mountains. So high, he explained, that they were virtually inaccessible. 'Some risk the climb though and take food in return for their prayers and healing.' Gyatso turned to address Eggy and Jack. 'One day I return,' he said, 'and then you will visit me, yes?'

'Oh, yes,' cried Eggy at once. 'We'll come, won't we, Jack?' But Jack had disappeared, called away suddenly by his new friend Edgar.

'Just look at that boy,' remarked Adelaide. 'He's very self-assured, isn't he?'

'Not usually,' said Eggy. 'To be honest, I'm quite amazed.'

'Nice young fellow.'

Eggy nodded. 'He's like a brother to me.'

Adelaide smiled. 'Well, you'd better make the most of your time together before he rushes off for his train. And I'll have a quiet word with Gyatso. I have something to ask him.'

'Do you remember when I told you I couldn't sleep?' Eggy whispered later. She took Jack's hand and led him up a flight of stairs. 'Up here is the old servants' lift, with the secret entrance to next door.'

'Is that where you saw Tabitha and the one-eyed man?'

'Yes, I'll take you next time. There will be another time, won't there?'

'Yes, if they invite me.'

'Don't be ridiculous, of course they will. Look how well you get on with Uncle Edgar.' She glanced up at him anxiously. 'Jack, he keeps saying there's going to be a war. Apparently there's a huge stockpiling of arms going on so it's only a matter of time.'

Jack frowned. 'Yes, he told me that too. It's like Tabitha said. You haven't told them anything about her, have you?'

'Heavens, no, she's our secret!'

Our secret! Jack smothered a grin. 'Talking of secrets, what would your old man say if he knew I was here?'

'Actually, I don't care a hoot anymore.'

'You quite like it here, don't you? I don't blame you if you do, Eggs.'

'Well, it's certainly better than I'd thought,' she admitted. 'Though I'd still rather be home.'

There were only two trains a day to Havenbridge and the last one departed at six.

'You'd better go,' Eggy sighed as the clock struck five. 'I'll come with you.'

Just as they reached the end of Dorlington Gardens, Eggy remembered she had left something behind. 'You carry on,' she shouted and rushed back to fetch it.

She quickly caught up with him again and they both paused to catch their breath.

'Sit on this if you want.' Jack placed his battered little case on the pavement and, glad of the rest, Eggy squatted, hugging her knees.

'How's Walter?' she asked and Jack told her how he was now reading every spare moment.

'And riding Starlight like he was born to it,' he added. 'We've given him a permanent job on the farm now.' In fact, he'd become one of the family. And the best news was he was still free of bruises. He knew Eggy would love to hear that.

'Oh, Jack, you're the best!' Eggy cried and wrapped her arms around him.

Jack's face reddened a little. 'His old man's a reformed character now - teetotal and working full-time. It's all since that party of yours, you know.'

'Ours, you mean.' Eggy's face glowed. 'You kiss Starlight's forehead like I do, don't you?'

'Like this?' Jack said boldly and stooped to place a kiss on her brow. As he did, Eggy slipped Uncle Edgar's golden sovereign into his pocket, happy that she'd remembered it in time.

'Does she miss me a bit?' she asked, still feeling the kiss wet on her brow. 'I wish I could come back with you.'

Jack nodded. 'Of course she does; even though she's got Walter fussing over her now.' He searched his pocket for his train ticket and found the golden sovereign instead. He puzzled a while, knowing he'd already spent some of it on the flowers earlier that day. He rattled his pocket. Yes, he'd even got the small change to prove it.

'It'll not be too long now till Christmas,' said Eggy. 'Give my love to Nellie and Loula and Walter, and anyone else you can think of.'

'Bottomley and Sligh?'

She began to giggle. 'Eew, can you imagine that pair, you know, *together*?'

'I'd rather not, thank you.' Jack shuddered. 'Think of all the hideous brats they'd produce!'

Eggy heaved herself up and smoothed her skirt. 'I'm not having any, that's for sure.' She hesitated. 'Are you?'

'Brats?' Jack picked up his case. 'Well, not quite yet.'

Eggy rolled up her sleeve and glanced at him earnestly. 'You do know I never want an ordinary life, don't you?'

The *Mark of Triandor!* Jack nodded and stroked her arm. How could life ever be ordinary again? He paused a moment, not knowing quite what to do next and since Eggy stayed exactly where she was he just patted her hand and murmured: 'Goodbye then, Eggs,' and hurried away.

Eggy hurried away too, fighting her instinct to turn and wave. After a moment or two it all got a bit much and she peered over her shoulder, stuck two fingers in her mouth and whistled. But Jack was already out of sight, weaving his way through a crowd of noisy shoppers and sight-seers to board the Southern Belle.

Chapter Sixteen

Aunt Adelaide's Absolutely Brilliant Idea

'Now here's a place I've always longed to visit.' Adelaide exclaimed, looking up from her book. 'Will you just listen to this, Eglantyne!'

Eggy leaned back and closed her eyes, lulled into silence by the music of unfamiliar words. It was all in German!

Adelaide glanced up and saw pleasure on the young girl's face. She had seemed rather flat since Jack returned. 'Shall I read that again but in English?' She composed herself and began to recite again. *'So, there it was - Limone, with its neat little gardens full of citron-trees, and rows of white pillars to protect them in winter. What a marvellous view we had as we cruised past Malcesine...'* Adelaide paused to pass Eggy the book. 'See, that's Malcesine - that's where my old school friend Anna Martinelli lives. Limone's only a short boat trip across the lake. Maybe we'll go one day.'

'Right, so who's *Go-ethe*?' Eggy enquired, attempting to read the author's name..

'It's pronounced *Gerter*, my dear. He was a world famous poet. I'll teach you some German, if you like.'

'Gosh!' Eggy stared at her in surprise. 'When I think how much I hated school...'

That night, the voices next door were even louder, loud enough for Eggy to know they were speaking a strange language she didn't recognise. Moonlight slanted through a gap in the curtains and she peered at the clock by her bedside. Past midnight; was she really the only one still awake? She sat up and reached for her diary.

I miss Havenbridge very much and wonder if Aunt Adelaide would agree to a trip home on the Southern Belle...

On the floor below, Adelaide was restless too. She touched Edgar's arm to see if he was awake. 'What if I took Eglantyne away?' she whispered. 'Europe, somewhere to broaden her mind…'

Edgar, a light-sleeper, agreed at once. 'What an absolutely brilliant idea. A Grand Tour will do you both good.'

'That's settled then. I'll tell her tomorrow.' Adelaide snuggled up to his back and yawned. 'By the way, do you know I love you, Eddie Trott?'

❀

'A tour of Europe, Eglantyne, what do you think? And then we'll go to New York in 1912. A cruise on the new Titanic, won't that be jolly?'

'Like a Grand Tour?' Eggy silently pinched her arm. 'Honestly? You really mean it?'

Adelaide nodded eagerly. 'It's how I met your uncle; on a train from Paris to Calais.'

'You met on a train? How romantic…'

'Yes, it was rather.' Adelaide smiled wistfully. 'It seems so long ago now. Eddie's very keen we should go. I'll show you some of Europe's most exciting cities: Paris, Vienna, Rome and Florence. You'll learn more in those few months than a whole year spent here at your desk.' Adelaide's pale face was now flushed with excitement. 'And then as a special treat we'll visit my old friend Anna on Lake Garda.' She stopped suddenly and picked up her pen. 'But I'm getting rather ahead of myself! Firstly, we need your father's permission. We'll take the Southern Belle at the end of the week.'

Eggy was unable to contain her delight. 'Loula will take one look at you and curtsey, just like you're the Duchess of York.'

'Our new Queen Mary, you mean? Goodness, Eglantyne, no one's ever mistaken me for royalty before.'

'There's just one thing though,' Eggy added. 'Would you mind very much not calling me Eglantyne?'

'On one condition then, Eggy,' her aunt replied. 'From now on you're to drop the formalities too. Just call us Adelaide and Eddie. We're friends, after all.'

Chapter Seventeen

Elsie Thomas

It was Loula who spotted them first. She took off her pinafore, tucked a stray lock of hair into a comb at the back of her head, and scurried down the steps to greet them.

'This is my friend Adelaide,' Eggy said proudly. 'She's very beautiful, isn't she?'

'Oh, my word, yes,' cried Loula. She attempted a little curtsey then flung her arms around Eggy's neck. 'How I've missed you, you rascal!' she laughed and ushered them into the dingy hallway. Here, she paused to ring a tiny bell on the hall table. Footsteps approached and an unfamiliar figure appeared; a girl of around Eggy's age, dressed in a maid's uniform. 'Thank you, Elsie. Fetch a tray of tea, will you, and then show Mrs. Trott and Miss Eglantyne to the Master's study, please.'

Eggy stared after the unknown girl. She was strikingly pretty with bright eyes and a cluster of ringlets springing from her white maid's cap. 'Who's that?'

'Elsie Thomas? She's been helping out since poor Millie Pickles left. Terrified of Ivy, Millie was. Not Elsie though,' Loula chuckled. 'Empty-headed but gives as good as she gets.'

Eggy wrinkled her nose in disgust. 'How is it that Bumley's still allowed to work here?' She turned to Adelaide. 'Shall I leave Father to you? He'll agree to our trip, as long as he doesn't have to pay.'

'Absolutely not,' Adelaide said firmly. 'You're coming with me.' And seeing she meant it, Eggy sighed and followed the alarmingly pretty Elsie into her father's study.

'Enter!' Theodore rose to greet them, kissed the air close to Adelaide's cheek and awkwardly patted his daughter's head. 'Still working hard then, Eglantyne? Good, good, how's the Latin and Greek?' He paused to stir his tea. 'No, I suppose girls don't…'

'All bright girls do Classics, Theo. And Eggy is no exception. In fact, Eddie and I would like to broaden her experience. We thought we'd organise a tour of Europe early next year.'

Theodore's eyes widened, imagining the appalling cost of such an extravagance.

'I've wanted this trip for years,' Adelaide explained, 'and Eglantyne will make a perfect travelling companion. Think of it more as a finishing school. She'll be adept in French, German and Italian by the time I bring her back…'

'There, that wasn't so bad,' said Adelaide, covering a yawn with her hand. 'Do you think Theo would mind if I took a little nap this afternoon? I'm rather tired after our journey.'

'He'll be relieved, Father loathes having visitors. Anyway, I shall be up at Cloud Farm.'

'In that case, I'll see you a little later.' Adelaide kissed her cheek. 'Oh, my, it looks like you have a visitor already!'

Eggy followed her gaze. There was Jack hurrying down the path, carrying a huge bunch of Michaelmas daisies, wrapped in old newspaper and tied with string. Taller somehow and broader, he walked with a new-found confidence. She scrambled to her feet, rushed outside, and placed two fingers between her lips. Just as she was about to whistle a girl flew up the scullery steps and ran along the path to greet him, linking his arm like she'd known him for years. It was Elsie Thomas.

She stared wildly for a moment and noticed little Emmeline, the stray cat, watching her inquiringly. 'What?' Eggy asked her mutinously as though she was responsible. 'Stop looking at me like that!' She picked up the cat and ran with her into the drab hallway and out through the front door, not stopping until she reached the Summer House.

It was warm and humid inside and smelled of mildewed books. Still clutching Emmeline, she flung herself down into a lumpy old armchair. 'It's all Bumley's fault,' she sobbed. 'If she hadn't terrorised poor Millie Pickles, that stupid girl wouldn't be here and everything would be exactly as it always was…' She stopped, hearing a noise outside, snatched up a random book and placed it on her lap.

'Eggs, is that you in there?' The door swung open. 'Ah, at last - I've been looking for you everywhere. I thought I'd surprise you.'

'Oh, you did that all right,' Eggy muttered without looking up. 'I saw you were busy.'

He stared at her, bewildered. The book she was reading, *Halsbury's Laws of England*, was the wrong way up. 'Aren't you coming for a ride?'

They wandered mutely through the garden, stopping occasionally to forage for late blackberries, and again by a little stone statue; a young girl holding a shell that served as a bird bath. Eggy dipped her fruit-stained fingers in the water, turning it faintly purple, and dried them on her skirt.

'I've never known you this quiet,' said a troubled Jack. He jumped over the fence into the fields. 'Aren't you glad to be back?'

Eggy murmured something inaudible and clambered over the fence to join him, hampered by her long skirt.

Jack frowned. 'Aren't we friends anymore?'

Eggy shrugged. 'I don't know.'

Arrow, sensing something amiss, snorted loudly.

'I see, Miss Trott.' Jack stared at her angrily. 'Not high-class enough for you, all of a sudden? You really are a stuck-up piece of…'

Eggy stared at him, horrified. 'Don't be so bloody stupid. It's not that at all.'

They rode across the fields and stopped close to the cliffs before taking the steep track down to the sea.

'Is it her?' Jack asked, glancing over his shoulder.

Eggy turned to see who was there.

'Elsie. She doesn't mean any harm, you know. She's just a bit…'

Eggy sniffed. '*Dim*, you mean?' It came out as more of a squeak which made her sound ridiculous, she knew. 'Dim but pretty, I suppose.'

'So what? Lots of girls are. Pretty, I mean, but none of them…' He hesitated, angry with himself. Say it, you idiot! Why the hell can't you just say it?

'I'm being a bit stupid, aren't I?' she murmured and Jack reached for her hand.

'You are rather,' he agreed and gave it a little squeeze. 'I've left some flowers for you with Loula. Race you to the end of the bay?'

❋

'It's about me and Jack,' Eggy said wretchedly, lowering her gaze so Loula wouldn't see how much she'd been crying. 'We had some words after I spotted him with *her*. Honestly, I've never seen him so angry. He even called me stuck up…'

'Her? Elsie Thomas?' Loula put down her knitting and frowned. 'Sounds like you owe him a proper apology.'

'Do you really think so?'

'I do. All that fuss over some daft young girl.'

'But she was all over him,' Eggy muttered. 'And I hated the way she kept touching his arm.'

'Means nothing,' Loula said dismissively. 'She'll flirt with anything in trousers, that one.'

'And to top it all, I ran into Ivy Bottomley just now. She had a horrible smirk on her face and said: *He's got a wandering eye*, you know.' Eggy pursed her lips. 'And she didn't mean a medical condition.'

'Your Jack?' said Loula, counting stitches. 'What nonsense she talks.'

'She hinted he won't have time for me anymore. Lou, the thought of never seeing him again…'

'He's got no time for himself, that poor lad, what with him teaching Walter and managing the farm. You'll see, I'm right,' she added, patting Eggy's hand. 'Just like I was right about London…'

Eggy smiled weakly. 'You know when he came to visit me?'

'In London?' Loula stopped knitting and peered at her inquisitively. 'He's never stopped talking about it, according to Nellie.'

'Well…' Eggy lowered her gaze again. 'Just as we were saying goodbye…'

'Go on.'

'It was awful. I couldn't bear him to leave…'

'Means you're growing up, my dear.'

'But I don't like it. I wanted everything to stay as it was.'

'Life never stays the same, my love. Having said that… I can't see anything pulling you pair apart.'

'That's pretty much what Tabitha said…' And, realising what she'd just said, Eggy gasped and covered her mouth.

Unawares, Loula swirled the remains of her tea and tipped

them into her saucer. 'Just look at this, my love.'

Eggy stared blankly at the mound of leaves before her.

'It's a bouquet of flowers,' Loula pronounced, 'and did you notice what he brought you today?' She pointed to the sink where she had steeped the daisies in water. 'And this here is an Oak tree,' she continued, 'which means you'll have a very long life.'

'I'd far rather have an extraordinary one.'

'Oh, you'll have that,' Loula laughed. 'Think of this trip you're having!'

Eggy rested her head on Loula's shoulder. 'I'd like a nice life for you too, Lou.'

Loula tilted her head and smiled. 'Believe me, I'm happy enough, my dear. And so will you if you to decide to be.' She lifted a finger and drew a heart around the tea leaves. 'No one can hold a candle to you, my girl, not even pretty, dim-witted Elsie.'

At this they hugged each other and laughed. 'Oh, and by the way…' Loula's smile faded. 'Did you happen to take that little photograph with you, the one of you in the silver frame? I noticed it's gone…'

Eggy shrugged. 'Why would I want a photograph of myself?'

The missing photograph played on Loula's mind for some days.

'It'll be that Ivy Bottomley again,' said Nellie, busying herself with a pile of ironing. 'Here, Jack, pass me another shirt, will you? Yes, she'll be after the silver, no doubt. Like a blooming jackdaw, that one.'

Jack felt his cheeks about to burst into flames and Nellie pretended not to notice, just as she'd pretended when she found it in his pocket one day.

Loula shook her head. 'What worries me is that people like her can do things just by looking at photographs; evil things, like prayers with bad intentions.'

'I don't believe all that silly nonsense,' Nellie said sensibly, 'and nor should you.' She glanced at Jack with an *Are-you-going-to-tell-her-or-shall-I* look in her eye and quickly turned the conversation to the latest film on at the Picture House.

Chapter Eighteen

The Blue Dress

'Poppy red,' said Isla, weaving Amelie's hair into a shiny neat braid. 'What a gorgeous color your hair is.' They sat together near the stream, making the most of the late September sunshine, and watching while Storm pottered in his hangar. 'By the way, those chapters you sent me…'

'Were they okay?' Amelie asked warily.

'I fell asleep listening to them every night.'

'Oh...' Amelie frowned. 'Was it really that boring?'

'Noo!' laughed Isla. 'Are you crazy? It's such an, I don't know, intriguing story -especially the Eggy and Jack, what's the word? Yes, *enigma*, I think. It's kinda *will-they-won't-they?* And hey, old Aunt Adelaide wasn't so old after all!'

'I'd like to know more about the house next door,' said Tim.

'We shall do soon,' promised Amelie. 'It's just that I don't understand…' She looked at them awkwardly. 'You know, Eggy and Jack and all the romantic stuff…'

Storm locked the hangar doors and came over to join them. 'Should soon be ready for our first solar-power flight,' he said brightly. 'Did someone mention Eggy and Jack?'

Amelie frowned. 'I thought they were just friends.'

'Ah, well, they were. But as they grew up things began to change between them. You'll understand when you meet some nice young chap yourself.'

Amelie looked alarmed. 'I hope not. Love stories are always sad.'

'Or cringe,' murmured Tim.

'They don't have to be sad,' said Isla. 'Or cringe even,' she laughed. 'My mom and dad are divorced but they still manage to be nice to each other. I guess relationships take a lot of understanding and hard work…'

Tim decided they were going to be late for lunch and set off back to the house, glad to avoid what might otherwise become a pretty intense conversation.

'All the same,' Amelie continued, 'I'd seriously love Mum to find someone new.'

'She so deserves to,' agreed Isla, lifting Amelie's new braid. 'There, don't move yet. Let me just fix this ribbon around it.' She moved back to admire her work. 'Yay, you look even more like Eggy now!'

They followed Tim back to the house, Amelie still musing over the tension that had arisen between Eggy and Jack.

'Maybe it was because Eggy's father was so absent,' Isla suggested. 'You know, it made her a bit insecure…'

Amelie smiled. 'You read my mind again.' She stopped at the little stone statue where the birds flocked to drink. 'I'd no idea this statue was so old,' she said, stroking the girl's head. 'Look there's a few blackberries left. Shall we go foraging later and ask Libby to make us a pie?'

Later, they came across Amelie's publisher, Lawrence Goodman, in the garden. He was chatting with Storm about the best time to plant tulip bulbs.

'Next month, you say? Right, I'd better buy some in,' said Lawrence. Then, seeing Amelie approach, his face lit up. 'I hear your new book's coming along splendidly,' he said cheerfully. 'Does this mean all your dreams have come true at last?'

'Not quite, to be honest,' Amelie replied. 'Firstly, I'd like to see *The Earth Watchers* as a film - for people who are too lazy to read books.'

Storm pulled up a large dandelion root and grunted. 'Hmm, it's the end of civilisation once we stop reading books.'

'Well, old chap, you'll be happy to know that people haven't yet stopped reading,' said Lawrence with a grin. 'Thanks to you, Amelie's first book, *Adventures of Wild Billy Storm*, is currently number ten in Publishers Weekly. We've also sold translation rights for The *Earth Watchers* in eight languages so far. So, Amelie…' He stroked his beard thoughtfully. 'Tell me about your other dream then. You said *firstly* so I'm assuming there's a secondly too.'

Amelie blushed, wondering how to raise the subject of her mother whose recent behaviour around Lawrence had become impossible to ignore; like dousing herself with perfume every time he came to visit. She glanced warily at Storm who was still pulling up weeds, unsure what he might be making of it all. There was very little Storm missed. 'I'm worried about Mum…,' she said.

'Worried about Lucy?' Storm looked up, startled. 'Good Lord, she's having the time of her life; meeting all those famous people, her talents finally being recognised.' He gave Lawrence an 'all-thanks-to-you-young-man' nod.

'I keep thinking about all she went through when Tim and I were young.'

Lawrence nodded gravely. 'Losing her husband and both of her in-laws at the same time? Yes, it must have been dreadful, for you too, Storm.'

'Indeed,' said Storm. 'Can't say I've ever got over it really; my darling son Ted and his wife, Joan. I adored them…' A tear threatened to spill onto his cheek. '…Not forgetting my fine grandson, Michael, the children's father. All gone in a flash and no chance to say goodbye…'

'Last year, I promised to buy Mum these,' Amelie added to lighten the mood. She picked up her backpack and pulled out a pair of long velvet gloves. 'Do you think she'll like them? Isla and I chose them.'

'My goodness!' exclaimed Storm. 'I'm certain she will.'

Lawrence agreed at once. 'She'll look a million dollars in those, not that she doesn't always, of course.'

Storm harrumphed and squinted at him over his spectacles and Amelie suppressed a giggle. Things couldn't be going better. 'The problem is,' she said, 'Mum never goes anywhere to wear them.'

'I'd no idea,' said Lawrence, 'but as luck would have it, I was considering inviting her to dinner. It's a Gala Ball at the Dorchester next Saturday. Annual publishing do and I'd find it horribly dull on my own. Do you think she might want to come?'

Amelie rushed forward and almost sent Lawrence flying, just as she had when he'd offered her a publishing contract at their Grand Ballroom Sale the previous year. 'Lawrence, she'd love to!' She turned to Isla who was looking delighted too. 'We'll take her to that posh boutique in Littlehaven, won't we Isla?'

'I can't wait!' Isla cried. 'You're such a dude, Lawrence.'

Lawrence smiled, amused by their enthusiasm. 'I'm glad that gets your approval.'

'You will look after her, Lawrence, won't you?' Amelie whispered when no one was listening.

He looked at her fondly. 'Sweet girl, of course I shall.'

'So, what did you say then? What did you say?' sang Amelie, bouncing up and down on her mother's bed.

‘I said yes, of course! But now I’m looking for something half-decent to wear. I was wondering about this…’ She took a dress from the wardrobe and laid it on the bed. ‘I bought it in a charity shop in Littlehaven, years ago, when I first met your dad. It’ll look perfect with your burgundy gloves, don’t you think?’

‘Mm.’ Amelie hesitated ‘It’s lovely...’

‘But?’ Lucy asked.

‘Isn’t it a bit old?’

‘But that’s part of its charm,’ said Lucy. ‘And I really feel I should wear it again.’

‘Right, then you must.’ Amelie stroked the old dress and tried to sound casual. ‘He’s nice, isn’t he?’

‘Lawrence?’ asked Lucy, careful to do the same. ‘You know, he reminds me rather of your dad. It’s his voice, I think.’

‘Well, Dad will definitely approve,’ said Amelie, bouncing on the bed again. ‘I just wish he could tell you so himself…’

Lucy gulped back a tear and gazed at her admiringly. ‘What have you done to your hair, darling? You look so grown-up.’

‘Isla did it for me. She says it makes me look like Aunt Eggy.’

‘It does rather.’ Lucy turned and stared at her reflection in the mirror. ‘So, what shall I do with mine?’ She swept her hair into a coil. ‘Up or down?’

‘Up. No, down. Oh, I don’t know…!’

Amelie had never seen her mother so excited. Not even last year when they stopped the End of the World and Lawrence’s hand rested on Lucy’s for a moment too long. And that’s when Amelie knew, absolutely *knew*! Some things were written in the stars.

It turned out to have quite a history, Lucy’s old blue dress. Storm recognised it at once as he stood watching her scrubbing at a red wine stain on the hem. Seeing it there, he felt tears sting his eyes.

His darling wife had worn it herself many moons ago but, never being one to harbour clutter, had cast it out on a whim to make more room in her wardrobe. 'It's only gathering moths,' she'd said. How it had maddened him.

'How could you, Louisa!' he'd berated her. 'That was Eglantyne's special frock, and her mother's before that. It's been in the family for years…'

It had been hard to forgive her at the time but now, at last, he could do so. It had returned home and all thanks to clever Lucy who had rescued it. A small miracle, he realised, and silently thanked her for putting his tormented heart at rest.

'Isla, I don't know why I'm so nervous,' Amelie confided. It was Saturday and they sat together, waiting for Lawrence to arrive. 'Or why Storm is so grouchy. He's been muttering to himself all day.'

'Why not ask him?' said Isla. 'He's out the front right now with Tim, chatting to Libby. Tim's telling her how to make pumpkin pie. He's found a recipe on his phone.'

'Come with me then, will you?'

They both ran out to greet him.

'Storm, what is it?' Amelie asked, without wasting time. 'You don't seem too happy. Is it Mum's dress, reminding you of Louisa?'

Storm shifted uncomfortably. 'No, my dear, it's not that.' He fumbled for the right words and finally said: 'It's just that I feel a little protective. I don't ever want to see Lucy hurt.'

'Hurt?' Amelie said, aghast. 'He wouldn't hurt a fly, would he, Tim?'

'Who, Lawrence?' asked Tim. 'Nah, no chance…'

'No.' Storm leaned on his old walking stick, the one he called Doris. Eggy had left it to him in her will. 'Lawrence is a very good man, like his name. What I fear though is…' He stopped then, hearing a car arrive on the drive. 'Well, another time perhaps?'

'Will I do?' asked Lawrence, climbing out of his car. He raised his arms and swivelled on the spot.

They could hardly believe how different he looked in his burgundy dinner jacket and rainbow-coloured bow tie! He'd even bothered to trim his beard.

Amelie nudged Isla. 'To think we once called him the Man in Black.'

'Jeez,' gasped Isla. 'You're sure looking hot, Lawrence!'

'Bit old for you,' Tim said wryly.

'I thought I'd better tidy up a bit,' he laughed, bowing elaborately. 'I hope Lucy won't be too bored tonight.'

'Oh, my goodness!' exclaimed Storm and they all swung round to see Lucy standing at the top of the steps. 'You look quite ravishing, my dear.'

'Indeed she does,' Lawrence agreed. 'Don't you agree, Tim?'

Tim looked up from his phone and nodded approvingly. Isla looked like she might burst into tears. 'You two look so cute together,' she said, grasping Lawrence's hand. 'I must have a photo of you both. That's it - stay right there with that potted palm behind you, just perfect.'

After the photographs, they all gathered round to wave them off - Tim, Isla, Amelie and Storm – and remained there long after Lawrence's car had disappeared. That was until Storm finally shouted: 'Chop, chop, you lot, Air Commodore Mrs. Lambe calls! We mustn't be late for combat,' and with that they ran off to wash their hands.

❀

Around midnight, a car pulled up on the gravel drive, its engine still running. An owl hooted and a car door slammed, footsteps, and a key in the lock. Amelie climbed out of bed and made her way downstairs.

'Hey, what are you doing up so late?' said Lucy, hanging her coat on the hall stand.

'I was too excited about your...' She nearly said *date* but stopped herself in time. 'How did it go?'

Lucy gazed at her with tired grey eyes and smiled. 'Wonderful, darling,' she sighed. 'Yes, it was really nice.'

They wandered into the big old kitchen where Lucy sank into her favourite chair. 'I haven't danced that much for years.'

'No Lawrence?' asked Amelie, filling the kettle.

'Ah, he had to get back to Charlie.'

Amelie nodded. 'Ah, I told him he should have a dog, living in that huge old house alone…'

'Dog?' Lucy laughed. 'Charlie's his partner.'

Amelie's jaw dropped. 'Don't tell me, not Charlotte, his new editor? She's ancient, forty at least.'

'Hmm.' Lucy gave a wry smile. 'You do realise I'll be forty in a year or two? No, filmmaker Charles Karlsson; he flew in unexpectedly from Sweden today.' Her voice cracked a little. 'They're getting married next year.'

'Oh.' Amelie's hand flew to her mouth. 'I feel so silly…'

'Not half as silly as me…' Lucy pulled off her velvet gloves and stroked them, as if to console them for having been taken on a wasted journey. 'Yes, I liked him a lot - even thought there might be a spark of something there…' Then, seeing Amelie's anguish, she stood up and wrapped her arms around her. 'Hey, now, it's not *your* fault, sweetheart! And we'll still be friends, Lawrence and me.' She took Amelie's hand and squeezed it. 'It's all right, truly.' She uttered a little laugh but Amelie knew it wasn't all right at all.

'Plus,' Lucy added, 'Charlie does seem rather nice.'

'You met him?'

'I spoke to him earlier on the phone. I'm sure you'll like him a lot.' She kissed the top of Amelie's head. 'You get to bed now. I just need a bit of time on my own.' She lingered a moment at the kitchen door. 'Things don't always turn out the way we'd hoped for but that sometimes means there's something better just around the corner…'

Outside, Lucy breathed in the cold night air and shivered, wishing she'd brought a shawl. She also wished she'd changed into more comfortable shoes. It was years since she'd worn heels. She stumbled off down the long dark path, past Storm's vegetable plot, past the children's playhouse, and had almost reached the footbridge when she tripped on some cobbles and fell, striking her head on the little stone birdbath. She lay there for a while, nursing her ankle and rubbing her head by turns, willing the pain to subside. What seemed like minutes passed and footsteps hurried along the gravel path behind her.

'Are you all right?' a voice asked softly.

Chapter Nineteen

It's All Gone Horribly Wrong

Amelie promised herself she wouldn't panic, at least not until the clock struck one, which it just had.

'It's all gone horribly wrong,' she bleated, tapping on Tim's door. 'I should never have encouraged her. Storm must have known all along; why didn't he just say? And why didn't *I* guess he'd have a boyfriend?'

'Go back to bed!' croaked Tim, still half-asleep. 'Mum's an adult, remember; adults make their own decisions.'

'But she's been gone far too long now and she's left her phone on the kitchen table.'

Tim groaned and pulled a hoodie over his pyjamas. 'Anything to shut you up, I suppose,' he grumbled. 'You shout Isla while I find my torch.'

'At least Isla won't be mean and grumpy like you,' snapped Amelie and scurried off to tell her the news.

'Try not to worry, honey,' Isla said kindly. 'Just wait while I grab a coat. I'm sure Lucy will be fine.'

They flew downstairs and found Lara and Freddie waiting at the kitchen door.

Amelie smiled, comforted a little. 'These two always know when they're needed! Pass me Lara's lead, will you?'

'Okay,' said Tim, joining them at last. 'How about I go straight up to Storm's hangar while you two check the playhouse?'

Amelie and Isla reached the playhouse and peered in through the window. Even without any lights on they could see there was no one inside. Moments later, Tim returned, shaking his head. 'Lara sniffed around the bird bath for a while and then we went up to the fields.' He shrugged. 'Zilch, I'm afraid.'

Amelie thumped her fist against the playhouse door. 'I'll never forgive him for this! He promised he'd look after her…'

'Lawrence, you mean - because he didn't tell her about having a boyfriend?' Isla smiled. 'I think they both got their wires a bit crossed, that's all. We all did.'

'I don't care. I'm calling him…'

'No, don't,' Isla said firmly, 'you mustn't. What would *they* tell us to do in a crisis? Which,' she added hastily, 'it isn't, of course.'

Tim mouthed Isla a thank you. 'See, Isla's right,' he said, giving Amelie's hand a reassuring squeeze. 'You remember when Storm nearly died last year? What did the Commander tell us then?'

Amelie nodded. 'Remember the power of your minds?' She unlocked the playhouse door and glanced around inside. 'To think this was once Eggy's summer house. It's funny to think of her sitting right here, reading that book upside-down…'

Isla shone her phone torch around until its light rested on the table. 'Look!' she cried, 'our maps are still here, a bit damp but exactly where we left them last summer.'

Tim brushed a dead wasp off his chair. 'Then I think this is a timely reminder.'

'Really?' said Amelie. 'A reminder of what exactly?'

'The extraordinary things we're all capable of,' replied Tim. 'You know, like preventing a Third World War…'

'Exactly,' said Isla. 'He's right, you know, babe.'

Amelie dusted off her stool before sitting down. 'Then finding

Mum should be relatively easy after that. Shall we sit in our triangle?' As she spoke a familiar sound echoed outside. 'Did you hear that?'

'Wind chimes again,' whispered Isla. 'That means *Tuló* must be near…'

Chapter Twenty

A Date with a Difference

Lucy heard the voice and tried to open her eyes. 'Lawrence, what are you doing here? Where's Charlie?'

'He's fine, my love, they both are…'

'It can't be…' Warily, she touched the man's face. It felt warm and living, every bit as alive as her own. The children had been right all along. 'Michael…'

'No, you're not dreaming,' he answered. 'But you have had quite a fall.'

A wave of pain reminded her. 'Have I died?' Her voice trembled, partly with fear but mostly excitement. 'I never thought I'd get to see you again…'

Michael reached out his hand and helped her to her feet. 'Easy does it, let's find you somewhere to sit down.'

They perched together on a tree stump. 'It's time to talk,' he said gravely, pulling her close. '*About That Terrible Day* as you call it, when we all disappeared.'

'Drowned, you mean.' She couldn't take her eyes off him. He was exactly as he'd always been, apart from his hair. She reached up to touch it. 'What happened?' Once dark it was now blond and reached to his shoulders.

Michael shrugged and gave a small laugh. 'It's how most of us look on Lumea.'

'I can't believe it's you. Show me I'm not imagining all of this…'

'You're not,' he said quietly. 'But I realise you're in shock. Wait while I explain…'

But Lucy couldn't wait. She had far too many questions. 'I lost three people I loved that day – not only you but and Joan and Ted. Joan was like a mother to me. I never even got chance to say goodbye.'

'I know, and it's why I've returned tonight. To tell you what really happened.'

As he spoke, a wave of tiredness swept through her, his voice lulling her into a deep sense of peace.

'That morning began like any other, calm and sunny with blue skies stretching as far as the eye could see. It was a perfect day for one last voyage before the start of winter. Our last ever, as things turned out.'

It was only as they rounded the bay that storm clouds appeared and dangerously high winds arose off the coast of Littlehaven.

'Ted was an experienced sailor, as you know, and he wanted us to turn back at once. But it was already too late. Half a mile out to sea already and our little boat got caught in the swell…'

Hearing this, Lucy came to and sat bolt upright. 'Stop it!' she sobbed, 'All these years, and I don't know how I got through them.'

'But you have, my darling,' Michael said gently. 'And what an amazing job you've done too. Tim, Amelie, even Storm - you've looked after them all. Here…' He passed her a clean white handkerchief. 'Do you know how proud that makes me?'

She looked up at him, still unsure if she was dreaming.

'You see?' he said, spreading his fingers into a starfish. 'Death didn't kill me.'

Lucy glared at him. 'I wish you wouldn't talk in riddles…'

'But I'm not, Lucy. We were saved.'

'Saved?' Lucy pulled away from him angrily. 'How can you possibly have been?'

'Lucy, you do know now that Mum and I are both Earth Watchers…?'

Lucy's anger subsided a little. 'Yes, the children told me…'

'I wasn't allowed to tell you before.' For a moment it looked like Michael's face might crumple. He closed his eyes, picturing them both, Tim now almost fourteen, Amelie twelve. 'I've missed you all terribly.'

Lucy said nothing, unable to make sense of it all. Did this mean that somehow he was back and their lives would continue as before?

'Let's make the most of whatever time we have left,' Michael said. 'Let me tell you what really happened…'

He'd had no idea at the time but there was major trouble brewing on Daktron, the furthest planet from the sun. This meant that all available Earth Watchers had to be called back on duty at once.

'But wait,' Lucy interrupted, 'you *weren't* available, were you? You were married with a family. Or had you forgotten that?'

'This was urgent, Lucy, more serious than you can imagine. We were on the brink of a major cosmic disaster, one that could have wiped out all life here on Luga. I'm no ordinary man…' He gazed at her intently. 'As Earth Watchers, our lives are never our own. We belong to the skies.'

Lucy frowned. 'But Ted wasn't an Earth Watcher. What happened to him?'

'No, which meant that, unlike us, he was given a choice: to come with us or remain here on Luga.'

'I still can't get used to that name.' Lucy's mind drifted back to the long weeks that followed the disaster: the coastguards' search, the thrum of helicopters overhead, television crews everywhere, and endless news reports. No one spoke of anything else for months on end.

'Wait!' she said suddenly. 'Kenny Pratt from the Fishing Tackle shop - he swore on oath he saw your bodies washed up on the beach. Was he lying?' she demanded. 'Or just drunk like people said?' Kenny was known to be a regular at the Hearts of Oak and wasn't considered too reliable a witness.

'Oh, no, he saw our bodies all right,' answered Michael. 'But that was before we'd disposed of them. You see that pile of dead leaves?'

Lucy followed his gaze. She and Storm had swept them up only days ago, ready for the compost heap.

'Watch closely now…' A beam of light shot from his palm and the leaves vanished before her eyes.

Lucy stared in astonishment. 'What was that you just did?'

'Just something to prove that solid things aren't really solid at all - where do you think all those ideas for Star Wars came from?' He looked back at his old home, barely visible now in the darkness. 'Do you still have my old telescope in the attic?'

'Of course we do. The children use it all the time.'

'I used to spend hours up there, looking for Lumea.'

Lucy glanced at him tenderly. 'They do that too.'

'It's the planet you call Venus,' Michael replied and a slow smile spread across his face. 'Lucy, have you ever wondered how we first met?'

'How could I forget? I was in the college bar doing random sketches for my final exhibition. Something made me turn and I saw you standing there, watching me work. You had such a striking face I knew I had to paint you.'

'I couldn't quite believe my luck,' Michael admitted with a laugh. 'I'd seen you around for a while but never dared ask you out. That wasn't our first meeting though,' he said quietly.

Lucy waited, certain she was in for yet another shock.

'Our first meeting occurred two million light years away, on a far flung planet right at the edge of our galaxy.' As he spoke, a spiral of stars appeared in the sky. ‘Look,’ he said, taking her arm. ‘See, just to the left of that brightest star…?’

Lucy wondered what Mrs. Lambe would make of all this.

Without warning, Michael waved his hand in the air and began to count. Just as he reached seven they were swept off their feet and found themselves rising over the fields beyond the garden.

Lucy clung to him, remembering her bumpy flight in Storm’s little aircraft the year before. But this was quite different. It was smooth and effortless and something told her she had begun a more extraordinary journey still. One she’d never want to forget.

‘Make the most of it,’ shouted Michael, ‘because you’ll have forgotten it all by tomorrow.’

They soared over rooftops and hills, gaining enough altitude to wave to an astonished airline pilot as they passed by. Soon they were cruising close to the International Space Station where aeronautical engineers immediately began to worry that their oxygen supplies were running low. Ever onwards towards that brightest star that guided them home.

At last, they landed, light as feathers, and Lucy gazed around at the spectacular view before them. ‘Well, this is certainly a date with a difference!’ She hadn’t even names for the colours she saw there, unearthly colours that she would never find in her paint box at home. Yet somehow here felt like home. ‘Why did we ever leave?’ she murmured.

‘Curiosity,’ Michael replied, ‘the evolutionary urge to explore. Our planet was already quite advanced so we had the technology to do so.’

‘What happened, and where did we go?’

‘Well, I discovered Lumea, where I’ve lived ever since, apart from my recent spell on Luga with you...’

‘And me?’

'You settled on Lumea's little sister planet - Luga, also known as Earth. It's what we'd already planned long ago. We knew we'd find each other again one day, just as we always shall. Lucy darling…' He turned to face her, his eyes bright with hope. 'Last year, Tim and Amelie and Isla did far more than save your planet, you know. That enormous Peace Gathering of theirs - it not only halted global destruction; it prevented a catastrophic war in Space.'

Lucy listened in awe, picturing Tim and Amelie back in Parliament Square. 'Seeing them there, addressing the crowds, I've never been so proud in all my life.'

'Nor me,' said Michael. 'Thcy did what no adult was able to achieve.'

And it was then that they found themselves back in the garden again.

'And that was merely the start though, Lucy,' he whispered. 'They'll never cease to amaze you.'

'I think I know that already,' Lucy said quietly. She frowned and turned to him anxiously. 'But what about you and me…?'

'My beautiful Lucy, it's time…' Michael cupped her face in his hands. 'I need you to remember this one very important thing: *Together or not, we are never apart.*'

'But you can't leave me…' Lucy clutched his arm. 'Not again…'

'I'll return for you one day, you have my word. But till then, Tim and Amelie need you here, and in time their own children will too. Oh, Lucy, trust me…' He squeezed her hand firmly, impressing it with his own conviction. 'If only you could see the life that awaits you. I always knew your talent would be recognised some day and see, already it is. Keep painting, my love.'

'You whispered that to me last year, didn't you? When I thought we were losing our home. You heard me…'

Michael kissed the palm of her hand. 'Yes, just as I heard you tonight. Lucy. I'm never more than a thought away.'

A swirling plasma-like tunnel appeared and he began to move towards it. 'This is it, I'm afraid, the Portal of No Return. But even though you'll forget all of this tomorrow; somewhere, somewhere deep down, you'll know.'

Lucy let go of his arm and watched helplessly as he vanished into the tunnel. And then, just as it began to fade, she rushed after him and disappeared from sight.

'I think I can see her in some kind of tunnel,' Amelie said, opening her eyes. 'But quite different from the ones under our house.'

'I saw that too,' Isla agreed. 'And I'm sure she's not alone. Whoever it is has quite a hold on her. What do you think, Tim?'

Tim's face had turned rather pale. He hesitated before speaking. 'Look,' he said slowly, 'I don't want to worry you...'

Amelie and Isla stared at him in alarm.

'It seems to me she's having a Near Death Experience…'

'A *what*?' said Amelie.

'I watched a documentary once on YouTube. It's like when you leave your body…' (He left out the bit about heart attacks and life-threatening accidents) '…and find yourself at the Portal of No Return.'

'Yes, I remember now,' said Isla, 'and there's no changing your mind once you go through it. Unless,' she added, 'there's some kind of trigger to call you back…' She gazed around frantically and spotted a photograph of Amelie and Tim. 'Yes, this is the one - you two in Parliament Square! I think it might just work. But how on earth do we get it to her?'

Tim thought hard for a moment. 'We need to project this onto her mind.'

'Lucy once told Mom how proud she felt, seeing you both there,' Isla whispered, clutching the photograph. 'She needs to have that feeling again…'

❃

Time passed. It could have been seconds, it might have been hours, but at some point they opened their eyes again. Freddie was clawing at the door and Lara, who never usually barked, suddenly did so. A face had appeared at the window and was peering in at them accusingly. 'What are you lot doing in here and why aren't you in bed?'

'Well, Mum, we could ask you the same,' Tim remarked, with as much annoyance as relief. 'Do you know how worried we've been?'

Lucy stared back at him, confused. 'What time is it?'

'Oh, Mum, you're shivering!' Amelie found a musty old blanket and wrapped it around her. 'And look, you're limping too. Come on, let's get you indoors…'

Together, they led her back to the house.

'I really don't know what all the fuss is about,' Lucy insisted. 'I'm absolutely fine, you know.'

'I'll call my dad anyway,' Isla said, ignoring Lucy's protests, and within minutes Dr Batty's car screeched to a halt on the drive.

Tim showed him into the kitchen where Isla was making tea. 'Thanks for coming, Andrew, I think she's had a bad fall. She seems, I dunno, a bit weird.'

'Don't worry, I'll check her over and send for an ambulance if necessary. You really should have called me before. I'd have happily helped you to find her.' He tested Lucy's pulse. 'Hmm, seems fine, a bit on the slow side but nice and steady…'

Amelie watched as he wrapped a cuff round Lucy's arm. 'What's that you're doing?'

'It's a sphygmomanometer[16],' replied Isla knowledgably.

Dr. Batty nodded. 'Yep, blood pressure's normal, that's a good sign too.'

Lucy, still wrapped in the musty old blanket, glanced up at them all. 'I'm so sorry to have caused all this trouble. Was I gone very long?'

Amelie frowned. 'Yes, long enough for us to worry. But where on earth did you go?'

Lucy was silent for a moment. 'You'd never believe me if I told you.' Then, she gazed up at them again and smiled. 'There again, you probably would.'

Chapter Twenty-One

The Grand Tour

Spring 1911

'So this is our itinerary,' Eggy explained while Adelaide checked their luggage. 'All the dates and places we'll be staying at. Our first stop will be Paris: Hôtel Lutetia, Boulevard Raspail.'

'What!' Jack stared at the list, horrified. 'But you'll be gone for almost a year!'

'Just think of it as my practice run for when we go travelling together. Adelaide says it'll go far too quickly.'

'Yeah,' Jack said, resigned. 'I'll probably be too busy to notice anyway.'

Eggy searched his face anxiously. 'You will write though, won't you?'

'I suppose so.' Jack grinned. 'Not that I'll have much to say.'

'And I will too, I promise you.'

And she did, the very moment they arrived; on a little black and white *Carte Postale*[17] that advertised the Lutetia. There was just enough room for her to scribble: *Here for two weeks. Wish you were too. Love from Eggs.*

She sent another to Loula and, simply because Adelaide insisted, one to her father who might like to know they had arrived. On a whim, she wrote one for *Joseph Trott, c/o Hadleigh House,*

Cloud Hill, Havenbridge, Angleterre, knowing it would probably never reach him.

Every few days a letter would arrive, written in Jack's spidery scrawl. Sometimes there was a line from Walter, telling her not to worry and how he was busy studying farming catalogues. It all worked splendidly until they reached Vienna. At the Hotel Sacher there were two letters waiting for them but both were for Adelaide. Eggy decided at once that she loathed Vienna, and therefore Austria as a whole, despite all the delicious *Kaffee und Kuchen*[18] Adelaide plied her with in an effort to cheer her up.

'I know there'll be something for you once we reach Italy. Look, I've just gotten some *Sachertorte*[19] for Jack. It's what our hotel is famous for. He likes chocolate cake, doesn't he? Yes, everyone likes chocolate cake. We'll post it tomorrow.'

'I don't know why you think I'm bothered,' snapped Eggy. She longed to tell Adelaide to shut up about him and leave her to brood but, as it turned out, she had been right all along. There, waiting at the Hotel Bernini in Rome were four letters, one from Edgar and three from Jack. Relief was mingled with annoyance. Why had she let him spoil her time in Vienna, precious time she'd never get back? She tore open all three letters at once…

Starlight was perfectly fine, Emmeline was too, but Jack's father was not. Poor Fred had suffered several funny turns during the past weeks, which was why he hadn't written sooner. The last letter was in lighter mood though, full of gossipy little things, mostly gleaned from the vicar. Straight-laced Miss Tribble had disgraced herself at the Church Fête with too much Elderflower champagne, and the Earl of Littlehaven had farted in his sleep during the sermon. The best news by far came right at the end and this Eggy wasted no time in sharing with Adelaide:

'Elsie Thomas has got herself into trouble. Enceinte,' she added, much to Adelaide's surprise.

Heartened by this shocking news, she began to enjoy the attention of a cheeky young waiter at Babbington's Tea Rooms at the foot of the Spanish Steps.

'How cosmopolitan we are!' Adelaide exclaimed. 'I never dreamed we'd be enjoying English afternoon tea in the Spanish Square in Rome, Italy, did you?' She peered at Eggy over her tea cup. 'You're really fond of that boy, aren't you?'

'Are you joking?' laughed Eggy as the grinning waiter arrived with a tray of pastries for *le belle signorine*[20].

'No, silly,' Adelaide replied. 'You know perfectly well who I mean. You two have been friends a long time, haven't you?'

Eggy smiled. 'Yes,' she said dreamily, 'almost half of my life.'

Adelaide signalled to the waiter for more hot water. 'We humans make some extraordinary connections at times. Take Eddie and me. Meeting on the way to Calais all those years ago; we kind of recognised each other at once. *Oh, it's you,* I said. The words just slipped out, you know?'

Eggy remembered the first time she met Jack. 'What did he say?'

'*Hello, my dear, I've been looking for you.*'

'How strange, but doesn't he mind you going away for all this time…?' Eggy asked, wondering if perhaps Jack minded a little too.

'Not at all, but that's because Eddie's not just my husband. He's also my best friend. No, he's just thrilled to see me happy again. And that,' she sighed, patting Eggy's hand, 'is all thanks to you, my darling girl. Sadly, we couldn't have children of our own. You've given me some kind of mission.'

'Are you sure you don't mean challenge?'

'That too,' admitted Adelaide and they both looked at each other and smiled.

Adelaide's lessons can hardly be called work, Eggy shared in her next letter to Jack. *I rather enjoy writing about the places we've visited, not to mention the funny things that happen, like Getting Lost in Rome. That was the title of my last essay. Somehow, we'd managed to lose each other in a crowd by the Trevi Fountains*[21]*. I'd just tossed a coin over my shoulder to make a wish when I realised that Adelaide was no longer there. I did panic a bit but remembered my 'Mark of T' and I'm sure it guided me back to the hotel. Poor Adelaide was in a dreadful state, as you can imagine. I don't think she'll ever let me out of her sight again.*

Sometimes we go to concerts or have evenings at the opera. This usually means getting all dressed up but I don't mind too much because Adelaide makes it fun.

'Let's pretend we're someone else,' Adelaide proposed one evening. 'Wear that gorgeous blue dress of yours and I'll introduce you as a Russian princess. What shall I call you? I don't know, Princess Tatyana or something? Here, take these…' She passed Eggy a pair of long satin opera gloves. 'Eggy, forgive me for asking but what's that mark on your arm?'

Eggy flushed a little. 'Oh, that, I drew it with a piece of shell,' she replied truthfully. 'And for some reason it never faded.'

'It's just that I've seen it somewhere before. You remember Gyatso from Tibet? It's exactly like one of his lovely mandalas.'

❀

In late summer they arrived in Malcesine, a little town on the eastern shore of Lake Garda in Northern Italy. Here they stayed with Adelaide's old school friend, Anna Martinelli. 'We're planning to move back to New York soon,' Anna confided one day. 'I'm concerned about the trouble brewing in Europe…'

It's been another beautiful day, Eggy entered in her diary that night, *only spoiled a bit by Anna. She's worrying about a big war starting in Europe and it's exactly what Eddie's been saying for a while. I dread to think what it all means...*

After a couple of weeks there, they ferried across the lake to Limone. Eggy and her aunt stood on the quayside, entranced. The mountains, the lemon and olive groves, the lake itself, everything was as Goethe described.

'He didn't mention stationery shops though, did he?' Adelaide remarked, spotting a pretty little *cartoleria* in the main square. 'Perfect, we can stock up on more pencils and notebooks. I imagine they'll sell phrase books here too. You might as well learn a smattering of Italian while we're here.'

What a relief it was to escape the heat that day, the hottest Eggy had ever known. The little shop was deliciously cool and fragrant. There were baskets of lemons everywhere, still with their leaves attached, and piles of fascinating new books – Italian mostly but a few in French and German too. There was even a newly-published edition of *The Secret Garden* by Frances Hodgson Burnett which Adelaide snapped up at once. Eggy browsed the display and claimed a blue marbled notebook and a Waterman fountain pen with a silver filigree overlay. It was the prettiest pen she had ever seen. Next she spotted a tiny phrase book for Jack. *For when we come to Limone one day*... she planned to inscribe that inside.

A sweet young woman behind the counter chatted to them in broken English while she wrapped their purchases in tissue paper and secured them with ribbon. 'You come again, sì?' she asked them, flashing a beautiful smile, and they promised they would.

'How wonderful, an ice-cream parlor, at last!' Adelaide cried. 'Look, over there!' She grabbed Eggy's hand and together they raced across the square like children. 'Italian ice-creams are the best in the world. Stay here while I'll get them.' She left Eggy seated on a bench while she wandered inside, murmuring to herself: '*Due gelati, per favore*![22]'

That evening, just as dusk fell, Eggy ventured out alone. Surprisingly Adelaide had agreed at once. 'After managing to navigate your way through the streets of Rome,' she said, 'I think you'll be safe enough here. Nothing untoward ever happens in little Italian towns like this.'

She sat down on the stone wall, gazing out over the water, watching the blinking lights and an occasional swan that appeared against the inky blackness. What was it about this little place that filled her with such a deep sense of contentment? After all the bustle and excitement of their travels it was good to be alone at last. Except… a stray thought dampened her mood. If only Jack could be there too.

She leaped suddenly, startled by a hand on her shoulder. 'Oh, my goodness!' Her hand flew to her heart as a wave of energy jolted through her body.

'It's only me,' said Tabitha. 'Do you mind if I join you?'

Eggy's hand still rested on her heart. It was beating wildly but she smiled all the same. 'No, I'm really pleased you're here. Sit down with me a while.' She moved over to give her more room.

'Thank you.' Tabitha gazed up at the mountains, barely visible now against the indigo sky. 'These mountains, Eglantyne; they serve to remind us all to aim high.' She raised her hand to the heavens. 'And one day,' she added, 'you'll visit greater mountains still.'

Chapter Twenty-Two

Hiraeth: the Place Where the Spirit Dwells

'Ah, you're there!' said Adelaide, making Eggy jump for a second time that evening. 'I thought I'd come down and join you.'

'It's like I've come home, Adelaide,' Eggy replied.

'Apparently, the Welsh have a word for that: it's called *hiraeth* – the place where the spirit dwells. We've nothing like it in English - apart from nostalgia, I suppose. The Germans call it *Sehnsucht*.'

'Yearning?'

'Oh my, what an incredible student you are!' Adelaide linked Eggy's arm.

They wandered through the Piazza Garibaldi and along the water front.

'Let's sit again by the lake,' said Adelaide, arranging her skirts on the wall. 'But please be careful, my dear! That water sure must be cold at night.'

That morning Eggy had offered to show Adelaide how to swim. She'd demonstrated by disappearing below the lake for what seemed like minutes before resurfacing with a silly grin on her face.

'Never, ever do that to me again!' Adelaide scolded.

'Don't worry, I won't,' Eggy giggled, dangling her legs above the dark waters.

Two more swans appeared, starkly white against the blackness below.

'Swan Lake!' cried Adelaide. 'That's it, Tchaikovsky – this can be your music lesson for today…' And with that she leaped off the wall and began to waltz along the promenade, much to the amusement of the passers-by.

'I've never seen you like this before!' Eggy laughed. 'I'm sure they'll think you're drunk. Please don't stop though.'

But Adelaide did stop and came back to watch the swans and the lights across the other side of the lake. 'I really wish Eddie were here. I lied to you,' she faltered. 'I told you we'd never had children but we did. A girl. Stillborn.'

'Adelaide, I'd no idea…'

Adelaide shrugged. 'Some of us aren't destined to be parents…' She glanced fondly at her niece. 'But you make up for all that. I think of you as the daughter I never got to know.'

Eggy squeezed her hand. 'I've a confession too, Adelaide. Before we met, I decided I'd hate you.' Shamefaced, she lowered her eyes. 'But instead, you're one of the nicest people I know.'

'Oh, Eggy…'

'I'm never having children either…'

'You might. Once you're married.'

'Married?' Eggy looked at her as though she had lost her mind. 'No, I don't think so…'

Chapter Twenty-Three

The Blue Rider

It was mid-December when they reached Munich for the last few days of their tour.

'This looks rather interesting,' remarked Adelaide, studying a poster on the hotel's notice board. 'Franz Marc and *Der Blaue Reiter*.'

'Does that mean The Blue Rider?'

'Mm, it's a new art movement, very modern. You like horses, don't you?'

'Of course! But why are these horses blue?'

'It's because he's an Expressionist painter,' Adelaide replied. 'It means he expresses his feelings through his paintings. The kind of thing your father would call pretentious nonsense. Why don't we go? It's literally round the corner.'

So they did and Adelaide was right. Eggy pictured the dismal set of watercolours in her father's study. 'I've never seen anything like these before,' she exclaimed. 'And there's definitely something about this one I love.'

'The two horses?'

'Yes, they remind me of Starlight and Arrow.'

'Then why not make a sketch of them? And if you make a note of the colors you can finish it back at the hotel. While you do that, I'll get us some coffee…'

❀

'Jack, we must go one day,' Eggy enthused. 'Promise me we'll go!'

It was Christmas Eve 1911 and they stood together in the kitchen garden, gathering herbs for Loula's Christmas dinner.

'What was that place called again?' Jack asked, plucking a sprig of rosemary from a nearby bush.

'Limone.' Eggy imagined them both there, looking out across the enormous lake. 'We could rent a house there like Anna's in Malcesine. But first you'll have to learn Italian. Close your eyes.' She handed him a small woven bag with the tiny Italian phrase book inside. 'Right, you can open them now. Look, it even shows you how to pronounce everything too.'

Jack glanced at it, flicking through the pages. 'Well, there's little chance of me going anywhere for a while,' he said bleakly, 'even with Frank and Walter helping out. But whenever you next go...' He broke off another sprig of rosemary and rubbed it between his fingers. 'You can take this with you so you don't forget me.' He smiled wryly. 'Mum says it's good for the memory.'

'You know I never forget you!' Eggy protested, stuffing it unceremoniously into her pocket. 'Actually though, Adelaide's planning another trip for us, to New York next spring. On the new *Titanic…*'

Jack nodded, stony-faced. Only one day back in England and she was already talking about going away.

'I'd like it much more if you could come too,' Eggy added. 'Wait here - I've got something else for you indoors.' She ran into the house and returned with her rolled up painting, secured with a piece of string.

Jack's eyes widened as he slowly unfurled it.

'You don't like it, do you?' Eggy waited, trying to read his expression. 'You can give it back, I don't mind. No, actually, I do mind, because one of them is meant to be Arrow. I copied it from a painting by Franz Marc.'

'Of course I like it, you idiot. Blimey, did you really paint this yourself? I was just thinking how I'd make a nice frame for it - but you have to sign it first.'

Eggy beamed. 'I will if you promise to come to London for New Year!' She planted a kiss on his chin. 'I'm sure Frank and Walter can spare you for a couple of days.'

So Jack stayed at Dorlington Gardens for two whole days and was even given his own room right at the top of the house. 'Here,' Edgar told him, handing him a key. 'Now you can come whenever you wish. Call it your bolt-hole, for whenever things get a bit much.'

He stayed there again in April when the sinking of the *Titanic* made headline news.

'Gosh, have you all seen this?' Jack gasped, reading Edgar's morning paper. 'It's only gone and hit an iceberg and sunk.' He stared at Eggy in shock. 'Thank God you two didn't go.'

'We've Eddie to thank for that,' Adelaide said soberly. 'He put his foot down for once.'

'What nonsense,' Edgar retorted, 'that's only because I'd planned to take you for our anniversary next year.'

'Fifteen hundred lives lost,' Jack read aloud.

Eggy peered over Jack's shoulder. 'I can't bear it. Over fifty of them were children…'

Edgar sighed and rose to his feet. 'Despite all this ghastly news, I'm afraid we must leave you for a while. We have an appointment in town.'

'And it's a perfect day for exploring,' Adelaide added, attempting to lighten the mood. 'Regent's Park is only a stone's throw away.

'That's if I can manage to stay awake,' Jack said, hearing the front door close. 'I hardly got a wink's sleep last night.'

'Was it the voices?' asked Eggy. 'I've pretty much got used to them now. Shall we take a look around while we can?'

She led him up a flight of stairs to the old servants' lift and glanced around her. 'Good, there's no one about.' She pressed a button on the wall and waited. 'I come here whenever I'm bored. It's where I saw Tabitha that time.'

Jack pressed his ear to the lift door. 'I think I can hear something.' A loud clanking followed and suddenly it slid open.

'Get in then,' said Eggy, giving him a little push. 'Don't worry; I've done this a dozen times.'

The door rattled to a close and soon they were left in darkness.

'Yes, sorry, I forgot to tell you about that.' Eggy grasped Jack's arm to steady herself. 'There'll be one big jolt and it'll come to a halt after that. Hold on…!'

It stopped at last and they stepped out onto the carpeted landing. Jack gazed around him in surprise.

'So, do you like it?' Eggy asked proudly, as though the house belonged to her. 'The House of Endless Possibilities…'

The same curious spectacle greeted them: rooms hastily abandoned, half-eaten food piled up on plates, clothes slung over chairs.

Jack shot her a worried glance. 'Are you sure no one will mind us breaking in?'

'What do you mean?' she laughed. 'We haven't broken in. And anyway, Tabitha says this is all from the future. Like the voices we heard. It's rather strange that Eddie and Adelaide haven't…'

A floorboard creaked and they swung around guiltily.

'You two certainly took your time!' a familiar voice cried.

'Hello, Tabitha,' said Eggy. 'I might say the same to you! I've been coming here for weeks and you've never appeared.'

Tabitha walked towards them, wearing silver breeches and a

tight-fitting cap. 'Not that time really exists,' she admitted. She spun around on the spot. 'Have you noticed anything different?'

They stared at her blankly. 'Your uniform, you mean?'

'Close…'

'Oh, it's your badge!' Eggy exclaimed. 'You've got it at last!'

Tabitha gave an elaborate bow. 'Yes, I'm now a bona-fide Earth Watcher and that's all down to you.'

They followed her to a small flight of steps at the end of the hallway and found themselves in a brightly lit corridor. Halfway along she stopped and ushered them into a tiny office.

'Sit down. I'm about to show you a glimpse of things to come.' She indicated a strange box-like object on the desk with a small keyboard and shiny glass screen.

'This is called a computer.' Tabitha ran her fingers along the keys. 'One day, every home on Luga will own one.' As she began to type three figures appeared on the screen, a young man and two girls. 'See these? They are from the twenty-first century. Over one hundred years from now. They're all Bright Hearts, like you.' She glanced at them sideways. 'A Bright Heart, you'll remember, is someone who comes to enrich life on this planet.'

'Heavens,' Eggy murmured. 'Is that what you meant by my 'future work'?'

'Yes - and Jack's future work too.'

Jack, whose one earthly ambition had been to fly a glider, looked uncertain. 'So then, what else do you need us to do?'

'In time you'll discover.' Tabitha placed a hand on his shoulder. 'A time when your own courage will astound you…'

It almost sounded like a threat.

'That girl,' Eggy said suddenly. For some reason she was unable to take her eyes off the screen. 'The one with the bright auburn hair…'

'Ah,' said Tabitha, 'that's Amelie. She and her brother are hybrids; that's to say half-Lumean and half-Lugan. Their father is a well-known Earth Watcher.'

Jack stifled a laugh. 'Have you seen those clothes they're wearing?'

Eggy blinked. The figures had begun to move, ever so slightly, as they grouped together for their photograph. 'Look, it's just like a movie...'

'That's a phenomenon known as *photo-animation*,' Tabitha explained. 'It only works for those who have eyes to see. If you listen very carefully, you'll hear them speak as well. Watch the boy, he's about to say something...'

'He is!' Eggy shook Jack's arm. 'Can you hear him? Come a bit closer to the screen.'

'I can!'

'What's he saying then?'

Jack gazed at her, astonished. 'He says: *Mum seems back to normal at last...*'

Chapter Twenty-Four

A Surprising Flight

'Jeez, will you two stand still, please?' Isla was beginning to lose her patience. 'Fine, now move in a bit, Amelie.'

Amelie rolled her eyes. 'Do I have to? You know how much I hate selfies.'

'Yes, you do have to, babe, so stop making a fuss. All the guys at my school think you're cute. Hot even, especially…'

'Hot!' Amelie repeated, horrified. She longed to ask *who* thought it but couldn't bring herself to.

'Yeah, Ben McKellen in Year Ten,' Isla continued. 'He's very nice-looking and incredibly bright. Not really my type though,' she added, glancing at Tim. 'You can meet him if you like….'

'No way!' said Amelie, doubly horrified.

'Oh, Tim, really,' Isla tutted, 'now your head's missing. Cool, hold it right there and I'll take a few more. I want them for Mom.'

'Why though?' puzzled Tim. 'We'll be seeing her next week.'

'You're still coming then?'

'Why wouldn't we? Mum seems back to normal at last.'

'She really is,' Amelie agreed, 'in fact, happier than I've seen her for a while. Have you seen her new painting yet?'

Isla nodded. 'You mean that one with the huge purple sky? I really like it.'

'Mum calls it amethyst,' said Amelie. 'Libby says it's 'never right' and must be down to the concussion. Hey, can we visit next door again?'

Isla thought for a moment and nodded happily. 'I've just remembered, Mom's working next Saturday so there'll only be the three of us. I'd love to show Storm one day too.' She stopped, hearing unsteady footsteps in the hall.

'Are you there, Isla?' Storm bellowed, entering with a jubilant smile. 'I have excellent news!'

Isla clapped her hands joyfully. 'Yay, is it about our trip to Italy at half-term?'

'No, my dear, but as a fellow pilot, you'll be pleased to know that our little microlight is now solar powered! No more running out of fuel and no carbon emissions. Therefore…' He glanced around at the little group. 'Who'd like to come for a wee spin?'

Isla hesitated. 'That last landing we had was a bit hair-raising, Storm. Do you mind if I sit this one out?'

'Fair enough,' he muttered, 'but I've something rather spectacular to show you.' He looked hopefully at Tim and Amelie.

'I'll come if you like,' Amelie offered bravely.

'Cheers,' said Tim, 'I'd rather not risk breaking a leg this early in the season.'

Amelie looked alarmed. At ninety-four, Storm was getting a bit old for flying but he didn't like to be told.

'Idiot!' Isla scolded and gave Tim's wrist a playful slap. 'He's only teasing, honey. You'll be fine, I promise.'

'That's settled then.' Storm rubbed his hands gleefully. 'Tim and Isla, you two climb up onto the cliffs; there's just a chance you'll see my surprise.'

'You all right there, Amelie?' bawled Storm as the little microlight gained altitude.

'I think so,' murmured Amelie, willing herself not to be sick.
They continued to climb and soon the sea came into view. Storm looked down and waved to two small figures clambering up the grassy slopes towards the cliff edge. 'There they are, bless them! Now, Amelie, watch out for the wheat fields and tell me what you see.'

Amelie dared to open her eyes at last. There, a thousand feet below them, were the fields.

'Voilà!' cried Storm.

Amelie looked; there, right in the centre, was a perfectly formed circle. 'Storm, do you know what that is?'

'Of course I do!' he cried. 'It's a crop circle. Thank heavens they're late with the harvest this year. We'd have missed it otherwise. Let's hope Tim and Isla can see it from the cliffs.'

'No, not just that; look, it's the *Mark of Triandor*! Don't you remember the drawing I showed you?'

'Good Lord, yes, I do! This must mean the Earth Watchers are back!'

'Yes,' said Amelie excitedly. 'I'm so pleased I came now - can we keep on flying for a bit longer?'

'Yes, let's cruise over to Littlehaven and back.'

They flew over the sea for a while and crossed Littlehaven Bay before finding themselves over open countryside again.

'What's that?' Amelie said suddenly. 'See those deserted old buildings with broken windows and graffiti-covered walls?'

'Hmm, looks like a disused industrial estate.'

'Seems like it's about to re-open,' Amelie observed. 'Did you notice that line of men in black hoodies, carrying boxes and machines and stuff?'

'Scruffy lot,' Storm grunted, 'never had hoodies in my day.'

'Can't we get any closer? Look, there's a couple of buses just arrived. With its windows all blacked out. They must be very important visitors then.' As she spoke an unsettling thought crossed her mind. What if they weren't actually visitors at all but people who didn't want to be seen?

They gained altitude again and flew back towards the coast.

'Ah, here they are again!' shouted Storm, and immediately wished he hadn't. The two small figures had almost reached the cliff top but suddenly Isla slipped and Tim reached out a hand to steady her. And, as Storm observed, he didn't let go. He guessed that Amelie had seen it too. He reached over and patted her knee. 'All is well, my dear, all is well.'

A sudden gust of wind blew them slightly off-course. 'Hold on,' he warned, 'we may be in for another bumpy landing.'

For a moment, Amelie went into free-fall. Her whole life was about to crash. Everything had changed and there was nothing she could do about it. A wave of nausea hit her. Then, just as quickly, she cast everything out of her mind – the disused industrial site and the blacked-out windows, and even Tim and Isla holding hands; everything, that is, except for the *Mark of Triandor*. As Storm had just said, all was well. It was all a nothing. Nothing at all.

Chapter Twenty-Five

Meeting Miss Wilson

'You won't forget, will you?' announced Amelie, packing her bag for school. 'Mum, Storm, it's Friday today, and I'm meeting Lawrence in London after school. Then me and Tim are staying at Isla's.'

'I'm pleased you two are friends again,' Lucy said happily. 'He thinks the world of you.'

'Lawrence?' Amelie smiled. 'There's someone new he wants me to meet.'

'Well, my dear,' said Storm, looking up from his newspaper. 'You'd better be prepared then.'

Prepared! For some curious reason Amelie remembered her old autograph book and ran upstairs to fetch it. 'Tim,' she called over her shoulder, 'when we get to London Bridge Lawrence will be there. If you don't want to come with me you can go on to Isla's without me. Lawrence says he can drop me off there later.'

'Let me introduce you to our youngest best-selling author,' Lawrence announced to the pretty young woman seated behind the desk. 'This is Amelie Joan Trott. Amelie, meet Miss Wilson, our new editor. Since you'll be working together I'll leave you to chat while I grab us some coffee.'

The girl rose from her desk and offered Amelie her hand. 'Never mind the formalities, please call me Tabby.'

Amelie tilted her head. 'I've a feeling I know your name...' With that she dived into her bag and fished out her old autograph book. 'Wait a moment…' She flicked through the pages. 'Yes, here it is… *Tabby Wilson…*'

'Wilson isn't my real name,' the girl whispered while glancing over Amelie's shoulder. 'It's one I use while I'm visiting Luga.'

Amelie gazed at her in disbelief. Despite what Storm had said earlier, she was hardly prepared for this. 'Tabitha! Is it really you? I never thought I'd get to meet you like this.'

'We'll have to be quick before Lawrence returns.' Tabitha lowered her voice again. 'You do understand that we Earth Watchers can only warn and advise?'

Amelie nodded mutely.

'Right…' She kept her eye on the door. 'As you know, the *Mark of Triandor* is for your personal protection but, and this is very important, *you have to protect it too*. It must never fall into the wrong hands.'

'Absolutely,' said Amelie. She rummaged through her bag again and found her little drawing. 'Unfortunately though, this one doesn't work. I've tried several times and nothing happens.'

'Show me…'

Amelie handed her the drawing.

'No,' said Tabitha, 'you've made an excellent copy. It'll work perfectly well once it's needed.' She took Amelie's hand for a moment and said: 'And it will be needed, very soon, I assure you. That's all I can tell you for now.' And with that she vanished, leaving Amelie wondering what on earth she would tell Lawrence.

'There you go.' Lawrence returned with three mugs of coffee and a plateful of shortbread biscuits. 'Here, have this while it's hot.' His eyes roamed the office for Amelie's new editor. 'Where on earth has she gone now? Strange girl, here one minute and gone the next.' He shrugged and sat down at the desk. 'Never mind, I think you'll both get on fine. Now…' He leaned back in his chair. 'I've something very exciting to share with you, Amelie. I've had a Professor Trickett on the phone from the British Library. Nice old buffer.'

Amelie looked blank. 'Should I know him?'

'Probably not but he's very eager to meet you.' Lawrence smiled proudly. 'Phineas Trickett is well-known for his research on ancient Tibetan mandalas; retired now but he has a particular interest in your Aunt Eglantyne's work. He tells me they met in the eighties; gave a lecture together at the Natural History Museum. I've taken the liberty of penciling you in for a meeting with him at my home next week. Are you up for that?'

'Yes, of course…'

'Excellent. So have your coffee and we'll go through some ideas for your new book cover. Then I'll get you over to Dorlington Gardens.'

Chapter Twenty-Six

Life is Just a Story

Isla was already at the door when Amelie arrived at Number Sixty-One. 'You okay, honey?' she called. 'You're looking a bit flushed.'

Amelie raced up the steps to join her. 'More than okay,' she said breathlessly. 'Wait till I tell you!'

'That's awesome,' Isla exclaimed, grabbing Amelie's bag, 'but we really need to hurry right now. The decorators are here tomorrow so now is our only chance to visit next door.'

'Whoa! What a mess!' Amelie gasped when they reached the top of the stairs. There were step ladders and paint tins everywhere. 'I see you've emptied out the lift.'

'We did it together,' said Tim, holding the doors open while the two girls squeezed inside. 'Are we ready?'

'You bet…' Isla steadied herself as the old lift jerked into action. 'Amelie's got some news for us, haven't you?' She gave Amelie a little nod. 'Come on then, girl, spill the tea!'

'It's my new editor,' Amelie announced. 'Lawrence couldn't have found me anyone better!'

'Why, who is she?' asked Tim.

'Tabby, Tabitha Wilson. But…' Amelie smiled mysteriously. 'That's only while she's living on Luga.'

Tim stared at her in disbelief. 'You don't mean like *Earth Watcher* Tabitha?'

'Yep, she's come to warn us about the *Mark of Triandor*.'

Amelie gave him a knowing glance. 'Just as I thought, we're going to need it very soon.'

'Does Lawrence know who she is?' asked Isla.

'Not yet, but he's already noticed how she disappears! Oh, and another thing, there's some famous professor guy who knew Aunt Eggy well. Apparently, he wants to meet me…'

Isla raised an eyebrow. 'Wow, you do move in illustrious circles.'

Just then, the lift shuddered to a halt and Amelie stepped out onto the carpeted landing again. 'I wonder if there'll be any more surprises in store.'

And to their immediate delight there were.

'Greetings, Bright Hearts!'

'*Tuló*!' Amelie's heart raced. It was their beloved ten-foot tall Commander, at last. Trembling, she raised her hand, placed it on her heart and bowed. It was little more than a year since she'd first met him on the stairs at Hadleigh House. Today though, he seemed taller than ever.

'Goodness, how you've grown, Bright Hearts,' he exclaimed, gazing round at the little group. 'Not simply in stature but in spirit too!' The light in his heart was so bright it almost hurt their eyes.

'I think maybe you have too, *Tuló*,' Amelie whispered and immediately felt foolish. But the Commander smiled kindly and stooped to touch her cheek. 'You may well be right, my dear.'

'Hello-again-my-friends!' They spun round, hearing Dorin's curious mechanical voice behind them. '*Tuló*-has-lots-to-share-with-us-today.'

They held their breath, hushed and expectant. Were they about to discover their next major assignment?

'Not quite yet,' the Commander replied and indicated five comfortable chairs, three of them arranged as a triangle. 'Do you remember when our friend Tabitha spoke about the *Mysteries*?'

'Tabitha?' Amelie said excitedly. 'Did you know I just met her in Lawrence's office…?'

The Commander gave a brief nod as if to say *but of course, I sent her there myself.* He drew up his chair. 'Today, I'd like us to consider the greatest Mystery of all.' He took a deep breath. 'Do you ever stop to wonder what *Life* is really about?'

'Sure,' said Isla. 'Like, all the time. I mean, who doesn't?'

The Commander rubbed his chin thoughtfully. 'I'm afraid most people don't, Isla. Lugans have lost the art of wondering.' He leaned forward curiously. 'So, what conclusions have you come to?'

Isla stared back at him, blank-faced, and Amelie prayed he wouldn't ask her instead. Tim shifted in his seat, blew out his cheeks while trying to sneak a look at his transonometer.

The Commander noticed all this and smiled. 'I'm afraid electronic devices aren't too good at answering questions like this. However…' He turned to Amelie. 'Maybe you are, my dear.'

'Me?' Amelie stared up at him, dismayed.

'Yes, since Life Stories are your speciality.'

'Honestly, I haven't a clue,' Amelie admitted. 'Unless, of course, you mean that Life is some kind of story…' She imagined a planet, many thousands of light years away, where an old storyteller sat, deep in thought. The tale he was about to write was vast and complicated, one with a mystifying plot and an endless cast of characters.

'Hey-not-bad!' said Dorin, tuning into her thoughts. He clapped his hands and hissed like a steam iron which was his way of laughing, they remembered.

'I've learned a lot since writing Eggy's story,' Amelie admitted. 'Not just about her life but what it means to be human.'

The Commander nodded. 'After ninety-seven years on Luga Eglantyne knew herself well,' he remarked. He took Amelie's hand into his own long-fingered one and added: 'So now, my dear, you're ready to learn from your *own* life.'

He turned to Tim and Isla and smiled. 'You're all creating an exceptional story, unlike any other that has come before it.' He raised his hands and cast an invisible blanket of light around them. 'This will comfort you all in times of need. Never worry what happens next – *everything* is for you to learn from.'

Amelie closed her eyes for a moment. Yes, she realised, there were lots of things that worried her these days: apart from her mother, there was Storm, her second-best friend. She could tell him anything and he'd always understand. But he would die one day quite soon and that was a *very* big worry. She frowned. And that wasn't all. She sat, biting back her tears. There was now another worry to add to her list: Tim and Isla. Just when you thought everything was going well, something always happened to spoil it.

'Are you all right, Amelie?' the Commander asked gently.

Amelie blushed. She knew he had heard her every thought. 'Yes, thank you, *Tuló*.'

'Don't despair, my dear. The future is glorious, I promise you. Your real home is elsewhere where the bigger part of 'You' lives. There, nothing is lost because nothing ever dies...'

They all glanced at one another, aware that tears threatened to fall. They knew that everything the Earth Watchers had told them today was true. It was just too easy to forget at times.

'We'll try to remind one another, won't we?' said Isla. 'When we get a bit lost.'

'Please do that,' the Commander affirmed. 'Let that bigger part of you *watch* quietly as your life unfolds. Then, you'll really begin to grow!' He stood up suddenly with a huge grin on his face. 'No wonder I'm so tall…'

They watched as the light in his heart grew brighter still. And when they glanced down they saw with surprise that their own hearts had too.

The Commander held out his hand and an old book appeared in his palm. 'As you'll see, today is just one small chapter in the Book of Life!' He carefully opened it and held it out for them to inspect. Instead of pages as they had expected, there was a tiny screen inside.

Tim watched with amusement. 'Oh, man! Look, that's Storm there, isn't it, on a trapeze? In his Royal Air Force uniform too!'

Amelie giggled. 'I think it's that time he worked in a circus…'

'What-a-curious-story-that-was,' remarked Dorin. 'Make-certain-you-ask-him-about-it!'

'Hey, Amelie!' Isla exclaimed. 'This one's for you.' There, coming alive on the screen, were Eggy and Adelaide, sitting on a bench outside their little *cartoleria*, eating ice-cream. 'Jeez, imagine having to wear those awful long dresses in the heat!'

'Seems like they're having a conversation,' Amelie observed. 'And just as though it's happening right now…'

'But of course,' the Commander laughed. '*Photo-animation* proves what we've always told you: *there is only ever Now*. These moving pictures are small episodes, stored in the Library of Life - just as your lives are too.'

Amelie's eyes widened. 'You mean we're being recorded right now?'

Oh, my God! thought Isla, stifling a gasp.

'Like, everything we say and do - forever?' asked Tim, as a wave of shame engulfed him.

'My friends, you have nothing serious to hide,' the Commander assured. 'Unlike those pesky Dark Hearts and the evils they perpetrate on Daktron…'

'Sure is nice to know Eli Dankstone's still there,' said Isla.

Chapter Twenty-Seven

The Worst Has Now Happened

1914

It was the summer of 1914 and Eggy was soon to return to Havenbridge. One evening, a grey-faced Edgar returned from his club in the City. 'I don't like it at all,' he muttered, sitting down without bothering to remove his coat. 'There's a chap at the Foreign Office called Gerald Smythe…'

'I remember him,' said Adelaide, pouring him a glass of sherry. 'Nice man, wife's a suffragette. Here, darling, sit down and enjoy this…'

'Well,' Edgar continued, taking a mighty gulp, 'seems like he's heard worrying news from Edward Grey. He reckons all the lamps are about to go out in Europe and we won't see them lit again in our life-time; figuratively speaking, of course.' He stared up at them wearily. 'War, in other words, ladies, and I fear he could well be right.'

Eggy's heart sank. 'Who is this Edward Grey?' she asked anxiously. Eddie dropped so many famous names she could never quite keep up.

'Sir Edward, Foreign Secretary. And he of all people should know. It's a dreadful business, chilling, in fact.'

That night, Eggy lay awake for hours, pondering over the news.

In the end, she switched on her bedside lamp and wrote in her diary: *All this talk about war, I don't like it at all...* She drew a little face with a downturned mouth.

Days later, she opened her diary again and this time added another face, this one with falling tears. *I don't understand any of it but I do know that Eddie was right; the worst has now happened...*

It was between late August and October that year when thousands of Belgians fled their homes, just as the German army planned to invade France.

Imagine, thousands of them are crossing on fishing boats and ferries this very minute; terrifying journeys, Eggy wrote in her letter to Jack. *There must be something we can do to help.*

'We can always find some room here,' suggested Adelaide, giving Edgar a funny look.

'Why, yes,' he answered at once. 'How many, a hundred or so?' He raised an eyebrow enquiringly and looked across at Eggy. 'I think now is the time to tell her, don't you?'

Adelaide nodded and clasped Eggy's hand in her own. 'Darling, it's about the house next door. We haven't known how to tell you this but it isn't really empty after all...'

'Oh, that,' said Eggy, relieved to know the secret was out. 'Don't worry, I've always known.'

'You knew?' Edgar peered at her over his spectacles. 'But how?'

'Purely by accident, I found a way in. That time I was late for dinner.'

'Good Lord! And we both thought we were going mad.'

'Yes,' said Adelaide, 'that was until we spoke to Gyatso.'

'He's familiar with these things,' Edgar added. 'He even lent us a book on Ancient Tibetan magic. How one can occasionally slip into parallel dimensions; extraordinary stuff really...'

'May I borrow it?' Eggy asked earnestly. 'May I? It's exactly the sort of thing I'm fascinated by.'

'Of course,' said Adelaide, relieved. 'It seems that you and I have been brought together for a purpose. And I don't just mean French verbs and Geometry.'

Very soon, one hundred and twenty Belgian civilians were brought to their secret location at Dorlington Gardens. The youngest was named Marina, born during the crossing, the oldest a great-grandmother of ninety-eight.

'Luckily, most of them speak French,' said Adelaide, 'though I'm doing my best to learn Flemish too.'

'I can try teaching them English,' offered Eggy and very soon she had them reciting their names and counting to one hundred.

Les Belges[23], as they became affectionately known, settled in very well in the house next door. Each family had its own small apartment though they often came together for communal meals to which *les Anglais*[24] were often invited.

All this delayed Eggy's long-awaited return to Havenbridge. However, the following year, a new danger threatened when the Zeppelin[25] raids began in earnest. At the end of May, a giant Zeppelin airship hovered like a dark menace over Dorlington Gardens, blotting out the moon. Explosions were heard all over the city, striking terror in all who lived there. For the first time in history, London was under attack from the air.

'You must return to Hadleigh at once,' Adelaide insisted.

'Then you and our guests must come too,' Eggy replied. 'We can easily take some in at Hadleigh and I'll find billets for the rest.'

'Hmm, your father won't be too keen about that,' remarked Edgar.

'Needs must,' Eggy insisted. 'Look, I'll go on ahead and organise things. I know Jack will help.'

Thus, Adelaide and Edgar prepared their guests for a mass exit to Havenbridge. 'We're taking you to a pretty little town on the South Coast,' Adelaide told them excitedly. '*Très jolie*[26]*! Un peu de vacances, hein*[27]*?*'

'So, why don't you wear this for the journey?' Adelaide suggested, offering Eggy a beautiful red velvet coat. 'Summer or not, it's none too warm today.' She stood back while Eggy tried it on. 'Oh, my, it looks so much nicer on you than me.'

Eggy could hardly believe it. She was actually going home at last! She would now spend every precious moment with Jack on the farm. They would need all the help they could get now the war was in full swing. A sudden pang of shame took her by surprise. She had plans and, for one dreadful moment, she was glad it had all happened.

Chapter Twenty-Eight

The Rise of the Daktrons

Jack was already there to meet her when she leaped off the train, dragging two suitcases with a rucksack strapped to her back.

'How could you know I'd be on this one?' she squealed, flinging her arms around him. 'They've put on lots of extra trains today because of everyone travelling south.'

Jack didn't mention he'd come down every single hour to check if she'd arrived. He stood back to appraise her. 'Gosh, you're looking well, Eggs!' And extraordinarily beautiful too but he kept that to himself. 'I love your new coat...' He smiled. 'And I see you're wearing my old trousers.'

'Much easier for jumping off trains,' she laughed. 'It's not safe in London anymore so our Belgians are coming down too. Thank heavens you're here to help.'

Jack gave her a peck on the cheek and picked up her suitcases. 'Here, let me carry those, you idiot!'

'We really must act fast, Jack - get Mrs. Fairweather and Isadora to form a welcome committee for them. Find extra accommodation...'

As they left the station, Jack took her arm and guided her across the road. 'I haven't told you my news yet.'

'What news?'

He stopped suddenly and grasped her shoulders. 'Eggs...' He looked into her eyes for what felt like eternity. 'I've joined up.'

She stared back at him blankly. 'You can't be serious…'

'We're leaving for France next week.'

'But the farm…' she spluttered. 'You're exempt from service because of the farm. You can't.'

'I have to, Eggs.' He cupped her face in his hands. 'I'm needed there.'

'You can't,' she repeated angrily. 'I had plans for us...' Tears of fury began to fall and she wiped them away with her glove.

'We've got Frank and Walter here now. They'll be company for Mum.'

How can you be so bloody selfish, Jack Hilton? She couldn't utter the words but the look on her face did. Her eyes darkened. 'Have you read the latest newspaper reports? You'll be killed…' Her lip quivered. 'And what if *you* killed someone? No, no, it's just wrong, horribly wrong…'

Jack reached out his hand, the one with the missing finger. 'It won't be for long though, Eggs, everyone's saying it'll be over by Christmas and once it is we'll go off and explore the world, if you still want. That's if you're not married by then…'

'Are you mad?' she screeched, beating his chest with her fists.

'Listen, this war could mean a new freedom for us both - a less ordinary life at last.'

'Rubbish!' Eggy stamped her feet. 'War never means freedom!'

Jack looked at her glumly, remembering the day she'd returned from London and accused him of doing Lord knows what with Elsie Thomas. 'I hate it when we fight.'

The first few drops of rain splashed on their faces and he took her arm again, urging her to walk a little faster. 'Please, Eggs, let's make the most of whatever time we have left…'

Next day, the rain held off and they rode over to Littlehaven to watch the tide coming in.

'What was that lake called?' Jack said suddenly. 'The one you like so much. Garda, wasn't it?'

'Yes,' Eggy replied despondently.

'One day, we'll look out over that lake together and remember today with a smile.'

'Hmm, if by some bloody miracle you're still alive.' The sound of hooves interrupted her and she turned. 'Tabitha!' Her heart lifted. At least she would talk some sense into him.

'Tether your horses, my friends,' Tabitha said briskly and pointed to Jacob's Cave at the end of the bay. 'The Commander is waiting to meet you.'

They reached the entrance to the cave and Tabitha shouted into the darkness: 'They're here, *Tuló*.' Her voice echoed around the rocky walls.

'Come through!' Another voice called back in response and there, seated before them on a large piece of driftwood, was the Commander. 'Excuse me if I don't stand,' he apologised. 'There's so little room here for people like me.'

They gazed back at him in awe. His head already touched the top of the cave. He smiled and beckoned them to him. 'You two Bright Hearts are bonded by your desire to help. I want you to understand this.'

Jack and Eggy glanced silently at each other.

The Commander let out a deep sigh. 'Unlike those Dark Hearted ones from a certain Planet called Daktron, as far away from light as it's possible to get. Not a place you'd ever care to visit.'

'Heavens no!' Tabitha shuddered. 'They only came to Luga knowing how rich the planet is.'

'Then colonised and established a base here,' the Commander said gruffly. 'They are responsible for everything that's wrong with your planet. Their hearts are incapable of love.'

'So, you see, we have a problem,' Tabitha said gravely. 'They have learned of a sacred diagram or mandala, one you are familiar with. Used wrongly, it would cast your planet into a hell beyond all imagination.' She turned to the Commander again. '*Tuló*, they are to be trusted, as you know.'

'Good.' He nodded. 'These Dark Ones worship Material Life, my friends: they seek gold, land, property, power. But, since all material things ultimately die, they have one great weakness…'

'FEAR,' added Tabitha. 'This is what drives them to steal and build empires; exert power over one another…'

'Firstly, they claim ownership of land, crying: *My house, my country, my King...*' The Commander reached out his long-fingered hand. 'Remember this, you two: *I, me* and *mine* are dangerous words! Use them sparingly. Such words lead to war.'

At last! Eggy glanced at Jack. 'Are you listening?' she hissed. 'War is wrong!'

But neither the Commander nor Tabitha appeared to hear.

'The Dark Hearts seek world domination and this will result in a dreadful loss of life.' Tabitha pointed to where their three horses were tethered. 'Not only human life but war horses; war dogs; animals used as machines.'

'Thank you,' cried Eggy, 'now please can you talk some sense into him?' She jabbed her finger in Jack's direction. 'He's only gone and signed his own death warrant.'

'Stop there!' the Commander said firmly. 'Jack is about to make a great sacrifice, my dear, and we'd ask that you do the same.'

Eggy stared back at him, confused. Why would no one listen to her?

The Commander's face softened a little and he reached out to touch her arm. 'Jack is incapable of killing,' he said gently. 'His purpose is to lend courage to his brothers and comfort them in their fear.'

'But he might die...'

'Eglantyne!' Tabitha gasped. 'Surely, you haven't forgotten? *Death will not kill you!*'

Eggy shivered, unable to shake off her doubts.

Jack took off his jacket and wrapped it around her shoulders.

'This young man needs your support,' the Commander continued. 'While he is immersed in war, you will have much work to do here.' And to Eggy's amazement he turned to her and bowed. 'And for this we thank you sincerely. *Together or not, you are never apart.*'

'We have a rather unusual gift for you both,' said Tabitha. 'It is this...' She put a finger to her lips and they all sat together for what seemed like an eternity, hearing only the soft crashing of waves against the rocks and the occasional call of a curlew.

'Silence,' she whispered. 'You will be surprised how powerful it is. Spend time in silence every day and you will come to know its power.'

They left the cave and stood together on the shore, neither willing to move. 'I'll be back sooner than you think,' Jack said brightly and Eggy rested her head against his chest. His heart thudded in her ears. Then, slowly, they untethered their horses. 'They'll never take you off to war, my boy,' Jack told Arrow, never taking his eyes off Eggy. 'You'll wait for me, won't you?'

Eggy's heart flipped though she wasn't altogether sure whether he'd meant those words for Arrow or for her. 'Come on then,' she sighed. 'Let's go and have some tea. I've already asked Loula to make your favourite cake.'

Chapter Twenty-Nine

Some Unusual Gifts

The day the volunteers were due to leave a storm threatened to break over the coast. It happened soon after Eggy left the house. No, she told herself, if she ran back for a brolly now the train would have already left. Drenched already, she tripped on a flagstone and landed in a puddle at the foot of Cloud Hill. She finally arrived at Havenbridge Station, muddy and bedraggled, just as Jack's train was pulling out. There he was, leaning out of a window at the rear, his eyes scanning the platform. She whistled and seeing her, he grinned and shouted, but his words were swallowed up by the roar of the train. She froze, unable to wave goodbye. It seemed much luckier not to for some reason.

Havenbridge town-centre was soon ablaze with flags, Belgian flags fluttering from flagpoles alongside the Union Jacks. 'Black's for humility,' Mrs. Fairweather explained, 'and yellow's for prosperity, I believe. Red is for victory, of course!' She turned to Lady Havenbridge who was supervising the Grand Reception in the Town Hall. 'So, what do you think, Isadora?' she asked. 'They should be here any moment.'

'Utterly divine,' Isadora Havenbridge replied. 'And your little band is a perfect touch.'

The band was in fact Mrs. Fairweather's hastily re-assembled string quartet since two of its players were now occupied on the Western Front, along with most of the town's brass band. Today, they were rehearsing *La Brabançonne*, the Belgian National Anthem, ahead of the refugees' arrival.

'Followed by *God Save the King*?' stated Lady Havenbridge, more as a command than a suggestion.

At last the Belgians arrived, all one hundred and twenty of them, plus tiny Jean-Louis Pratt, born during the very first raid at Dorlington Gardens. They were shepherded by Adelaide who not only spoke fluent French but had now mastered enough Flemish[28] to say *Welkom*[29]! and *Kom met mij mee*[30]!

'I agree with Eggy, you know,' Adelaide said firmly. 'They are not refugees anymore. They are our guests.'

❋

'They've settled in surprisingly well,' remarked Edgar, 'considering they've kept pretty much to themselves elsewhere in the land. It must be dreadfully hard for them.'

'They've even set up a little school here,' Eggy added. 'I'm continuing to teach them some English.' It was certainly taking her mind off things a little. There had been virtually no news from Jack since he left and she made sure she didn't have a moment left to brood.

However, Adelaide couldn't help but notice how pale and worried she looked. 'Eggy dear, what a wonderful community you've created here. I see they have their own Medical Centre too.'

'Yes, Dr. Fairweather has given one of their doctors a room in his house.'

'His name is Alain,' said Adelaide, 'and what a lovely young fellow he is, good-looking too. If you ever need any medicines, I'm sure he'd be happy to help.'

'Adelaide!' Eggy knew precisely what Adelaide was suggesting and laughed. She'd even caught him glancing at her a few times. 'The war will be over soon,' she said firmly and Adelaide knew not to mention it again.

It was around this time that Tabitha returned, armed with more unusual gifts. 'A few seeds, from Planet Lumea,' she explained, and presented Eggy with five small bags. 'I'll show you how to make special medicines from them. Then, should sickness ever strike you'll be well prepared.'

Eggy potted the seeds exactly as Tabitha instructed and was surprised to find how rapidly they became seedlings. She checked and watered them every day and when Tabitha returned a few weeks later they had grown strong enough to turn into tinctures.

'They all have their own special *signature*,' she began, pointing to each little plant in turn: '*Wormwood, Blood Root, Gravel Root, Gelsemium*, and this one is my own favourite, *Angelica Archangelica*... You must ask Loula for a little brandy to preserve them in.' Tabitha tilted her head and studied Eggy thoughtfully. 'It's just a little something to take your mind off your worries.'

Chapter Thirty

The Musical Box

1916

'Oh, this awful, wretched war!' sighed Adelaide, leafing through a copy of *The Times* without ever bothering to read it. 'When will there be good news?'

It had been raging for two whole years now with no sign of an end. Eggy had become increasingly unsettled, watching for the postwoman to arrive and rushing to the door four times a day. Maybe there'll be something later, she always told herself.

'Let's take a trip to Littlehaven,' she announced, pretending to be brave. 'We'll have tea at the Marine Hotel and I'll show you my favourite shop.' Taking charge made her feel surprisingly powerful and grown-up.

'Come on,' she commanded, as they both stepped off the train that afternoon. 'It's only a short walk to the centre.'

'Do you love him, Eggy?' Adelaide asked unexpectedly and Eggy pretended not to hear. Adelaide smiled. 'Silly question, of course you do. And you know he loves you too.'

'He's never said so.'

'Oh Eggy, do wake up! I've seen the way he looks at you. But he's terrified, partly because you hate the idea of marriage, and not least because of your father. The poor boy fears for his life.'

'Not enough to stop him going to war.'

'I know.' Adelaide took her arm. 'After the war though; do you think you'll settle down together? Or go abroad perhaps?'

'That was the general idea.' Eggy's eyes were clouded with anxiety. 'But there's something else that bothers me…'

'Having children?'

'Yes, how did you know? I'm not brave enough, Adelaide.'

'I think he'd love you enough not to mind,' Adelaide said gently.

'Do you really?' Eggy looked up, her face blotchy with unshed tears. 'I can't imagine my life without him.'

'Then next time, be brave enough to tell him. It's easy enough: *I love you!*'

Eggy's face brightened. 'I think I will.'

They walked to the end of Station Road and turned into Chapel Row. The scent of lavender and rose greeted them even before they crossed the cobbles. 'Does this place remind you of anywhere?' Eggy asked with a smile.

'Our little *cartoleria* in Limone!' Adelaide shaded her eyes and peered at the window display. The shop was full of fancy soaps and trinkets; notebooks and lace handkerchiefs. 'Look, there's even a sweet little musical box!'

There, right at the back of the window stood a tiny wooden stage with velvet curtains and just as Adelaide spoke, the shop girl came to the window to wind it up. 'Do you like it, Eggy?'

'I adore it!'

'Listen! It's Beethoven, I think – yes, *Für Elise*! What a perfect gift for anyone called Elise; or even Elsie, I suppose,' Adelaide teased.

Eggy caught the twinkle in Adelaide's eye and began to laugh at herself.

Just a week after their little outing, Eggy had an unexpected visitor. Everyone knew where to find her these days: holed up in the potting shed at the end of the garden, where the orchard met the fields. The new seedlings were now ready to replant, but Loula had warned there'd be no more brandy for a while. Eggy pondered over the next batch of tinctures and how on earth she might preserve them. Perhaps sherry would do instead, or gin, as Adelaide suggested. Either way, she hoped Tabitha would reappear soon. Just as she thought this, a shadow fell over the pots. She turned, and dropped her trowel in surprise. 'Jack!' She lunged at him with such a force it almost toppled him. 'You might at least have warned me,' she said awkwardly, looking down at her grubby old riding breeches.

Jack grinned and kissed the top of her head. 'Since when were you ever bothered about wearing old clothes?'

'Gosh, what happened to your hair?' she gasped. 'Your curls, all gone…'

'Army regulations – they'll soon grow back.'

Eggy blew a wisp of hair from her eyes and laughed. How wonderful he looked in his uniform. 'You'll still do, I suppose.'

He fumbled in his rucksack, hindered by a roughly bandaged finger. Soon he produced a clumsily wrapped package which he tucked under his arm. 'What's up then?' he asked, seeing the look of horror on her face.

'Your finger!' Eggy grasped his hand and he winced.

'Yeah, another one gone,' he said, as though losing another finger was nothing at all. 'I saved a rabbit in a trap.'

'But that's terrible, Jack – even though it matches your other hand now.'

Seeing her anguished face, Jack let out a howl of laughter. 'I really am sorry, Eggs, I was joking. It's only a small cut, I promise.'

Reassured, she tiptoed to plant a kiss on his cheek. 'I'm so proud of you, saving that rabbit. I've saved a few too. Rabbits are for companions, not food. I've told Lou so she doesn't cook them anymore… same as chickens.' She gazed at him solemnly. 'You've still got everything safe, haven't you?'

'The *Mark of Triandor*? Yes, of course, and this too…' He patted his webbing[31] and pulled out a blue and gold gemstone. 'I haven't needed either of them just yet.'

'Good, I'm glad you've kept them both safe. That means you will be too.' She wanted to say more, things she'd promised Adelaide she'd say, but somehow the words just wouldn't come. (Somewhere she'd read that girls should never, ever, make the first move. What would a suffragette make of that? Her mind buzzed. Why, oh why, was life so bloody complicated?)

Jack interrupted her thoughts. 'They're my lucky mascots,' he said, returning the Stone of Power to his webbing, remembering, with a pang of guilt, Eggy's little photograph that lay hidden in there too. 'Thanks for your letters, Eggs.'

He wanted to tell her how he read them every single night, how he dreamed of times they'd spend together after the war, exploring Paris and Vienna, and that place by the lake she liked so much. He promised himself he'd learn French and Italian one day too. (Not German though because of the war.) 'Eggs,' he began, 'I'm wondering if…' His brow glistened with sweat. 'Eggs, would you…?' As he spoke, the carelessly wrapped package slipped from his under arm.

'What's that you've been hiding?' Eggy asked suspiciously.

'Close your eyes and I'll show you.' He waited then placed it into her soil-stained hands. 'Right, you can open them now.'

She tore open the wrapping paper and stared at it in disbelief. It was the musical box, shaped like a theatre with velvet curtains that opened and closed, and drawers for hiding small treasures. The very one she'd seen in Littlehaven only the week before. 'How did you know?'

There was a key at the back and when she turned it the same music began to play. *Für Elise*! 'Is this really for me?'

'Who else?' Jack laughed. He kissed her brow, hesitated a moment, then picked up his rucksack and prepared to go. 'Next time then, Eggs, next time. And I'll try to get longer, I promise…'

'No, don't go yet,' Eggy begged, 'this is the most beautiful thing I've ever seen…'

Goodbyes are always the worst, thought Jack and a sudden panic overtook him. What a bloody coward I am! 'I love you, Eggs,' he declared at last, 'I really do!' But he was already halfway across the fields before the words would come out. A bead of sweat reached his chin. Next time he'd tell her properly; if there ever was a next time

Eggy had become so engrossed with the little musical box that when she raised her head, he had already gone. She flew to the door and watched him disappearing over the fields. Even when she whistled he didn't turn his head.

That night, she placed the musical box on her dressing table. The top drawer had a tiny key inside which opened all the others. They were empty apart from the bottom one which rattled a little, and there, right at the back, lay a tiny sapphire ring; very old, by the look of it, its gold band worn thin. She tried it on, surprised to find it fitted perfectly then slipped it back into the drawer.

Dearest Jack,

Did you know there was a ring inside? It's the prettiest one I've ever seen but I shan't wear it until I see you again.

Now, if anything should ever to happen to you while you're away, I'd never forgive myself if I didn't tell you...

She stopped then, hearing Loula call, and slipped the unfinished letter into her diary with the little sprig of rosemary he'd given her long ago, and joined Loula in the sitting room. They sat companionably by the log fire, Loula knitting socks for the boys in France and Eggy winding wool.

'It'll all be over soon,' Loula said cheerily, counting stitches.

Chapter Thirty-One

No More Than a Bad Dream

And Loula had been right but not in quite the way she had intended. Weeks later, a letter arrived by the evening post. Eggy hugged it close before running upstairs to read it in private.

Dearest Eggs,
I think of you endlessly, especially at night when it's relatively quiet though to be honest, it rarely is. Maybe one day this war will be no more than a bad dream...

That same night she was shaken from sleep by a deafening roar. A flash of light followed, and she heard Jack's voice calling, pleading for help. She touched her arm at once, willing its power to reach him wherever he was, willing him to do the same. 'You'll be fine, my love, you will. Just remember *The Power in You*!'

Weeks passed and no news came. 'You'll hear something soon,' Loula promised, knowing how hard she was taking it.

One day, a young man arrived at Cloud Farm and introduced himself to Nellie:

'Hello, Mrs. Holland...' He removed his cap. 'I'm Sam. I promised Jack I'd call in on you while I was on leave...'

Walter, washing his hands at the sink, stopped what he was doing and ran upstairs.

Sam clutched his cap between his knees and searched in his

pockets. 'How are you, Mrs. Holland? I'm sure you know by now.'

Nellie didn't. She was peeling carrots at the time and her knife slipped, cutting her deeply.

Sam took out a clean white handkerchief, leaped up and wrapped it tightly around her thumb. 'It happened so fast,' he stammered, 'honestly, he wouldn't have known a thing.' It was all he could find to say, even though he'd been practising it for days. What he couldn't tell her, couldn't bear to recall, was that poor Jack had been caught in an explosion; propelled into the air like some worthless piece of debris; a human cannonball. Tears filled his eyes. The truth was there'd been smoke and dust everywhere, and orders came to retreat immediately before they lost any more men. He'd never, in all his life, forget that terrible day. Sam hung his head. His was the burden of having survived.

'You can be very proud, Mrs. Hilton,' he croaked as handed her the letter. 'I found this in his things. He'd started it minutes before…' Sam grimaced, holding back an explosion of grief. 'He was always talking about you and how much he missed his Sunday dinners.' Sam made that bit up since Jack rarely spoke of home. Too wrapped up with concerns for others; keeping the lads' spirits up with his daft jokes. Always comforting the young'uns, away from home for the first time in their lives and scared witless. He'd teased him once about him having a sweetheart at home. 'Bet you got a picture of her in there!' He'd tried to ferret in Jack's webbing and Jack had sent him reeling.

Nellie slipped Jack's letter into her apron pocket for later and carried on preparing the dinner. Once Sam had gone she sat down with it in her lap, holding back her tears lest they spread the ink across the paper and ruined it.

Dearest Mother,

Like Eggs says, France is a special place. How's Dad

doing these days? Tell him I've been made up to a Lance-Corporal now. And you - how are you, Mum? is Walter looking after you? I'm hoping to be back on leave soon. Looks like I'll have to finish this a bit later though. Sergeant Major's on his way. Don't you go worrying about me because I'm happy enough...

And there it ended. A wave of pride softened the shock – Lance Corporal! She thought of Eggy who wouldn't have had the news yet, and wondered if the little photograph had been blown up with him too. 'Walter!' she shouted, hearing muffled sobs from upstairs. 'You'd better come down for your dinner.'

Walter couldn't. He flung himself down on his bed. He had intercepted the telegram two weeks ago. Read it and torn it up. He buried his face in the pillow along with his shame. How could he ever tell her that now?

Eggy had just returned from Miss Tribble's haberdashery shop where she'd purchased more wool for Loula's 'Boys at the Front' sock enterprise. 'Grey is so boring, isn't it?' she remarked to Miss Tribble. 'Would you pop in some red, please - just to liven them up?'

Ivy Bottomley greeted her at the door, though greet was not exactly the right word. A sly grin appeared on the woman's face. 'Well, well, so it's happened at last,' she remarked gleefully, arms crossed over her chest. A chill wind ran through Eggy's heart. What could she possibly mean?

Ivy Bottomley ran a finger across her throat. 'Dead and gorn,' she sneered. 'Popped 'is clogs.'

'Gone, who's gone?'

Eggy hurried from room to room to find Loula. She ran outside, searching blindly until she discovered her hiding in the Summer House. It had become Loula's own little bolt-hole since Eggy left all those years before. Seeing her there, framed by the door, Loula let out a great howl.

'It's not true?' Eggy gasped, praying for it not to be. But Loula said nothing. Her face was blotchy and tear-stained and all she could do was stare, stare down guiltily at her shiny black shoes.

'So that evil blabbermouth told you,' she at last. 'That was my job not hers.' She cursed under her breath, words Eggy never dreamed she'd hear coming from Loula's mouth. Then she placed a hand, soft and velvety from pastry making, on Eggy's arm. 'Don't worry, my love, it was very quick, he won't have suffered at all.'

'No,' Eggy cried fiercely. 'He's missing, not dead; I'd have known if he'd died! And I shall continue to wait for him to walk through that door, any door, a bit the worse for wear maybe, but alive all the same.'

'That's grief talking,' murmured Loula. 'I was the same when my Arthur was taken.'

'What a terrible thing to say!' Eggy screeched. 'How dare you take away all my hope?'

Later though, she thought of Nellie and gathered an armful of roses from the garden. She waited till it was dark and laid them at the farmhouse door with a little handwritten note. She'd made several attempts, none of them quite right, so in the end she abandoned them all and simply wrote: *For Nellie, my other Mother, from Eggs with love.*

'I told you not to, you stupid bloody fool!' she ranted at the sea next day. But the sea offered no comfort at all; its vast, empty horizon only added to her despair. A chill gust propelled her closer to the edge of the water. The *Mark of Triandor*! It didn't work then, did it? It was all a hoax, and as for *Death will not kill you!* What crazy talk was that? She watched the waves and imagined herself beneath them, surrendering to the tide; remembering the day he'd saved her. How she wished he hadn't bothered. 'I can't bear it,' she told the sea.

'Yes, you can,' it seemed to reply, 'just as countless others have borne it before you.'

That night, Tabitha appeared in a dream.

'What is it you want from me, Eglantyne Trott? Is it comfort or courage?'

Eggy didn't answer but looked down in awe as a wave of golden light blazed from her own chest.

Tabitha spoke again, more gently this time. 'Why do you think you're known as a Bright Heart, my darling?'

Chapter Thirty-Two

Phineas Trickett

'Imagine how hard it was back then. Like with no cell phones or video calls.' Isla fought back her tears. 'That last bit really got me didn't it you, Tim?'

Tim was about to reply when Amelie said: 'It was awful writing it. Tim's lucky, he never cries. Not even when there's a sad film on and everyone else is.'

'That doesn't mean I don't feel anything. I just don't cry,' said Tim. 'Well, hardly ever.'

'Jeez, never knowing if your loved ones were safe or not. And you, Storm, how did you cope in the war with no contact for weeks at a time?'

Storm nodded soberly. 'Sometimes it was years, my dear.'

'And poor Jack, what could have gone wrong with his Stone of Power?'

Amelie frowned. 'I don't know. Or the *Mark of Triandor* for that matter - no wonder Eggy lost heart.'

She didn't want to admit it but it had worried her for a while, even to the point of doubting it herself. She gathered together a stack of papers on her desk and squared them neatly with her hands. 'Anyway, no doubt we'll find out in due course. I'm taking a few of Eggy's diaries to Lawrence's house to show Professor Trickett.

Come on, Freddie, my little muse. We're going for a ride.'

Freddie stretched, leaped off her lap and followed her outside. She steered her bicycle onto the driveway and tapped Freddie's wicker basket affixed to the handlebars. 'Hop in!' she instructed and he jumped in at once.

They were halfway down Cloud Hill when Amelie spotted a stout elderly man coming the other way. He stopped to wipe his brow and gazed wearily about him.

'Can I help you?' she asked.

'Thank you, my dear, I'm looking for Laurel Lodge,' he replied, peering at her through thick bottle-glass lenses. 'Years since I've been here.'

Amelie peered back. 'You're not by any chance…'

The old man smiled. 'Trickett, my dear. Phineas Trickett. Should I know you?'

'Amelie Joan Trott,' said Amelie, dismounting. 'We can go there together.'

'Not on that thing, I hope,' he laughed. 'Long time since I've been on a bike.'

'No, I think Freddie might object.'

Phineas Trickett stared nervously at the cycle basket where Freddie reclined. 'Hmm, I'm more of a dog man myself.' Freddie opened one eye and glanced at him with disdain. 'Mm, handsome chappie, I suppose,' Phineas appeased.

'We're here now anyway,' said Amelie, trying not to laugh. How could anyone be scared of Freddie?

They trudged up the long, winding drive together.

'So good to meet you at last,' said Phineas.

Amelie gazed at him warmly. 'I've been longing to meet you. How amazing that you knew our Aunt Eglantyne…'

'What a marvellous woman!' Phineas patted her head. 'You've

brought her diaries for me, I believe?' He clasped his stubby little hands together excitedly. 'I can't tell you what this means to me.' He lowered his voice a little. 'Eglantyne and I shared a special interest in Tibetan Magic. She even let me into a little secret. What am I saying? A rather big secret if you know what I mean.'

'I think so.'

Phineas nodded and reached into his pocket. He took out a packet of cigarettes and looked at her apologetically. 'Dreadful habit, I know. Don't ever be tempted, my dear…'

'Don't worry, I won't,' said Amelie and sneezed violently. 'I'm a *lerjick.*'

Phineas drew on his cigarette. 'Unfortunately, my office was ransacked recently. Years of research notes stolen, including the…' He cleared his throat. 'Well, you know what I mean…'

'The *Mark of Triandor*?' She rang the doorbell and waited.

'Exactly, it broke my heart. Knowing you have a copy has lifted my spirits. All is not lost.'

'Yes,' Amelie whispered, 'it's quite safe with me.'

'Good,' he replied, 'and you must stay safe too. There are those who'd love to get their hands on it.'

'Did you know she had it inscribed on her arm?'

'Yes, I happened to notice it. That's when she shared it with me.'

Amelie suddenly put aside her doubts. 'Well, I'm thinking of doing the same.'

'Hey, what are you two doing here?' Amelie cried, surprised to see Isla and Tim at the end of Lawrence's drive.

'Waiting for you, of course,' said Isla. 'We just caught sight of your famous professor leaving. What a cute little guy…'

'Phineas?' Amelie laughed. 'Yes, he's rather sweet, isn't he? Poor man was terrified of Freddie though!'

Tim raised an eyebrow. ‘Scared of a cat?’ he said disparagingly. ‘So, how did it go?’

‘Wonderful!’ Amelie’s face glowed. ‘But he was a bit upset when I explained he couldn’t keep the diaries. I’m only up to the end of the war…’

‘First or Second?’ asked Isla.

‘First,’ replied Amelie, ‘when the Spanish Lady arrived.’

Chapter Thirty-Three

The Spanish Lady Arrives

November 1918

Armistice came and Adelaide suggested a little party to mark the end of the war. 'Only a quiet one,' she said, knowing that Eggy had little to celebrate with Jack 'still missing.' No one dared to argue with her. But sadly, Adelaide's plans were soon thwarted when the Spanish Lady arrived.

For Eggy influenza almost came as a relief. She spent most of her time in the potting shed now, replanting seedlings in the herb garden, gathering them once they were fully grown, and creating special tinctures, according to Tabitha's instructions. They were needed more than ever now. Tabitha must have known all along.

'Still missing?' Loula feared Eggy was losing her mind. She spoke to Dr. Fairweather about it.

'She just won't accept he's gone, Doctor,' she said wearily. 'I really don't know what to do.'

Dr. Fairweather frowned. 'Not unusual, I'm afraid; it's a common reaction to loss. She'll get over it in time, like thousands of others have.'

Shyly, Loula reached out to touch his arm. The poor man had lost his only son in the war; mentioned in dispatches for bravery.

❀

'Adelaide, you and Eddie must stay on with us,' Eggy insisted. 'You'll be far safer here than in London.' What she meant was she couldn't bear to lose them too. Yet, as it turned out, even in a small town like Havenbridge, no one was entirely safe. People were dying in huge numbers, children especially. Tabitha's herbs couldn't have come at a better time.

The Spanish flu wasn't really Spanish after all since it most likely began in America, according to Tabitha. 'This is just another kind of war,' she warned. 'And unless Lugans change the way they live it won't be the last either. The medicines will help a little.'

Eggy worked day and night making more tinctures. She also decided to train at Littlehaven Hospital as an auxiliary nurse. How life changed during those two dreadful years. There was mask wearing, distancing; and so many curious theories as to how it all began. Many believed it was spread by German submarines, others blamed foreigners, any foreigners from pretty much anywhere in the world; anyone who wasn't British.

Ailing Fred Holland finally gave in to the flu, leaving Nellie to fight yet another battle at home without her beloved Jack. But at least she had young Walter. He managed to survive it all right but eight of his brothers and sisters didn't.

Loula, who had refused to leave the house for weeks, was obliged to venture out for bread one day since Billy Birch's delivery cart failed to arrive. Poor Billy, she brooded, yet another dear soul gone. Would there be anyone untouched by this terrible disease? She returned from town in tears, shocked by all the changes she'd witnessed. 'The sight of folk wandering about in them god-awful masks…' It was all too much for her. 'I thought I'd landed on another planet,' she wailed. 'How long do we have to keep this lot up for?'

'For as long as it takes,' Dr. Fairweather told her sternly. He had come back to check on a maid, isolating in one of the attic rooms.

'For all you know I could be carrying the dreaded germs.' Loula stepped back, putting another few feet between them. 'Bloomin' Germans, they started it all, same as the war. Here, Doctor, you hop in the servants' lift, eh? Save you climbing all them stairs.'

Eggy reprimanded her later. 'The Germans didn't start it, Lou. It's more likely because of the way we've all been living, killing one another off and wrecking the planet. Luga's fighting back, like she has done many times before.'

'You and your funny ideas. And please stop calling it Luga. It gives me the creeps. Earth is Earth and that's an end to it.'

But that wasn't an end to it at all and Loula began to wonder…

There's a strange kind of beauty in it all, Eggy wrote after a long shift on the wards. *Despite the suffering, there's a real sense of everyone pulling together, the like of which I've never seen before in my twenty-two years. I'm so proud of Havenbridge. I just hope no one ever has to go through this again.*

She was kept busy at the hospital, often going without food or sleep for days. Busy enough to keep grief at bay. But that night exhaustion overcame her and it was impossible to quell the rising tide that came in its wake. 'He's dead!' she realised. 'I've finally got to face it, like everyone else has.' Her throat ached with unshed tears. 'I just bloody well hope the Spanish Lady gets me.'

Her wish was granted, and just as the last stock of tinctures ran out. Her aching throat became a wheezy cough and next morning she awoke with a fever. As the days passed delirium set in. But the nights were the worst. It felt like every bone in her body had been broken, her chest was on fire. As for the *Mark of Triandor*, what was the point in even trying? It hadn't saved Jack so why should it save her now?

Loula, doubly masked, brought her some onion broth. 'Try a

little,' she begged. 'Please try, Eggy my love!'

The following night, in her delirium, Jack came close. She closed her eyes and at once felt a cool breeze on the back of her neck. '*I'm here*,' he said.

I must be dying, she thought. Her nightdress was soaked, even the bedsheets too. 'Have you come for me?' she whispered.

'*Not yet*,' she heard, and immediately sank into a deep and dreamless sleep. In the morning her chest had cleared, her bones no longer ached and the raging fire had quelled.

'It's a miracle,' declared Loula, attributing it to her onion broth.

❋

We discover who we are at times like these, wrote Eggy.
I've found it hard to forgive myself – for not being able to save my Jack's life like he saved mine. I just hope I helped him a little. Strange times indeed, since even I went to church one day. Kneeling there, I was struck by the light slanting from the stained glass windows. I saw rainbows dance on the stone floor and imagined having one at Hadleigh, - on the little landing where I sometimes like to sit. I shall have the old window pane replaced by a colourful figure; something to celebrate the end of the war. Yes, a figure of Tuló, perhaps. Adelaide knows a gifted young artist called Jennifer Newall who works with stained glass. Yes, I think I'll commission her.

❋

'Look at this,' Eggy gasped, reading the newspaper headline one day. 'Fifty million people have already lost their lives from the flu. That's more than from the war itself.' Adelaide and Edgar were about to move back to London now that life had returned to some kind of normal. Not that it ever would be normal again, would it, she sighed, and Edgar agreed.

'No, I'm afraid we haven't seen the end of it,' he said sadly.

'Mark my words - there'll be more horrors to come.'

They certainly hadn't seen the end of their grief. It was now three years since Sam's ghastly visit and Nellie and Loula continued to wear black. Walter was inconsolable. He had lost a brother and a friend; someone who trusted in him and wanted him to do well.

It always hit Eggy when she least expected it, like one evening while she walked Nellie's dog across the fields. 'He's not coming back, is he?' she cried aloud, loud enough it seemed for Tabitha to appear.

Silently, Tabitha shook her head. 'It's not possible, my dear.'

'I miss him so much. I can't seem to move on...'

And Tabitha replied, as she always did: 'Together or not, you are never apart.'

'Why didn't the bloody *Mark of Triandor* work? Tell me, dammit!?'

'Trust me, my dear - it always works but not always in the way we expect.' Tabitha gazed at her with such compassion that Eggy couldn't stay angry with her for long. 'Jack has achieved his mission but you still have much here to do.'

'You mean, I've got to get on with the rest of my life?'

'Yes, dear one, it's best that you do.'

But with no Jack and Adelaide and Eddie now back in London again, Eggy was adrift. For years she'd tried to keep everyone and everything alive: her patients, her herbs, and more than anything, her hope. Even when life was at its most uncertain, she had kept soldiering on. Now that the worst was over, it had somehow lost all meaning.

Eggy had many admirers; soldiers she had nursed back to health, sent home from the Front to convalesce. One was called Charlie, a raffish young officer in the Buffs[32] regiment. Secretly, she found him rather intriguing – not to mention good-looking.

'Oh, for heaven's sake, Eggy,' Loula cried. 'I'd be after him myself if I was twenty years younger!'

'Have dinner with me,' Charlie demanded one day. They were sitting together in the hospital gardens, Eggy showing him exercises to strengthen his injured arm. Suddenly, he leaped up, plucked a rosebud from a nearby bush and presented it to her. 'What a beautiful creature you are!'

Eggy was flattered, but furious too. She thrust it back at him, suggesting that he might have first asked the rose bush's permission. Bewildered, Charlie returned to the bush to mumble an apology. Unused to rejection, he confided all this to a mutual friend: 'What is it with that girl? She's prickly as the blooming rose bush.'

It was after this last encounter that Eggy made a decision. She was never going to settle down. Charming and entertaining as Charlie was, he just wasn't Jack. She smiled, remembering his golden sovereign bet. The day they saw the glider which actually wasn't a glider at all.

Chapter Thirty-Four

A Surprise Visitor

A steady crunch of boots on the gravel drive usually signalled the arrival of the delivery boy. This was followed by the infernal cacophony, as Theodore described it, of the outside bell. It reverberated through the whole house and never failed to cause alarm, even though the war had long since ended and the deadly flu had passed out of their lives.

The past few years had left an indelible mark on them all; especially those who had witnessed the horrors of war first-hand. Though silent, their grief and guilt merged into one unspeakable memory. 'One can only guess the torment those poor souls re-live each day,' Loula remarked sadly.

Since no one came to answer the bell that day, Eggy went herself. When she opened the door she found a young man waiting there with his back to her. He was wearing army uniform. 'Hello?' she asked nervously. An impossible thought had occurred to her. Could it be Sam come to admit he'd made a dreadful mistake and that Jack was alive after all, recovering from the flu and on his way back home?

He turned sharply to face her. 'It's me, Eglantyne,' he announced. 'At least, I'm assuming that's who you are. I'm your brother.'

Joseph! Eggy's heart sank.

'Well, are you going to let me in, or what?' he demanded irritably

Eggy frowned. 'It's just that it's been so long…'

'And in all that time you never wondered if I was dead or alive?'

'Of course I wondered.' It was true in a way. She had given him an occasional thought but more from curiosity than caring. She hoped he wouldn't be stopping too long. He seemed far too like her father, terse and difficult. 'Why didn't you write?' she said.

'I did, many times.'

'Oh.

'To get straight to the point, Emily's having a baby…' He waited for her to say something but since she didn't, he continued. 'Emily's my wife. And since that mean bastard stopped my allowance, I've no means of supporting her.' He sighed impatiently. 'Apart from my measly army pay, I've nothing. Emily's got her heart set on the sea. So…' He looked around, taking in the old familiar environment. 'This place should be big enough for us all to avoid one another.'

'Oh…' said Eggy again, horrified at the sound of this new arrangement. She picked up the little brass bell on the hall table. 'Come into the sitting room, I'll ring for some tea.'

They sat together in awkward silence until footsteps approached.

'Dear Lord, preserve us!' Joseph bellowed, as Ivy Bottomley entered with a tray. 'I thought you'd be enjoying His Majesty's Pleasure[33] by now, Bottomley.'

A little snort of laughter escaped Eggy's mouth.

'Mrs. Bottomley-Sligh to you, you cheeky blighter…' She raised her hand, ring finger erect. Like an insult, he observed.

Once she had left the room Joseph and Eggy exchanged glances and began to laugh helplessly, and by the time they regained their breath, they knew they'd become friends.

'Gawd, how I loathed that old witch.'

'Me too, Joseph,' she said, thinking how someday she would tell him more.

'Call me Joe, won't you? And you can be Eggles or Eggs or something.'

'No,' she replied sharply. 'I'm known as Eggy. Only Jack calls me Eggs.'

'The boy from the farm? Oh, I remember. I rather liked him. Not a boy anymore now, of course…' Then, seeing her face change, he stopped. Oh dear, not anything anymore then, poor chap. There'd been millions lost in the trenches, not to mention killed by the wretched flu. 'Emily will love it here,' he said, looking around at the cheerless room. 'Just needs a bit of fresh blood. You'll like her, Eggy – not that I know the first thing about you! Insane really, isn't it?'

'Why did you fall out with the old man?'

'Oh, that.' He frowned and bent to re-tie one of his bootlaces. 'It was when I discovered Mother's will. She'd left me a fair old whack and I needed some of it to go to Paris.'

'Paris? You've been to Paris too?'

Joe nodded. 'With my best pal, George - his family kindly paid for me since the tight old wretch refused. That was it then, I'd found my new family.'

'The same people who took you home for the holidays?'

Joe bit his lip, struggling to control his sorrow. 'George was like a brother to me, Eggy. He survived, if you can possibly call it that; had shell-shock ever since…'

Then Loula arrived with a fresh pot of tea. Seeing Joe, she trembled with joy and almost dropped the tray. 'You're home at last, my angel! This is the best surprise for years. I'd better go and attend to your room.'

But first, she smothered Joe with kisses, hugged him so tight he wondered if she would ever let him go.

'You're the one person I've missed,' he told her, hugging

her back.

She returned later with a silver dish on which she had placed a pile of mail. Right at the top was Eggy's postcard from Paris.

He's very handsome, Eggy decided, observing him while he searched through his letters. Can brothers ever be thought of as handsome, she wondered?

Joe's return and the appearance of an obviously pregnant Emily sent Theodore into a rage. This was followed by weeks of silence during which Eggy found herself a go-between in their communications. One evening during dinner she could stand it no more.

'How dare you, Father! As if you haven't treated my brother badly enough already, you horrible, selfish old wretch…'

The room held its breath. No one dared move, save Theodore who thumped his fist on the table, threw his glass of wine at the wall, and stormed out of the room.

'Thanks Eggy,' murmured Joe, patting his sister's hand. 'That was very brave of you.'

'Perhaps someone should go after him,' suggested Emily. 'He looked rather pale.'

'No, leave him,' said Eggy, 'he needs to dwell on this for a while.'

Hearing the commotion, Loula poked her head around the door.

'Eggy's torn Father off a strip,' Joe explained. 'Not before time. He's gone off in a sulk.'

'He didn't look at all well,' fussed Emily. 'I hope he's not having a stroke.'

'I'll go after him,' said Loula.

She found Theodore, head in hands, on the front steps in the rain. 'Here,' she said, wrapping her shawl around his shoulders. 'You'll catch your death out here. Whatever she said, I'm sure she didn't mean it, you know....'

'She meant every word, Mrs. Bellamy. She despises me; they all do.' Tears began to flow down Theodore's cheeks. 'I never thought I'd hear her stand up for her brother like that…'

Loula rubbed his back, encouraging him to say more.

'It all started over Lillian's money, you know. I never did figure out what to do for the best. I kept thinking of my poor little girl with no money of her own. So I started saving whatever I could…'

Loula listened, aghast. Of course, he didn't know about Lillian's private legacy. And now she was left with a promise she could never break. Whatever could she tell him? She paused, hoping for the right words to come.

'Don't worry, my dear,' she said at last. 'Eglantyne will be looked after. She's very resourceful. Why not put the past behind you all and make a fresh start? A new life is about to bring joy to the family.'

To Loula's surprise, Theodore took her hand and kissed it. 'Whatever would we do without you, Mrs. Bellamy?'

And so began a brand new chapter in the Trott family's history when everyone decided to get on. Joe shook his father's hand, saying: 'No hard feelings, old chap,' and Eggy, now knowing the truth, pinched his cheek and smiled when his uncivil grunts became replaced with *Pleases*, *Thank yous*, and *How kinds*.

It was soon their first proper Christmas together and not long before baby Storm was born. Eggy and Emily were sitting together making paperchains, while Joe installed a large fir tree in the Morning Room, which Emily had renamed the Garden Room because of its lovely view.

Eggy had splashed out on gifts for them all, including a train set for the new baby.

'Bit young for a baby, isn't it?' said Joe, patting Emily's rounded belly. 'And what if it's a girl?'

'And why wouldn't a girl love it too?' retorted Eggy. 'I would for one.'

'It's perfect, Eggy,' laughed Emily. 'What a lovely thought.'

'What are you calling it anyway?' asked Eggy.

'Lillian if she's a girl,' Emily replied.

'And William if he's a boy,' said Joe. 'Billy for short.'

'Billy,' echoed Eggy. 'Well, if Loula's tea leaves are correct you're about to have a huge, bouncing boy.'

'Superstitious old nonsense,' said Joe.

It was New Year's Day, 1924. The best thing by far was the absence of the Bottomley-Slighs. Ivy had now taken employment at a public house in Littlehaven while Reginald was imprisoned for causing malicious damage to a railway compartment on the Southern Belle.

'A drunken brawl with the ticket collector,' said Loula who had heard this from the vicar. 'All over his non-existent ticket…'

That night, she wrote in her diary:

Life has become a little easier. Joe is training as a lawyer and has joined the family firm: Theodore Trott & Son, Family Solicitors. The house is no longer cold. Log fires blaze in every room and the sound of Emily's laughter warms everyone's heart. Emily is all I could wish for – a sister and more. And very soon there will be a new little person to join the family...

February 1924:

The sun shone for the first time in weeks and I suddenly remembered my little musical box, tucked away in my wardrobe. Would I manage to look at it again and risk a deluge of tears?

I raced upstairs to fetch it and there, right at the back of one of its tiny drawers, found the little sapphire ring.

Would anyone notice, she wondered? Yes, Joe would, he never missed a thing.

Nevertheless, she slipped the ring on her finger and, on a joyful whim, slid all the way down the bannisters, just like she did as a child. For some reason no one ever did notice the sapphire ring, not even Joe, but then, of course, he had other things on his mind.

Chapter Thirty-Five

A Storm Arrives

February 1924

Unable to sleep one night, Eggy crept downstairs to make some cocoa. She was just on her way back when Tabitha took her by surprise.

'You're going to have to be very brave tonight,' she whispered. 'Remember, your Stone of Power? It will eradicate all pain.'

'Oh, Lord, Tabitha, whatever can you mean?' Eggy exclaimed, just as Joe collided with her on his way down.

'Who the hell were you talking to?' he said wildly, gripping her arm. 'Are you off your nut? Quick, Eggy, I need your help. There's only a maid in there with her…' A gruesome scream ripped through the house. 'I'm not allowed in apparently.'

'Emily? But it's not due yet!' Eggy blanched. The baby wasn't expected for another month. She'd even planned to be well out of the way when it happened. Oh, Lou, why did you have to visit your sister this week? She stared at Joe with terror in her eyes. 'Supposing she dies…?'

Joe glared at her fiercely. 'How could you!'

'I'm sorry. I didn't mean it, it's just…'

'Mother, you mean?' Joe nodded wretchedly. 'I've got to do something to help her. Dr. Fairweather's on his way but it's taking him forever.' Outside, the wind rose and rain slashed against the window panes. 'Eggy, you know how Emily adores you…'

A crash of thunder sounded directly above them. This will be the bravest thing I've ever done, thought Eggy, as another terrible howl came from upstairs. 'I'll go,' she said and rooted in her bodice for the little blue and gold crystal.

'Here,' she whispered, pressing it into Emily's hand. 'Hold onto this, it will help, I promise.'

And somehow, it actually did. Emily yawned peacefully, longing to close her eyes. 'Why is it little ones always seem to come in the night?'

The next rumble of thunder was followed by a flash of sheet lightning. Fifteen minutes later, Dr. Fairweather came leaping up the stairs three at a time, just as the not-so-little-one was about to emerge.

It was a miracle, thought Eggy, waiting with a clean white towel in her hands. A bit messy but a miracle all the same! Yet how was it possible for a baby to make so much noise?

'A thunderous arrival!' exclaimed Dr. Fairweather.

'Yes,' Eggy laughed, 'we must call him Storm; wild Billy Storm!'

Apart from shouting a good deal Storm was also very wrinkly. Despite this, Eggy was glad he'd joined their newly assembled family. She put her lips close to his ear and whispered: 'Welcome, old chap! You look like you've been here many times before…'

Unfortunately, Storm's sudden arrival tested Theodore's recently found patience to the limit. 'Can't you bloody well do something with it, Loula?' he complained one morning. Storm had been bawling interminably outside Theodore's window for hours. 'Please, Loula?' he added sheepishly. (Having dispensed with formalities, he now insisted she call him Theo.)

'Teething, Theo,' said Loula, rocking Storm's pram. 'It's a very nasty business. Lovely boy though, isn't he, your first grandchild?'

Theodore harrumphed and said he hoped it would be the last.

However, exactly one year later Margaret Lavender (Maggie) made an appearance, followed by John Henry the next. Although Eggy adored them all, Storm always remained her favourite.

On Storm's third birthday Theodore tripped over his little train set. 'Who left this bloody mess on the floor?' he raged, forgetting himself, and immediately blamed Eggy for giving it to him. At which point Storm rose to his three-year-old feet, folded his arms across his chest and bellowed: 'Go away, Grandfather Trott, I don't like you at all.' He glared at an astonished Theodore. 'Eggy is the nicest person in this room, apart from me.'

That same year, an exciting letter arrived, forwarded from Dorlington Gardens by Adelaide. Eggy had been feeling a bit down lately, caught off-guard by fleeting reminders of Jack. She tore it open to find an invitation from Gyatso to visit him at his monastery in Tibet. Adelaide whisked her off at once to Harrods, for a short and shiny bob which was the fashion at that time, and several pairs of new trousers for ease of travel. 'I shall be travelling to places where women aren't allowed,' said Eggy. 'Will I pass for a boy all right?'

Seeing his aunt with short hair, Storm erupted violently and complained that she didn't look like herself anymore.

'Shush, boy! That's the general idea,' Eggy explained, tapping the side of her nose. 'It's my disguise, you see. The less I look like a woman the easier my journey will be.' As she spoke, she removed her precious sapphire ring, threaded it onto a piece of cord and hung it around her neck. There it lay, together with the little blue and gold crystal, resting against her heart.

'Oh, Eggy! I wish I were half as brave as you,' said Emily.

'And you're going all that way on your own.'

'Me, brave?' gasped Eggy. 'But you've had three babies, remember.'

'That's nothing, is it Storm?' Emily said sweetly, gazing at her chubby little son. 'I'd gladly do it all again, especially since your little crystal worked its magic. I still don't understand how. But I've just had an idea. Why don't we have a pretend Christmas Dinner since you'll be away for the real one?'

'What, in July?' Loula gasped. Wasn't that blasphemous? But things were about to get much worse.

'Remember, there's to be no dead animals, Lou,' Eggy said firmly. 'Not even if Joe or my father beg and plead. We're to be a totally meat-free household now.'

Loula left the recently renamed Garden Room in a huff. Sometimes Eggy was quite the dictator and impossible to reason with. Everyone knew they'd die without meat and she, Loula, would be held responsible.

'Don't worry, I'm not a meat person either, Aunt Eggy,' Storm piped up, emptying his box of locomotives onto the floor.

Emily winked at Joe. 'That stubborn little boy will do anything his Aunt Eggy tells him. I don't know how she does it.'

'Good for you, Billy Storm, you're a very clever boy and I love you!' Eggy picked him up and swung him around the room. 'I'm not too keen on brats normally,' she joked, 'but you'll do, I suppose. And I'm very pleased you like your train set. Maybe your own children will play with it in years to come.'

'Eggy!' laughed Emily. 'You're such a fibber. You're wonderful with children and you know it.'

Eggy smiled and wandered into the kitchen to make peace with Loula. Storm had taken the edge off her sadness.

'Wherever do you get these silly ideas?' Loula grumbled,

mourning the loss of roast duckling and angels on horseback. 'Whatever will people think?' She took out her frustration on an old copper pan, polishing it until it gleamed.

'That you're a very thoughtful person who loves animals. Don't worry, I'll find you some delicious new recipes…'

Loula capitulated and created an enormous bean and vegetable lattice pie, garnished with roasted potatoes and parsnips, baby carrots and Brussels sprouts. This was followed by a Christmas pudding (suet-free), set aflame with a ladle of brandy, and finally, dishes of petits fours (these supplied by Adelaide and Edgar who were their guests of honour). It was, they all agreed, a proper family Christmas at last, even though it was five months too early.

Storm agreed to give his grandfather another chance and invited him to play with his trains, provided he didn't lose any of the tiny figures. His favourite was the station master with the flag.

'I'll be a station master when I grow up,' he said proudly.

'What about a pilot?' Eggy suggested, picking up his toy glider. 'I once had a friend who wanted to fly one of these.' She looked up and caught Loula's eye. 'The war put a stop to that.'

'This really is the nicest pretend Christmas ever,' Emily pronounced, raising her glass of champagne.

'Indeed,' Theodore agreed, much to everyone's delight. He really had mellowed at last but was also showing odd signs of dementia. 'Lillian, my love,' he announced, grasping Eggy's hand, 'what a splendid day it's been.'

And thereafter, whenever Theodore asked: 'Is that you, Lillian?' Eggy would simply pat his arm and say, 'Yes, darling, I'm here.' And in a strange kind of way, it felt like she really was.

Chapter Thirty-Six

Children of the Mountain

Together or not... It was in Tibet that Eggy really began to sense Jack's presence again. Impossible though it was she was certain he was thinking of her too.

Dressed as a monk she managed to enter the city of Lhasa which at that time was closed to foreigners. Here, she was met by a mountain guide called Pasang, who suggested she might shave her head since her golden hair would immediately draw attention. She did so gladly but soon found that even bald-headed monks weren't entirely immune from danger.

There were snakes, mountain bears, and one night, a prowling band of robbers. While they both slept, one of these snatched the sapphire ring from around her neck. She was awake in a flash, rolled up her sleeve and drew the *Mark of Triandor* in the air. Sparks flew from her fingers and a lightning bolt of electricity struck the ringleader. He dropped the ring at once and yelped in agony as his hand began to sizzle.

Pasang reached for his knife but stared in surprise as Eggy let out a great roar: '*The Power in Me*!'

For a moment she was unsure where those words had come from, until a long shadow fell across their path. She spun round and recognised the Commander.

'It was indeed the Power in You!' he cried. 'When needed, the *Mark of Triandor* acts like the Hand of God; it will create or destroy in a flash.'

Out of danger at last, Eggy and Pasang gave silent thanks for their visitor and continued up the mountainside to Gyatso's monastery. It was here she spotted a small mandala[34] hanging in her private quarters.

'You know about this then?' she asked one of the senior monks, showing him the the underside of her arm.

'Is *Mark of Triandor*,' he replied in his broken English, 'word for Nameless One…'

At that moment Gyatso arrived to greet her. 'Tell me, how is your good friend Jack these days? I hoped he might come with you.'

'Dead,' Eggy answered bluntly, 'even though I've tried not to believe it.'

Gyatso nodded solemnly. 'Death does not kill us. Whatever happens we're always alive.'

During Eggy's months at the monastery she became Gyatso's personal student. He taught her meditation and yoga and once encouraged her to venture out alone. Thus, one evening, half-frozen and exhausted, she fell into a snow drift. Seconds before passing out she remembered a breathing technique Gyatso had shown her. Within minutes, her body heat had risen sufficiently to melt the snow around her. She awoke at sunrise to the clamour of voices and broadly smiling faces.

'Why do you think I allowed you to go off alone?' asked Gyatso. 'It was a test, and one you'd already proved yourself capable of. Are you ready for your next challenge?'

'Why not?' said Eggy. 'If you think I can do it, what have I got to lose?'

'I will now teach you how to fly,' Gyatso promised.

'How Jack longed to fly,' she murmured. 'If only he'd had the chance.'

Well, it wasn't quite what I expected, Eggy explained in her diary. *There were no gliders involved. You may not believe me but I'm telling you, there are people here who can actually fly, unaided. It requires years of patience and another complicated breathing technique. The monks here devote their lives to this practice. I'm delighted to say I had a fleeting experience of it myself: a sense of weightlessness when my feet lifted a few inches off the ground. (I told Gyatso that I'd rather rely on the* Mark of Triandor*, since it takes far less effort!)*

'You're very privileged to have been entrusted with it,' he told me in return, 'since it is only to be used in exceptional circumstances.'

Before she left Tibet, Gyatso accompanied her down the mountainside to a small village where a hundred or so children had gathered to greet them.

'This is our school,' Gyatso said proudly, pointing to a tiny barn. There were no desks inside, just benches for the older students while the little ones sat cross-legged on the cold, damp floor.

'Would you care to teach them an English song or two?' he suggested.

Eggy shook her head. 'You haven't heard me sing yet, have you? However, I could always try a few rhymes.'

This idea was a huge success and by the end of that day she had them all reciting little verses. In return she learned to say *tashi dele* and *Kah-leh phe* (hello and goodbye) and could even count up to one hundred in Tibetan.

'Once I get back to England I will send you some money,' she promised. 'How much will you need to set up a proper school building? No, don't bother to answer that. We'll do whatever it takes…!'

And thus the foundation stones for the *Miss Marigold School* were laid.

'Marigold is my middle name,' Eggy explained. 'I think it's a lot easier to say than Eglantyne.'

'Thank you.' Gyatso placed his hands together and bowed deeply - something that reminded Eggy of the Earth Watchers' salute.

'I'll come back to visit you all one day,' Eggy promised, 'though it may not be for a while. I think I'm needed at home right now.'

And she was right. Poor Theodore was about to suffer a stroke and died shortly before her return.

Chapter Thirty-Seven

It was Christmas 1933 and Eggy, long returned from the East, had made eight-year old Maggie a set of paper dolls with costumes from all around the world. She also created a little cardboard box wardrobe to store them in, labelled 'Maggie's Mannequins[35].' She had taught Storm, now nine years old, to count to one hundred in Tibetan and allowed him to hold her Stone of Power. 'Shush! It's a secret,' she warned. 'You mustn't tell a soul…'

'Gosh!' Storm turned it over in his hands. 'I'll never own anything as magical as this!'

'Young Storm – you must *never* say never!' replied Eggy, patting his head. 'Magical things happen all the time. I'll tell you about the time I learned to fly if you like…'

Just then, Joe came in and seeing them together, gave Eggy's cheek a peck. 'What terrific pals you two are. We've missed you, Sis.'

'And I you…' Eggy smiled at him sadly. 'I'm sorry you've had to deal with everything while I was away. Father and so on. Seems like we're orphans now, you and me…'

Joe sighed. 'Weren't we always?'

In the spring of 1934, the Commander appeared with a young boy called Dorin. He spoke with a strange mechanical voice and explained that his sister Tabitha had now been assigned to a post on Planet Trankon.

Eggy felt a pang of sorrow. 'Does that mean I'll never see her again?'

'Never-say-never,' Dorin replied with a grin. 'But-meanwhile-you-have-me-I'm-afraid. Tuló's-sent-me-to-assist-you.'

'We've news concerning your future work,' the Commander continued. 'You'll find we've created some tunnels beneath your land, somewhere for you to cultivate special fruits and vegetables, enough to feed hundreds for decades to come.'

'Underground produce - without sunlight?' asked Eggy. 'How can that possibly work?'

'Plasma light,' the Commander replied. 'Think of it as an underground greenhouse.'

'It-is-how-we-eat-on-Zalnea,' Dorin added. 'The-plants-contain-vast-amounts-of-protein-so-no-animals-need-die.'

'Dorin,' said the Commander, 'why don't you let Eglantyne see it for herself?'

The entrance to the tunnels lay beneath her little potting shed. Eggy unlocked the door and Dorin bent down to remove a piece of old rush matting. Underneath, was a hatch which, once opened, revealed a long flight of steps. Dorin beckoned and Eggy followed him down.

The tunnels were far more extensive than she had imagined, and opened into a vast network of passageways. It seemed that an entire town lay beyond Hadleigh House without anyone ever knowing!

'You-may-share-with-all-who-are-open-to-the-Mysteries,' whispered Dorin.

'You must mean my aunt and uncle,' Eggy replied. 'They're due to arrive tomorrow.'

'Adelaide, Eddie, honestly, it's like a small town down there,' Eggy whispered, once they found time alone. 'We can start growing high protein fruit and vegetables there. It seems we'll be needing them in a year or so…'

'They'd also make rather useful air raid shelters,' commented Edgar and Adelaide cast him a warning glance.

'We don't need any more reminders of war, thank you, dear.'

The following year, Eggy and Adelaide travelled again to Italy to visit Anna and Luigi Martinelli. The Martinellis had recently returned from New York and now occupied a small lakeside villa in Limone.

'*Benvenute*[36]!' Anna greeted them. 'Welcome back! I hope you enjoy your dinner tonight.'

Eggy glanced at Adelaide who said: 'Anna, I don't want to cause a fuss but we don't eat meat anymore…'

Anna smiled. 'Don't worry, dear. Our chef's preparing us *pasta agli spinaci*. Trottole[37] Spinach, in honour of you both!'

'I feel like I've met up with a forgotten part of myself,' Eggy remarked. 'A part of me that's been blithely living a life of its own here without me... I feel almost complete again.'

Yes, almost, Adelaide mused. She still misses her Jack. 'I think I know what you mean, darling. People are so warm and friendly here. By the way, Anna, who's that extraordinary fellow down by the harbour, mending nets?'

'Oh, you mean the crazy guy?' laughed Anna. 'He's not warm and friendly at all.'

'Giacomo, he's called…' said Luigi and tapped the side of his head. '*Andazzo*! Totally mad.'

'He spoke to me earlier,' said Eggy, 'not that I could understand a word he said.'

'And have you noticed how white his hair is? And his teeth

all yellow and rotten.' Anna grimaced. 'Like some ugly old mongrel dog.'

Or a pirate, thought Eggy, who had spotted a scar over one eye

Luigi nodded. 'Poor chap, he was born in France, an imbecile, according to what's-her-name in the *cartoleria*.'

Eggy's face lit up. 'Oh, you must mean Signora Bartoli with her sweet little girl, Martina? I got talking to them today.'

Anna clapped her hands. 'That's the one, she knows all the gossip! But seriously, Luigi, the man's hardly an imbecile. He may be French but he speaks perfect Italian.' Anna loved the odd bit of gossip herself. 'I've heard his real name is Laurent. And by the way…' Her tone became serious now. 'I've also heard murmurings of another war.'

'Wouldn't surprise me at all with that monster running the show in Germany,' said Luigi. '*Orribile*!'

'Herr Hitler?' Adelaide shuddered. 'If I were Jewish I'd be out of there like a shot. We've had a few arrive in London already, haven't we, Eggy?' What Adelaide didn't mention was they had accommodated a hundred or so German Jews in *the house next door*. 'There'll doubtless be more.'

The following day, they spotted Giacomo again. He spun round as though he knew they were watching and stared back at them glumly.

It's you again, thought Eggy. You poor lost soul. She shifted her gaze to the lake. 'What if we never get chance to return here, Adelaide?'

'Never say never,' Adelaide replied, taking her arm. 'Whatever else happens, you'll come back, I promise.'

Chapter Thirty-Eight

The Secret Weapon

1938 -1940

Eggy returned from Italy to find that her now elderly Starlight had died, put to sleep after an episode of colic. Walter was broken-hearted for Arrow too had gone. 'He'd no one left to live for,' reckoned Nellie who, like Walter, felt much the same.

Three years later, in 1938, a new horror came to light. In Germany, thousands of Jewish homes and businesses had been ransacked; scores of hospitals, synagogues and schools destroyed. It was *Kristallnacht*, the Night of Broken Glass.

'But why?' sobbed Eggy, looking up from her newspaper. 'Why would anyone do such a dreadful thing?'

Dorin's voice answered her at once: 'Racism-my-friend. It-exists-at-the-very-core-of-the-Dark-Hearts'-charter.'

December 1938

Ten thousand Jewish children have now arrived in Britain, Eggy wrote in her diary. *It's all part of a rescue programme called Kindertransport (children's transport). At least another hundred are now safe in the 'House Next Door' and others, here in Havenbridge, where we've found them foster homes. Walter's sweet mother made room for a little brother and sister, called Josef and Rosa. Isadora, who always longed for children of her own, has welcomed another six. The rest we've taken to the tunnel town where Walter and I have hastily set up a school. Eddie was right! We'll call them air-raid shelters if anyone asks! 'I'm doing all this for Jack,' Walter said, and he had us both in tears. 'And for you,' he said kindly, 'since you it was you who found me.'*

❀

The following year, a miraculous crop of vegetables appeared in the kitchen garden: gigantic potatoes, carrots, and cabbages.

'And tomatoes as big as pumpkins!' Fifteen-year old Storm pulled one off the vine and weighed it in his hands.

'We shan't starve then, Storm!' said Eggy. 'Lou's making us a vegetable and lentil pie for lunch. What's the time? I'm ravenous!'

Storm consulted his new watch - one Eggy had given him for his birthday. 'Just turned a quarter past eleven…'

There was a sudden commotion in the kitchen and they turned to see Loula standing in the doorway, her face as white as the flour on her hands. 'I think you'd better come in. Mr. Chamberlain's on the Home Service[38]…'

Eggy and Loula stared at one another in horror. 'Not again…'

It was Sunday 3rd September 1939 and war had begun. From that moment all places of entertainment were closed and any gathering of crowds was strictly forbidden. 'Except for churchgoing,' added Loula.

In London, Adelaide and Edgar had been listening to the wireless too and eight minutes later, they heard air raid sirens. Luckily, they turned out to be a false alarm.

❀

We're now into 1940 and the raids have begun in earnest, wrote Eggy. *For safety, Adelaide and Eddie have joined us here. So too have dozens of evacuee children from the East End which means, once more, I've had to set about finding homes. Nellie has found space for a couple and Isadora has added to her tribe with another half-dozen. Emily has persuaded Joe to take in a whole family here. They're called Lambe and are from Stepney. We call them the Little Lambes.*

'You really should write a book,' Loula commented one day. 'You always said you wanted an extraordinary life, and it certainly has been so far.'

Eggy smiled. 'Once all this is over maybe I shall. That's unless someone saves me the trouble!' She remembered her precious diaries, stashed away in a drawer - they had far too much sensitive information for prying eyes to find! She gathered them all up and hid them behind a panel in her old wardrobe, remembering how, thirty years ago, she had once hidden the *Mark of Triandor* there too.

It was mid-November and dusk had fallen early. Dorin arrived at Eggy's little potting shed and they stood there, chatting for a while. He had come with a message from his sister, Tabitha.

'Eglantyne,' he announced, 'do-you-remember-the-secret-weapon-she-gave-you?'

Eggy nodded. It was the day before Jack went off to war. 'You mean Silence, don't you?'

'Used-daily-Silence-will-end-the-war…' Dorin gazed up at the stars, alive and dancing on that clear night. 'Hurry-home-now-and-await-the-bells…' His voice became a whisper, like the first stirrings of birdsong in the early morning air. 'Enjoy-your-minute-of-silence.'

Eggy looked at her watch. It was five minutes to nine. She ran indoors and found Loula about to switch on the wireless for the Nine O'clock News. At one minute before the hour the bells of Big Ben rang out and signalled a minute of Silence, just as Dorin had described.

Chapter Thirty-Nine

Nice Mr. Cornthwaite Takes a Nap

'The Big Ben Silent Minute[39]? Good Lord,' said Storm, 'millions of us took part, every evening at nine. Long after the war, some high-ranking German officer suggested that this was, in fact, the Allies' secret weapon that brought it all to an end. Pity we don't continue it now.'

'But we are doing,' Amelie cried gleefully, 'and it's going to be every night at 9pm GMT. We're starting tonight - me, Isla and Tim. We've even got Mr. Cornthwaite and the whole school involved…'

'What a wonderful idea,' said Lucy. 'We'll join you then, won't we, Storm? I must say, darling, you do seem a lot happier at school this year.'

'I am,' said Amelie, 'mainly because of nice Mr. Cornthwaite. We call him Dave.'

'Dave?' Storm frowned over his spectacles.

'Amelie's got a crush on him,' Tim cackled.

'I haven't!' Amelie yelled back at him, red-faced.

'Is that the poor guy I spoke to at Parents' Evening?' asked Lucy. 'Looks like he hasn't slept for years?'

'Yes, that's him,' said Amelie, still red-faced, 'and no, he hasn't. It's because of his kids.'

'So he was telling me,' said Lucy, 'a tribe of unruly under-fives! I imagine he comes to school for a rest.'

‘Yes, especially since I found a solution.’

Storm raised an eyebrow. ‘Care to expound…?’

‘The Silent Minute, Storm. We’ve been doing a practice run in Maths, or Math, as Isla would say. It’s like a rehearsal really. Everyone closes their eyes and thinks about creating a better world. Meanwhile, I keep an eye on the clock and ring Aunt Eggy’s little Nepalese bell whenever it’s time to stop - the one Aunt Eggy brought back from Nepal. We do much more than a minute though. We generally wait till Dave wakes up.’

‘You mean he falls asleep at his desk?’ barked Storm and enquired whatever had become of the world, as he frequently did, though no one ever came up with an answer.

Amelie nodded eagerly. ‘Yes, the very moment we begin. And since we haven’t the heart to wake him, I carry on with my writing and the others go on Tik-Tok, or make paper aeroplanes ready for the next class. It’s working in everyone’s interests.’ Then, seeing horror in Storm’s eyes, she added:

‘Miss Snarkey came in one time and screamed at us for being *too quiet.*’

‘It’s normally like a madhouse,’ Tim explained.

‘But since Dave carried on sleeping,’ said Amelie, ‘I had to think fast. “Sir’s working on a very complicated equation,” I said, and she left without a word.’

Chapter Forty

Storm Entertains Herr Hitler

'Storm, tell us about that time you joined the circus…'

It was another warm September day and Isla had flopped down on the grass next to Tim, waiting for Amelie to arrive. 'Dorin told us to ask you.'

'Ah, yes,' he chuckled, locking the hangar doors behind him. 'It was when I was shot down over Eastern France. By luck, a group of travelling circus performers happened to see me land…' He settled on a nearby tree stump and leaned on his favourite old stick.

'I see you've got Doris with you,' said Amelie, joining them. 'I knew you'd worked in a circus once but you never said where it was.'

'Did I not?' said Storm. 'Well, you'll recall that when I landed, the first thing I saw was a brilliantly coloured stone. It was just like the one Eggy handed me when I was young…'

The circus folk watched as the young airman untangled his parachute and picked himself up. It was just as though he'd done nothing more than trip on a flagstone! They gathered about him, checked him from head to toe for any injuries then led him off to a nearby encampment where they offered him food and a bed for the night.

Luckily, Storm knew just enough French to discover that his rescuers were facing a challenge of their own. A party of high-ranking Nazi officers was due to arrive in a few weeks, amongst them the Führer himself. And they had been instructed to entertain him.

Storm shook his head. 'I was baffled. You see, despite his hatred of the Jews and Romani people, Hitler loved the circus. I took a good look at them all. They were, I assumed, either one or the other but had cleverly bleached their hair to disguise their appearance.'

'Monster,' one man cried, hearing the Führer's[40] *name. He spat on the ground. 'He likes to think we'd risk our lives simply to entertain him.'*

Unfortunately these circus folk had just lost their main attraction, an acrobat who had broken his leg in rehearsal. They had found a replacement but he badly needed an assistant. Seeing Storm there gave them an idea.

'The replacement spoke English of sorts,' said Storm, 'though his voice was extremely odd. I assumed it was his Romani accent. He stepped forward suddenly, placed his hand on his heart and said: *You-will-do-for-the-job!* Well, you all know who that turned out to be….'

Isla smiled. 'Your old Earth Watcher friend, Dorin!'

'Yes, Isla, except he was my new friend at that point. Not only had he just saved my life as an airman, he'd placed a Stone of Power exactly where I would land.' Storm grinned. 'Well, how could I possibly refuse? I began six weeks of intense training with him, learning to fly from one trapeze to another without a safety net; and eventually landing on my feet, unharmed.'

Amelie gasped. 'How high up would that be?'

'Ooh,' said Storm, 'forty feet maybe?'

'Sheesh, that's nearly twelve metres!' said Tim. 'Weren't you a bit like scared?'

'Ruddy terrified!' admitted Storm. 'But I soon learned to trust him. That was until he disappeared on another mission and I was left to entertain Adolf myself!' He searched in his wallet and produced an old black and white photograph: a circus performer hanging from a trapeze. 'Look, this is me…'

'Yay!' murmured Isla. 'Isn't that the one the Commander showed us? The *photoanimation…*?'

'I carry it to remind myself what it means to be brave. Me on a trapeze - dressed in my own RAF battledress, pretending to fall from a burning plane - while Herr Hitler and his cronies sat watching. As it turned out, they loved it. I was the star of the show.'

However, after Storm's little stunt he was obliged to swallow his pride and turn to the Führer with a Nazi salute. He was then invited to perform in Berlin to celebrate German victory at the end of the war.

'No damned chance of that!' Storm muttered. 'However, I did stay on there for almost a year. I finally reached home, just before VE[41] Day was announced.'

'But that wasn't quite the end of the war, was it?' murmured Amelie.

'Victory in Europe Day?' Storm reached for her hand. 'No, my dear, I'm afraid not. There were even worse things to come…'

Chapter Forty-One

This Must Never Happen Again

August 6th 1945

Eggy awoke that morning with a terrible sense of doom. She pulled on her dressing gown and stumbled downstairs to find Loula fast asleep at the kitchen table. 'Are you all right?' she asked, shaking her gently. The wireless was playing quietly in the background and Eggy leaned across her to turn up the volume.

'What time is it?' Loula yawned and glanced at the clock. 'Goodness, I hardly slept last night. Turn that noise down, will you, dear? I've got such a head this morning.'

'My God, Lou, will you just listen?' Eggy stared at her in horror. 'An atomic bomb has been dropped on Japan.' Her voice trembled. 'In Hiroshima. I believe? I swear I felt it happen, soon after midnight. I daren't think what this will mean.'

'The end of the war?' said Loula with another yawn. 'And not before time.'

'End of civilisation,' Eggy murmured, unable to hold back her tears. 'This must never happen again, Lou. Imagine if these weapons get into the hands of the Dark Forces. Lives wiped out in a flash - what the hell have we done?'

Meanwhile, the world celebrated.

The Earth Watchers marked the ending of the war by sealing the tunnels. 'Should the Dark Hearts ever discover them they would use them for their own evil purposes,' the Commander warned. 'Had Britain been invaded, these tunnels would have become slave labour camps.'

Once news of the tunnels got out a myth arose about nuggets of gold hoarded there, brought in by smugglers. In fact, any gold had once belonged to the Jewish guests who had hidden their valuables away for the duration of the war. The Earth Watchers had now replaced them with artifacts of extraterrestrial life. Little items for future generations to find; reminders that Lugans are not the only life-forms in the Cosmos!

'You know, these two World Wars you have lived through, Eglantyne,' the Commander continued. 'They were in fact one. The years between them were simply a Pause; a gathering of the breath before the next onslaught. Man against man,' he said sadly.

Eggy's beloved Uncle Edgar died in 1949 and, unsurprisingly, Adelaide joined him a few months later. Eggy recalled with shame the way she had spoken of her before they finally met. What a wonderful friend and companion she'd become – one who had fueled her love of distant places. A year later, in Adelaide's honour, Eggy resumed her travels.

❃

I can feel you with me, my darling Adelaide, she wrote in her diary. *I've been spending some time in Nepal, a land I love dearly, and have set up a small orphanage there. I also returned to Tibet to revisit my school, the Miss Marigold School. How marvellous it was to see Gyatso again (we talked about you a lot) and oh, those children's smiles! They will doubtless be the sons and daughters of those I met the first time.*

In South America I discovered some excellent little craft

villages. I've now created a business called 'The Fair Shares Trading Company' and have put Loula in charge, since she's as passionate about it as I am! These people need all the help we can give them, especially the women and children. But now, I must begin my journey home...

❀

The Fair Shares Trading Company! Loula was in her element. Tibetan lamps and paintings had now arrived at Hadleigh; rugs and wall hangings, silver jewellery too, oh, and saris, and brightly coloured cushions, the most beautiful she had ever seen.

'Oh, my!' she exclaimed, busily organising everything into categories. 'This really has given me a new lease of life.' She had already made space for them upstairs in the Ballroom, in time for Eggy's return.

Eggy finally arrived home, two days before her sixtieth birthday. She was horrified to find poor Loula, now aged eighty-six, had fallen down a flight of stairs, carrying a box of cushions. She had stubbornly refused to use the lift, believing the exercise would do her old legs some good. Eggy was frantic, cancelled her birthday celebrations at once, and sat by Loula's bedside all night.

'Yet another one gone,' she sobbed and comforted herself with the thought that she'd very soon be joining her.

'I'm-afraid-not,' Dorin said gently. 'You-have-far-more-to-do-here...Including,' he promised, 'a-lecture-on-Tibetan-Magic-with-Professor-Phineas-Trickett...'

Chapter Forty-Two

Dame Eglantyne Trott

Storm had been having a bit of a clear-out after complaints from Mrs. Lambe that all his wretched dust and clutter was causing them a health hazard.

'Bloody woman,' he began before Amelie reproached him.

'Storm, you do realise that Libby's husband's grandfather was one of the evacuees living here during World War Two? He was called Norman: one of the *Little Lambes.*' Amelie made him sound like nobility. Lord Norman Lambe, peer of the realm.

'How could I forget? That boy was a young devil,' growled Storm, remembering how he'd run rings around poor Loula and tormented their long-suffering cat.

However, after much cursing and harrumphing, Storm finally capitulated and discovered, buried beneath all the mess, an old newspaper cutting from The Times. It was an obituary for Dame Eglantyne Trott: explorer, philanthropist and feminist; one that he had removed from the newspaper in line with her wishes.

'Eggy made it to the New Year's Honours List in 1992, you know,' said Storm, handing Amelie the cutting. 'But she was quite insistent that no one should find out.'

However, after much persuasion, he and Louisa had been allowed to accompany her to the Palace. Walter came along too and

Doris, of course, her beloved walking stick with the silver handle. Doris had come to Eggy's rescue in 1973 when, aged seventy-seven, she unwisely slid down the bannisters and injured her knee.

'Hold on, will you?' said Amelie, scribbling notes. 'You're going much too fast.'

'Righty-ho,' said Storm, 'let's take a wee break. I've found some interesting photos for you. You can include them in your book.'

'Oh, wow, I will – just look at Great-grandma's hat!' Amelie giggled. 'What does she look like?'

'Never mind laughing, it cost me a flaming fortune, that outfit did. Sit down, my dear.' Storm patted the sofa and cleared a space. 'I have a video too. Walter made it for her. Why don't we watch it together?'

'No! You're making a video for me?' Eggy had exclaimed. 'Oh, Walter, you're such a brick! When all this nonsense is over we'll walk along the Mall for a bit then drive to The Dorchester for afternoon tea…!'

She soon amazed them all by standing in the middle of the road, waving Doris and whistling for a taxi. They all fell into the taxi, giggling like children.

'Dame Eglantyne Trott!' Eggy sat, watching the crowds through the taxi window, remembering Jack and the time she'd pretended to sing *Let Me Call You Sweetheart* at the Royal Albert Hall. She smiled gratefully. Seated next to her was a small girl, dressed in a white pinafore dress. She blinked and the child was gone.

Back at Hadleigh, letters of congratulations arrived; cards from unknown well-wishers and admirers. There was one though that really took her attention; from an elderly man, judging by the shaky hand.

Nothing acts like a dame, or attracts like a dame! Dammit woman, why the hell didn't you marry me?
Yours, Charles Easton

Heavens, thought Eggy, it's that good-looking officer I snubbed all those years ago; and it seems he still remembers me!

She placed his card with the others then spotted something on her foot and stooped to pick it up. It crumbled a little in her hand but still retained its shape; it was a tiny pressed rosebud. The one she'd rejected along with his invitation to dinner. Had he really kept it all that time, hidden between the pages of some book? An unexpected tear splashed onto her hand. 'Dame Eggs indeed…' she sighed. 'Oh, Jack, my darling, what would you have made of all this?'

Chapter Forty-Three

Three Can Be a Difficult Number

‘I thought I’d make a copy of the *Mark of Triandor,*’ Amelie announced, rolling up the sleeve of her hoodie. ‘It’s like Eggy’s but in permanent ink. That way it won’t fade.’

Isla smiled. ‘Cool, it would easily pass for a tattoo. I’d love to have one myself but Dad would go mental.’ She glanced at the clock. ‘Is Tim around, by the way? The match starts in an hour.’

‘He’s been locked in the bathroom for hours,’ said Amelie, intent on her drawing. ‘Sounds like that could be him…’

Tim walked in with a huge smile on his face. He was wearing a new black tee-shirt and faded jeans and had brushed his hair in a way that made him look like he was going somewhere special; which, of course, he was, he reminded them, since it was his favourite team.

‘Jeez, Tim!’ Isla gave him a nod of approval. ‘You look awesome!’

Amelie glanced up and caught the look that passed between them. Tim’s cheeks were aflame. She froze. Whatever it was she’d just seen, she couldn’t now *un-see* it. It had clouded an otherwise perfect afternoon. *This* wasn’t supposed to happen. She wasn’t even sure what hurt more - losing her brother or her best friend. Both were as bad in their own way.

‘Shall we go then?’ Tim said at last. ‘We’ll be late otherwise.’

'Sure,' said Isla, gathering up her things. She looked at Amelie, aware of her silence. 'Are you okay, hun?'

At that moment, Freddie leaped onto Amelie's lap and she buried her face in his fur, just in time to conceal a small tear that had already spilled onto her cheek. And just as she'd noticed that something or other between them, Storm sensed something in Amelie too. When she dared to look up again she caught his rheumy old eyes gazing at her with such love and concern that she put Freddie down, ran over to him and fell into his waiting arms. The smell of his old tweed jacket was as comforting as hot chocolate and marshmallows on a cold wintry night.

'Shall we go for a walk?' he whispered.

She nodded mutely and together they walked into the garden.

'Three can be a difficult number, my dear,' he began. 'It's a powerful mathematical structure.'

'That's what the Commander told us last year.' She looked at him wildly. 'Why did they have to go and spoil everything? We were fine as we were.'

'And you still are.' He put his arm around her shoulder and the warmth of it consoled her a little. 'Who knows what memories those two souls share?'

'Past lives, you mean?'

Storm nodded. 'I imagine you've known one another since time began. As we all have.' He stopped suddenly and lifted her chin. 'They both love you dearly, you know.'

'I just wish I didn't feel so…' Amelie struggled to find the right word.

'Rejected? Abandoned? Insecure…?'

Amelie bowed her head. 'All of those. I've always felt odd, like I don't fit in. And let's face it I never had any friends before Isla came along; apart from you.' She wiped her nose on her sleeve.

'It's bad enough them always playing football and video games and stuff, but now this... I feel more left out than ever.'

'But folks are queuing up to be your friend these days! Anyway, those two will need you more than ever now. Please don't abandon them by shutting down your heart.'

So, even Storm had noticed.

'You and Isla have a special bond,' he continued, 'one that Tim can't ever be part of. She looks up to you a lot, even though you're a good bit younger than she is. You must know how she adores you.'

A look of surprise passed over Amelie's tear-stained face. 'You really think so?'

'Yes, really, and Tim does too. Oh, you should have seen the look of pride on his face when you spoke at that Press Conference last year. He'd do anything to protect his little sister. You'll never lose either of them, I swear.'

Amelie couldn't hide her grin. 'All the girls at school fancy him.'

'And how does that make you feel?'

'I think it's funny.'

'But I bet you're a bit proud too, aren't you?'

Amelie nodded. She was.

'So why not be happy that your best friend likes him a lot too? However,' Storm added with mock gravity, 'you just wait till the boys start flocking around *you* in a year or two! Oh, my -Warrior Tim will be there, not letting any of them get too close, as I shall be too!' He waved Doris in the air. 'Just let them try!'

Amelie giggled. 'I can't see that ever happening.'

'Oh, but it will, you mark my words! And when you do meet someone it's very important that they're also a good friend.' He breathed a great sigh. 'Louisa and I were lucky like that…'

Amelie linked his arm. 'I do love you, Storm,' she whispered. Suddenly, she remembered the Commander's invisible blanket and felt unusually safe.

'As I do you, darling girl…' And they continued their walk in silence, Amelie trying to get her head around having a boyfriend some day and Storm wondering if lunch might be ready. All that serious talk had given him quite an appetite.

Just then, Amelie's phone pinged. 'It's from Isla,' she gasped.

'Go on then,' said Storm. 'See what she has to say.'

'This…' A huge grin spread across Amelie's face:

Hey, girl, I forgot to say this - Mom's given me £25 to buy a dress for my aunt's wedding and I haven't a clue where to start. Please say you'll come shopping with me. I so need your help!! XOXO

'Clothes shopping? What, me?' Amelie looked up and saw Storm grinning too.

Yes, okay, she replied at once. ***That'll be fun! XXX***

Chapter Forty-Four

A Return to Limone

October 2019

It was the October half-term and their long-awaited holiday had finally begun. As soon as they stepped off the ferry they were struck by the abundance of flowers that greeted them. They seemed to be growing everywhere, even between cracks in the walls.

'Bougainvillea, wisteria, clematis,' Storm listed. 'This place has hardly changed at all.'

'And the lemons!' cried Isla. 'They're everywhere.'

'It's exactly as I imagined!' breathed Amelie, not knowing quite where to look next. 'There's even a little cartoleria! I wonder if it's the same one Aunt Eggy visited?'

'It is.' Storm turned away to face the lake, squinting a little as he looked across to Malcesine.

'And a Gelati Vegani shop too!' Isla squealed. 'How cool is that?'

Tim searched for spare change in his pocket. 'My shout – just tell me what you all want…'

'Cool, did you say, Isla?' said Storm, awaking from his reverie. 'Of course it's cool! It's a ruddy ice-cream shop.'

'Why are you so rude today, Storm?' Amelie scolded and Storm's face crumpled a little.

‘I can’t stop thinking of the last time I was here.’

‘Oh, Storm honey, is there anything special you’d like to share?’ said Isla, never one to bear a grudge. ‘I see you’ve brought Doris, Eggy’s old stick. What a lovely thought.’

‘Share?’ Storm repeated.

‘Yes, we’ll all just listen and not interrupt.’

‘Isla, you sound like one of those life-coach people on TV,’ remarked Amelie. ‘You know, you’d make an amazing counsellor if you don’t like being a pilot. In fact, you could easily do both. You know, put nervous passengers at ease…’

‘Sure,’ said Tim in a voice very much like Isla’s. ‘This is your Captain speaking. We’re currently cruising at an altitude of forty thousand feet, quite a drop, eh, with absolutely nothing between you and the ground. Enjoy your flight…’

‘Oh, shut up already!’ Isla giggled. ‘I was only trying to get Storm to open up a bit.’

‘And I shall do, my dear,’ replied Storm, somewhat chastened. He patted Isla’s hand. ‘Let’s sit down over there on that bench and I’ll try to explain.’

They all followed, grateful to relax awhile in the warm autumnal sun.

‘Here we go then…’ Storm leaned on old Doris, ready to begin.

‘Wait,’ Amelie said, searching for her pen. ‘I need to write some of this down.’

Chapter Forty-Five

Old Giacomo and the Box of Eggs

September 1993

Storm and Louisa had decided to accompany Eggy that year, believing she might, at a spritely ninety-seven, need assistance with her travel plans.

'Oh, do stop fussing, you two!' Eggy laughed. 'I can manage perfectly well on my own. I have Doris remember!' She swung her old walking stick in the air, narrowly missing Storm's head.

'Careful with that damned thing!' he grumbled, snatching it out of her hand.

'You'd better be kind to her,' warned Eggy. 'I'm leaving her to you in my will.'

❀

'It's all gone by in a flash, hasn't it?' sighed Louisa, sipping her breakfast espresso. 'I've become rather attached to this little place. Best coffee in the world.'

'To be honest, it's depressing me this year,' Storm said gloomily. 'Overrun with Normans and Bettys.'

Louisa shot him a warning glance. 'For goodness sake, Storm, keep your voice down, will you?'

'*So what*, Norman and Betty are perfectly nice names, silly boy,' Eggy remarked, winking at Louisa.

‘So what?’ Storm blustered. ‘Just take a look at them, will you? White socks and sandals, the British abroad; grown men dressed as toddlers and even the women aren’t much better. Not like Italian women. See how elegant they are?’

‘I see…’ said Louisa, raising an eyebrow and pretending to be put out. ‘You’re in a very strange mood today.’

Storm surveyed the elderly guests over the top of his spectacles, forgetting, as Louisa was quick to remind him, that at sixty-nine, he too was technically a Norman.

‘You’re not including me, I hope,’ said Eggy who liked to imagine she was still that same agile young woman who once climbed the little lanes with ease. The reality was somewhat different, of course. Apart from Storm and Louisa, there were three of them on this holiday: the youthful, energetic Eggy, her now struggling older self; and Doris.

‘Look at you, Eggy,’ Louisa crooned, ‘you’re as young and glamorous as ever.’

‘As you are too, my darling,’ Storm said politely. He rose from his chair and helped Louisa to her feet. ‘I think it’s time for our trip across the lake. Do you fancy coming with us, Eggs?’

Eggy froze. It had jolted her. ‘What did you just call me?’

‘Eggs?’ Storm shrugged. ‘Oh, Eggy, how silly of me…’

‘Anyway,’ Eggy replied, still ruffled, ‘the answer is no, thank you all the same. As it’s our last day I’ll just mooch about here for a bit, collect some olive branches for Ted and Joan, and young Michael, and then who knows?’ Thinking of their family back home, she smiled and waved them off cheerily. ‘See you back here at six for dinner.’

Her smile faded as she watched them leave. She toyed with the remains of her toast and glanced around the half-empty dining room. Last week’s tourists would now be back at work; their little ones setting off for school. She rather missed their noise this year, now they had gone. Seeing the waiter approach, she pushed her plate aside. 'Grazie, Giovanni.'

She reached for her shawl and draped it around her shoulders, picked up Doris and walked outside to take in the view. A morning mist still hovered over the lake, the fierce heat of summer mellowed by the onset of autumn. Slowly, she made her way up the winding hill to her favourite haunt, a quiet lakeside beach that reminded her of home. Havenbridge seemed another lifetime away today.

Storm had been right. The place was swarming with Normans and Bettys; retired teachers, by the look of them.

Many of the familiar faces she'd come to expect had disappeared now, apart from Martina in the cartoleria and Elsa, the nice Austrian lady who owned the dress shop. She laughed to herself. And poor old Giacomo! There he was, leaning against a wrought iron gate, looking very frail and gaunt this year. She was a little surprised to see him again, half expecting him to have left the planet years ago. But the little town had a tradition of longevity. Her surprise grew when he suddenly greeted her.

'*Bongiorno, Signora*!'

Only a gruff hello, but it was a greeting all the same. She fluttered a wave and continued on her way.

Her ankles had swollen from the heat and she paused to sniff a piece of rosemary growing out of a crack in the stone wall, rubbed it between her fingers and breathed in its scent: *Rosemary for remembrance*. Jack had once handed her a sprig; it had perfumed her pocket for weeks.

'This is what happens when you're old, Eggy,' she cautioned. 'That strange ability to recall things from eighty years ago while forgetting what the hell you had for last night's dinner.'

At the edge of her vision a little girl danced in the sunlight; it was the one who'd joined her in the taxi on the way to the Dorchester.

'*Come sta, Signora*?' At her favourite café the waiter was clearing crumbs from the tables and laying out fresh covers for lunch.

How am I, she wondered? I really don't know. '*Molto bene, grazie*,' she replied pleasantly but it wasn't quite the truth. She was weary, very weary.

She ordered her usual caffè espresso and sat overlooking the bay. A little Moleskine notebook lay open before her. Oh dear, only two blank pages left. She must treat herself to a new one at the *cartoleria* in town. She picked up her pen and began to write: *Silence today, broken only by the pleasant thrum of boats crossing the lake*.

A gentle breeze blew over the water and soon the mist began to lift. So too did Eggy's spirits. A bright flash of sunlight blinded her for a moment as the little girl returned, dressed in an old-fashioned pinafore dress and carrying a hoop. Fascinated, she smiled. *It's you again!*

She finished her coffee and continued up the lane to the olive groves. The girl with the hoop trotted alongside her. 'Come on, old slowcoach!' she teased, racing ahead. 'You'll never catch up with me now!'

Old Giacomo was slightly ahead of them, carrying a bag of provisions. Just as they reached him he tripped on a cobblestone and a box of eggs fell to the ground.

'Oh dear,' said Eggy, laying Doris aside to help him to his feet. 'It's you again!' She looked him up and down to assess any damage. 'Hmm, you seem fine to me, just broken eggs.'

'Eggs?' he repeated, not knowing English, and she smiled wryly. First it was Storm, now crazy old Giacomo.

'Are you all right, my friend?' she asked, touching his arm.

'*Sì, grazie*.' He squinted at her and continued on his way. After a few metres he stopped and waited for her. '*Grazie mille, Signora.*' He reached out his hand to touch hers and then she saw it. A little stump where a finger had once been. '*La guerra.*'

She knew just enough Italian to understand. The war; it had been blown off by shellfire. Some men lost their faces, he said.

She held on to his hand a little longer than was polite, imagining it for a moment to be Jack's. Just long enough to offer up a silent prayer: *I love you, Jack. Forgive me for not telling you while I had the chance.*

A plane flew overhead and the old man glanced up at the sky. '*E stanno arrivando,*' he muttered.

They are coming. 'Yes, more tourists,' said Eggy, 'they will be coming in just as I'm leaving.'

'*Sì, Signorina.*'

Signorina! Young lady, it had been some time since anyone had called her that.

'You, very beautiful.' He gave her a broad toothless smile and his old face lit up. '*Vuoi sposarmi?*'

Astonishingly, he kissed her hand and Eggy - now far too old to blush - did so.

'Marry you?' she laughed. 'Grazie, Signor, I'd be honoured.'

She could have been saying anything to him, of course, *like why were you always so grumpy and rude*? He would never have known.

They stood there together for a while, gazing out over the lake.

Chapter Forty-Six

Jean-Jacques Laurent

At this point, Amelie stopped and placed a hand on Storm's arm. The old stick he'd been leaning on, the one Eggy had left him in her will, had suddenly given way. 'I think Doris wants us to listen,' she said. 'It's about grumpy old Giacomo.'

Storm, grateful for the interlude, said: 'Yes, my dear, of course. Do carry on…'

'Well, you'll remember Anna, Adelaide's friend, and all the gossip about Giacomo being mad?'

They nodded, remembering his yellow teeth like an old dog and his mumbling.

'In fact,' said Amelie, 'very little was known about him, except that he'd lived in Limone for most of his life. Sixty years, according to the oldest inhabitants, all close to a century themselves.'

As a young man Giacomo worked on the boats, sailing to and from Malcesine; and later in the olive groves and *limonaie*. Not that he had ever needed to work apparently. Anna had been right. His real name was Laurent, Jean-Jacques Laurent, the adored only son of wealthy horse breeders who lived in Bouzincourt. Sadly, they both died in the early 1930s and with no other family, the devastated young fellow left behind his life of luxury and trekked southwards; carrying only a battered old suitcase, stuffed with francs - thousands upon thousands of notes, enough to last him a lifetime.

Having crossed the border into Switzerland, he finally reached Italy. Here, he occupied himself mending fences, milking goats, and picking up the language as he went. He finally settled in Limone and became known as *Giacomo Laurenti*.

He was a gruff, secretive man. On rare occasions though, usually after a bottle or two of wine, he would speak of his life in France, what little he could still recall, since his memory had begun to slip away. 'Too much bad Italian wine,' he would snort, raising his glass. *Salute*[42]*!*

There was a story he liked to tell; about a soldier his family had once befriended during the Great War. ('War?' he'd yell, sometimes in Italian, sometimes in French. 'What the hell is so great about war?')

A shell had exploded close to Bouzincourt where they lived, Giacomo told. Somehow the fellow had escaped and walked undetected as far as the local church, two kilometres away. Here the curé[43], an old priest, took him in, threw a cassock[44] over his uniform and gave him directions to a nearby safe house. And that was how he came to find the Laurents. Monsieur Laurent emptied the young man's pockets and burned his uniform right away, along with all of his papers. Madame Laurent dosed him with *tisanes*, special medicinal teas made with herbs. It seemed the poor man didn't even remember his own name anymore. 'Who am I?' he kept asking, 'and why am I here?'

'Questions we all might ask ourselves,' commented Madame Laurent wisely. '*Choc d'obus*,' the couple agreed. Shell-shock. They cared for him like a son.

Once the war ended the young man remained there with them for some time, training horses and generally helping out on the farm. Sometimes, at weekends, they would all travel to Senlis where

Monsieur Laurent's cousin owned a couple of old bi-planes.

'Yes, it was there we all learned to fly,' Giacomo said proudly. 'There's nothing in this world like the thrill of your first flight!'

But soon, everything fell apart because Monsieur and Madame Laurent died and the young soldier disappeared too. 'I often wonder what happened to him,' Giacomo said. 'Everyone gone, nothing to live for anymore…'

Chapter Forty-Seven

A Bright Yellow Notebook

Eggy carried on up into the olive groves and found three small branches, laden with fruit. 'Would you mind very much if I took these?' she asked the tree courteously and immediately thought of Charlie Easton, wondering what might have happened if she'd married him. '*Grazie mille*[45],' she replied with a bow and tucked the branches into her bag.

That evening she entertained Storm and Louisa with her account of old Giacomo and his box of eggs. And how taken aback she'd been by his missing finger, blown off in the war. 'All those memories come to haunt me; yes, even the rosemary…' She twisted the little sapphire ring on her finger while the sound of *Für Elise* played quietly in her head.

Eggy took the lift up to her room. It was always the same, Number 106: *la camera della Signora Trott*[46].

The day slipped into darkness, much earlier than last week, and she pulled on her coat. She might just make the *cartoleria* before it closed.

Her old friend, Martina was still there, engaged in conversation with some Norman and Betty from the hotel. And somewhere at the back of the shop an old musical box was playing. Martina had been a small girl when Eggy first noticed her in the shop. Mrs. Bartoli owned the business in those days and little Martina, her daughter, had peered at her from behind her mother's skirts. Martina ran the place now, old Mrs. Bartoli having retired years back. A slender beauty still, her colourful presence filled the little shop. There wasn't anything Martina didn't know about her specialist papers and gift wraps, or the beautifully bound notebooks, and artists' pencils and pens.

Glancing up, she spotted Eggy right away and sang out her name, '*Eglantina*!' She ran over and kissed her warmly on both cheeks, patted her face like a child. '*Bellissima! Ancora così giovane*[47]*!*'

'Yes, young enough to have a proposal apparently!' laughed Eggy.

'You meet rich young man, yes? You say sì, I hope!' Martina handed Eggy a bottle of her favourite *limoncello*[48]. '*Auguri*[49]*! Congratulations...*'

Eggy found herself a new notebook, bright yellow to remind her of Limone. 'More memories,' she murmured to her little companion who had barely left her side that day. The girl even took her hand and helped her up the hill. At the top, Eggy stopped abruptly, feeling a sudden ache in her heart. 'It's been a good life, hasn't it, my darling?'

Chapter Forty-Eight

Are You Ready for the Journey?

In Room 106, she closed the shutters and settled down at the glass-topped dressing table that served as her desk.

'You're still here, I see.' The little girl was pulling silly faces, crossed eyes and a poked-out tongue. 'You can stay if you wish but you mustn't interrupt me. I have things to do.'

The girl ran a finger along her lips to seal them.

Eggy poured herself a tot of *limoncello* and opened her bright yellow notebook:

Looking back, I've been lucky. Two horrendous wars and a two-year pandemic, yet somehow I survived. The Dark Hearts haven't beaten us yet!

I do worry about the future though. Not mine but yours, dear Reader. I'm afraid we've left this place in rather a mess for you.

Do I have any other regrets? Well yes, quite honestly, I do...

My darling Jack: eighty years you've been gone, and today was filled with your memory. Daft Storm calling me Eggs, and then the scent of rosemary. Later, I stood by the lake with old Giacomo, wishing it could have been you. If only I'd been able to save you as you once saved me...

Just then, Storm and Louisa knocked on the door to bid her goodnight.

'Sleep well, my loves,' said Eggy, blowing them both a kiss

'Thank you for a splendid holiday. Run along now and I'll see you bright and early in the morning.'

'And that was it really,' Storm sighed. 'I'm not sure what happened after that.'

'But I am,' Amelie said calmly. 'May I carry on?'

Whether it was the *limoncello* or the surge of memories that were flooding her head but Eggy felt suddenly overwhelmed. Her suitcase was already packed, her clothes laid out for travel the next day. *But supposing I'm not ready,* she brooded, *or the taxi forgets to come?* She dozed fitfully at the little glass-topped table and then suddenly awoke. The young girl was watching her curiously.

'Gosh, is it morning already? I'd better hurry then,' she said, glancing at her watch. And it was then she noticed her arm. The *Mark of Triandor*, such a vital part of her for eighty-three years, had vanished. *The Power in Me!* It had gone. After a brief moment of panic she fancied she heard a voice:

It's no longer needed since the Power is already within you.

'Is that you, Tabitha? Oh, my, what an extraordinary day this is turning out to be!'

And then for some strange reason the taxi arrived early. She spotted it, pulling in to the hotel car park. 'Oh Lord, Storm and Louisa aren't even here yet. I'd better go and fetch them.'

'No, come with me.' The young girl took her hand and led her to the door. Eggy smiled as a sudden surge of energy filled her. Skipping past the lift, they flew down the stairs together until they reached the entrance hall where the receptionist was tidying her hair in a mirror.

'*Bongiorno*[50]*, Signora*!' they shouted but she appeared not to hear.

Outside, Eggy stood for a while, surveying the view. The sun had risen over the mountains and it promised to be a perfect day for their flight. 'I'll miss you,' she whispered, wondering if she'd ever return. Seeing her, the taxi driver tooted and she waved, then stuck two fingers in her mouth and whistled. 'All right, all right, I'm coming!'

The taxi door was already open and she clambered inside. 'Drat!' she muttered. 'Would you believe it? I've left my luggage behind; and my Doris too!'

'No-worries-Signora,' said the driver in perfect but strangely mechanical English. 'You-won't-be-needing-them-now.' He turned to face her.

'Dorin!'

He smiled. '*Sei-pronto-per-il-viaggio-finalmente*[51]?'

'Am I ready for the final journey? Why, yes,' she answered, looking up at the great mountain overlooking the lake. 'I think I am.'

Chapter Forty-Nine

Martina Bartoli Arrives a Little Too Late

Storm reached out and squeezed Amelie's hand. 'Darling girl, what would we ever do without you? There's not much left to tell you now except that it was Francesca the maid who sounded the alarm.'

Francesca had come early that day, hoping to catch her favourite Signora before she returned to England. What a special lady she was - always telling her to sit down and put her feet up, while she quizzed her about the children and her lazy, good-for-nothing husband who gambled away her earnings.

'No, Francesca!' she would insist: 'please leave the bedding, once a week is enough…' And then, bless her heart, there was always a generous tip at the end of her stay. Yes, there it was again this year, on the bedside table, an envelope stuffed with six thousand *lire*[52] notes, enough for her to treat herself to a new dress and a pair of shoes. But that was not all. Francesca uttered a wail of sorrow

Storm and Louisa came running at once and found Eggy slumped over her dressing table.

They stayed on for a few days more so that arrangements could be made for her body to be flown back with them.

On their final morning, they sat together in the hotel bar overlooking the lake, Louisa endlessly checking her watch, her purse, her tickets, her passport, while Storm gazed staunchly ahead, refusing to give way to tears.

'Should be here soon,' they both murmured and allowed themselves a smile.

'*Imprenditore di pompe funebri*[53], that's a new phrase I've had to learn,' said Storm, still trying to be brave.

'Funeral Director?' Louisa hazarded a guess.

Storm nodded. 'I'm grateful he's arranged for Eggy's… I mean, for everything to come with us.' He couldn't bear to say remains. Remains were what filled her suitcase: clothes, toiletries, notebooks. He wondered where Eggy was now.

Louisa patted his hand. 'She'll be with her loved ones, darling, having a ball.'

Storm looked at her fondly, grateful she knew him so well. After forty-one years together it was hardly surprising. 'Good grief,' he said suddenly, 'what's that bloody racket now?'

They swung round to see the hotel receptionist involved in a heated telephone conversation. '*Sì, sì, presto*[54]…' she repeated while beckoning to them with her free hand.

'Not a problem with our taxi?' Storm asked anxiously.

The receptionist shook her head. '*Mi scusi*[55], Signor, Signora…' She covered the mouthpiece and rolled her eyes. 'Is Signora Bartoli. She arrive...'

Storm and Louisa looked at each other, mystified. Martina Bartoli?

'That's Eggy's friend, I believe,' said Louisa, 'from the little *cartoleria* in town. I wonder if she knows yet…'

Storm sighed. 'I hope she doesn't want to load us up with more stuff. We've no space left in our luggage…'

'It's too late now anyway, darling. Our taxi's here…'

They picked up their cases and made their way down the steps, each with the very same thought: would this be their last time here too?

'No!' Storm uttered resolutely. 'She'd want us to return.

Chapter Fifty

A Love Story That Never Was

‘And you have returned,’ Tim said gently, ‘with us.’

‘And for that I can’t th ank you enough…’ Storm blew his nose loudly and Doris slipped to the ground. ‘I’m missing that pair dreadfully, you know.’

‘But you still have Doris,’ said Amelie, retrieving his stick. ‘She’s here for you too.’ Her eyes drifted towards the *cartoleria*. ‘I wonder what happened to Signora Bartoli? It sounded like she really wanted to see you.’

‘Martina?’ Storm followed her gaze. ‘She must be well into her eighties now. Maybe I’ll take a look. I could do with a few postcards anyway.’

‘I’ll get the ice cream then,’ volunteered Tim, eager to escape for a while. ‘I don’t know about you but my head’s buzzing.’ He dug his hand in his pocket again and fished out a pile of coins. The swear box had come in very handy that week. ‘What are you having, Isla…?’

‘*Nocciola*[56]*, tesoro*[57],’ Isla said with a little wink. ‘Can I come too? That story’s really gotten to me.’

‘Sure.’ Tim put an arm around her shoulder.

Amelie pretended not to notice his awkwardness or the catch in Isla’s voice. She so wanted to give them a hug. Storm was right; it was difficult for them both.

'Mine's *caffè*[58],' she said, 'three scoops, *grazie mille*.'

Tim laughed. 'Three! You're such a greedy bugger, Amelie Trott.'

Amelie wondered if that counted as a forbidden word but decided to let him off. 'No more than you are.'

'Okay, so that's three scoops of coffee,' Tim repeated, counting on his fingers, 'a *cioccolata*[59] for me, plus a hazelnut for Isla, and you'd like your usual *vaniglia*[60], wouldn't you, Storm?'

'Correct! No fancy stuff.' Storm took a deep breath and wandered over to inspect the postcard carousel outside the shop. He chose two of the lemon groves and one of Malcesine across the lake.

'Do you happen to know a Signora Bartoli?' he asked the young man at the counter who stared at him blankly and replied: 'I ask for you.' He disappeared into the back of the shop and returned with the manager.

'*Buongiorno, Signor*. Martina Bartoli, sì…' She scribbled an address on the back of his receipt. 'You find her most evenings.'

'Ah, Via Santa Maria,' read Storm. 'That's at the other end of town, I believe; perhaps we'll take a stroll up there tonight.'

They found Martina watering window boxes outside her little stone cottage. Hearing English voices, she turned, took one look at Storm and dropped her watering can in surprise.

'Signor Trott-a?' she cried and apologised at once for soaking their feet. She flung her arms around his neck and stroked their faces in turn, except for Tim's. He managed to dodge away just in time. Martina's old eyes glistened with tears. 'I think I never see you again! You come inside, yes? I have so much to tell…'

She led them into a tiny sitting room and brought them a jug of fresh lemonade.

'Do you mind if I make a few notes?' asked Amelie, delving into her bag for a pen.

'*Certo*[61],' said Martina and brought her a little table to rest her notebook on. 'Please do.'

'That night she die…' Martina closed her eyes and murmured a little prayer. 'I go outside to close the *persiane* at the shop. How you say that?'

'Shutters,' said Tim, much to everyone's surprise. The transonometer had many interesting uses apart from ordering ice cream.

Martina nodded gratefully. 'I hear someone try the door and I shout: *Sorry we close…*'

It was then she'd glanced down to see an old sepia photograph at her feet. She stooped to retrieve it. '*Ei, Signor*!' she shouted. 'Is yours, yes?'

A few metres away an old man staggered up the cobbled lane towards her, clutching at the rail on the wall to stop him from falling.

'You know this person?' He gestured to the photograph in her hand and his craggy old face twisted into a smile.

Martina squinted at it. It was a girl, someone from way back, sixty years or so, but as for her identity, she hadn't a clue.

'You find her, yes?' For one magical moment the years fell from the old man's face; his features slipped back into place and a fresh-faced young man stared back at her. '*Grazie mille, Signora.*'

Martina had only one thing on her mind at that time: tired and hungry, she wanted to go home. She nodded and stuffed the photograph into her pocket.

The old man reached out his hand and slipped a child's tiny marble into her palm. 'For you, Signora. *Buona notte*[62]!'

Pazzo, thought Martina. Mad, but harmless.

Martina's story was suddenly interrupted by Doris *tap-tap-tapping* on the tiled floor.

'That's Eglantyne calling,' said Storm. 'She's obviously keen to tell us something.'

'Oh, *santo Dio*[63]!' Martina looked like she might faint and murmured a little prayer again.

But Amelie was unable to contain herself any longer. 'That man, it was Giacomo, wasn't it? Do you have that photo still?'

'I find, Signorina…' She went away, returned shortly and placed the old photograph into Amelie's hands. 'I realise later - is Eglantina.'

'Martina, do you mind if I say something for a moment?' Amelie passed the photograph to Storm. 'It seems that someone else may have died that night too…'

'Yes,' Martina admitted sadly. 'Old Giacomo…'

'Who was formerly Jean-Jacques Laurent?' Amelie nodded thoughtfully. 'And whose family rescued a soldier?'

Isla stared at the little photograph. 'Wasn't this the one Jack stole that day? Jeez…'

Storm wiped his brow with a large pocket handkerchief. 'So Jack didn't lose his life after all.'

'No,' said Tim, 'but he *did* lose his memory. Hey, we've had so many clues…'

At that point, they all began to shout over one another, swapping clues and piecing them all together:

'Yes, of course - when Jack's friend Sam saw him tossed in the air like a piece of debris that must have been…'

'The *Mark of Triandor*?'

'Exactly, he was lifted up, protected from the worst of the explosion…'

'Yes, and the elderly couple - they weren't his parents at all…'

'Yeah, they found his papers though and re-named him Jean-Jacques.'

'Jean-Jacques, Giacomo… Oh, poor Jack, he'd totally forgotten who he was!'

'Until that last day when he was with Eggy and he asked her to marry him…'

'Oh, man, why didn't we see it before?'

'I did, as soon as she saw his missing finger! I knew he was Jack.'

'Okay, why didn't you say so, already?'

The noise got louder and louder, and Storm had to bellow 'Shut up!' and somehow they all did, apart from Isla who added one last piece to the puzzle.

'Remember at the beginning how Jack said he longed to fly? How awesome he got his wish in the end.'

Martina frowned and touched Storm's hand. 'Some *limoncello*, Signor?' she offered, understanding none of this.

'No thank you, my dear,' replied Storm. 'I need to keep a clear head.' He cast around at their faces, one by one. 'Imagine though, all those times they will have passed each other in the street. Not knowing…'

Amelie shook her head in disbelief. 'It's like a love story that never was.'

'Yeah,' Tim murmured, 'but the good news is this. Eggy *did* save his life after all. And in the weirdest way, she still got to see him again!'

'I can't bear that both of them died without knowing,' said Isla and Martina, who must have somehow guessed, began to weep.

'She was incredibly beautiful, wasn't she?' Isla whispered, gazing at the photograph once more. 'And I'm sure Jack was good-looking too. He must surely have met other girls?'

'*Ma sì*[64]!' Martina winked. 'There were a few.' Not that anything lasted, she added in her faltering English. His heart was elsewhere. And with this she began to wail.

'Other girls, eh?' Storm gave a wry smile. 'I wonder what Eggy would have to say about that!'

And without warning, Amelie uttered a series of words that had never passed her lips before; forbidden words.

They all stared at her in horror.

'*Cosa c'è*[65]?' demanded Martina and was immediately told she was really better not knowing.

Storm tutted and said he hadn't heard language like that since his RAF days and Tim clutched his sides laughing, barely able to breathe. 'Blimey, that's worth at least fifty euros for the tin!'

'No, Tim,' Amelie replied astutely. 'It's reported speech. And it's Eggy's way of saying she wished she'd never turned the lovely Charlie down.' Her face broke into a smile. 'She didn't mean it, of course. Jack really was the only one for her.'

Just before they said their goodbyes, Martina opened her handbag and produced a small box. 'Is the little *biglia*[66] Giacomo give me…'

'It's the marble,' said Tim, remembering.

Storm lifted the lid of the box and there it sat on a miniature velvet cushion. His mouth opened but no sound would come out.

'It's a piece of Lumeanite, isn't it?' Isla whispered, shaking his arm. 'A Stone of Power.'

'It is! Martina, have you any idea how important this is?' Storm murmured, turning it over in his hands. 'Because of this little stone he'll have become totally invisible while he made his escape…'

'I don't ever want to leave this magical place,' said Isla, her eyes brimming with tears.

Tim put an arm around her shoulder and gave it a little squeeze. 'We'll come back for a match one day, seeing as we're both Italian supporters now.'

'Yes, but supporters of opposite teams!' wailed Isla. 'The woman in the shop gave me the wrong freaking shirt.'

Tim grinned. 'We'll try not to fall out over it.'

'It's okay for you two,' Amelie said gloomily. 'What have I got to look forward to now?

Isla linked her arm. 'Don't forget we've got our shopping trip when we get back.'

'Good,' said Amelie, 'as long as we're not shopping for football shirts.'

Chapter Fifty-One

A Visit to Little Heaven

'Come on, let's get the Tube to Oxford Circus,' said Isla. 'There'll be loads of shops there to choose from.'

'Lawrence said he'd take me home. Do you mind if we call at his office when we're done?'

'Cool, are you buying something too?'

Amelie nodded eagerly. 'Yes, I'm celebrating.'

'Celebrating? You mean you've finished your book?'

'Yep, it's all in here.' She tapped her rucksack. 'Eggy's life story at last.'

Isla jumped up and down, squealing with joy. 'I'm so proud of you, babe! Let me give you a hug.'

Amelie beamed. Everything was back on track at last. No more awkward feelings, no more being left out. It really was okay. 'I suppose I ought to contact Phineas though.'

'Your sweet little professor?'

'Yes, I think I've kept him waiting long enough. But let's go and have some fun first…'

However, their shopping trip wasn't quite as much fun as they had hoped. Everything Isla liked was either a size too big or too small, and whatever Amelie found caused Isla to shake her head and say, 'Not really you, babe.'

'Shopping's not really me,' admitted Amelie.

'So, let's go for a smoothie,' Isla suggested, 'while we figure out where else to go.'

'There's a new shop opened in Littlehaven,' Amelie remembered. 'Not the big posh one, but where you end up with a whole bagful of stuff for about ten pounds. Nice stuff though - not rubbish. One of the girls in Tim's class was raving about it and wanted me to go with her.' She didn't mention it was Tilly Muldane who was stalking Tim and only wanted to be her best friend so she could get to know him better. 'I think I'd rather go with you though.'

Isla gave her another hug. 'Let's call it a day then and try Littlehaven next week.'

'Cool! By the way, I really don't mind.'

'Mind?' Isla looked at her curiously. 'About today, you mean?'

'No, about you and Tim. I did at first but not anymore.'

Isla's conker brown cheeks reddened a little. 'I never want anything to change between me and you, right?'

Amelie nodded. 'Nor me. I understand, really…'

'Well,' Isla said glumly, 'that's nice because I don't. And I don't think Tim does either.' She took a deep breath and let it out slowly. 'And it looks like me and Mom will be on the move again soon.'

'Back to Washington?' Amelie's face fell.

'Just for a year - I told Tim earlier and we've agreed to stay friends and see what happens; in the future, I mean. Anyway,' Isla added sensibly, 'we're a bit young for dating, aren't we?'

'You've thought about it a lot then,' said Amelie. 'I'm glad we've got all that stuff out of the way.'

Isla grinned. 'Me too…' The two girls linked arms and hurried off to meet Lawrence.

❀

The following week, they took the bus to Littlehaven, armed with two colourful canvas shopping bags. Lucy had run them up especially so they wouldn't come back with a load of horrible plastic ones, she said.

'The shop's right near the bus station so we won't have far to walk,' said Amelie, happily taking charge. It was like that time Eggy took Adelaide shopping and they saw the musical box. 'Look, there it is, *Little Heaven*. That was the original name for the town, you know.'

There was a dark blue van parked outside and two men in overalls were running backwards and forwards with deliveries.

'Gosh, it's heaving in here,' said Amelie, elbowing her way through a crowd of shoppers. For a moment, her heart sank. Tilly Muldane was there with a group of friends but fortunately they were about to leave and hadn't spotted her.

'Your friend's right, though,' Isla commented, pulling an armful of dresses off the rails. 'There's almost too much to choose from. What do you fancy?'

Amelie said she wanted a pair of jeans like Isla's with holes in the knees. She would, of course, have to endure a barrage of sarcasm from Storm who always wondered what was wrong with the world.

'I quite like this pink dress,' said Isla. 'What do you think? Not too Barbie, is it?'

'It's pretty, go and try it on.'

'I will!'

'Oh, that was amazing!' Isla declared as they made their way to the bus station.

'And look how much we've ended up with!' Amelie peered inside her bag, and began to count. 'Two pairs of jeans, a hoodie, a tee-shirt…'

It was then that Isla's expression changed. 'How come this stuff is so cheap though?' Suddenly, it dawned on her and she shook her head violently. 'Oh, no, what have I done? Mom's always telling me not to buy cheap clothes, unless they're from a thrift shop…'

Amelie looked at her, confused. 'Is that like a charity shop?'

Isla nodded. 'These will have come from sweatshops,' she muttered. 'It's where desperately poor people work, some of them only our age and younger. They sew clothes all day for peanuts, mostly in East Asia. And then…' She turned around and stared angrily at the shop. '…they're sold over here.' She tipped out her bag, scattering its contents on the pavement. 'I don't even like it anymore,' she shouted, picking up the pink dress. 'I'm taking it back!'

Amelie had never seen Isla angry before. Maybe it was all the stress or her period or something. 'But Isla, you can't, our last bus is here already.'

'You do realize we're lining the pockets of criminals…'

The bus pulled up and, reluctantly, Isla stuffed everything back into her bag and clambered aboard.

'I wish we hadn't gone now,' Amelie said quietly. 'I'm sorry, it's my fault.'

'No, it's not,' Isla sighed. 'I meant every word but I'm sorry I got so angry. It's all the stress, I suppose, thinking about leaving here and everything…'

Amelie nodded. 'It won't be easy for us either. I'll miss you loads. And Tim will too,' she added kindly. 'But it won't be forever, will it?'

Isla nodded back. '*Let's make the most of whatever time we have left.* Now, where have I heard that before?' She smiled ruefully and opened her bag again. 'I wonder where all this stuff was made…' She turned the pink dress inside out and inspected the label. 'That's weird, this isn't even imported. It says *Made in the UK.*'

The bus driver swerved suddenly and Amelie clung to the handrail in front of her. 'Woah! Did you see that other bus?'

Isla glanced over her shoulder in time to spot another bus veering off to the right. 'That was a close call!'

Startled, the other passengers shook their fists and cursed: 'Stupid bugger, overtaking on a narrow road like this!'

Lucy was waiting at the front door as they came up the drive. Her face was troubled. 'I'm glad you're back. There's been a tragedy in Littlehaven today. Did you see anything? It's been on the news…'

'Tragedy?' Isla and Amelie stared at her, aghast. 'No, not a thing…'

'Some people were drowned.' It had clearly evoked a host of painful memories and it showed on her face. Amelie and Isla realised at once.

'That's awful,' said Isla. 'I'm so sorry - we'd no idea, Lucy.'

'Are you all right, Mum?' Amelie asked, falling into her arms.

Lucy didn't reply. Instead, she kissed Amelie and glanced down at their bulging canvas bags. 'Come on then, you two, show me what you bought!'

Isla held up her new dress with little enthusiasm.

'Oh, Isla, that's perfect for a wedding. Come in and show me the rest.'

They followed her inside and Lucy began to rummage through Amelie's bag. 'Oh, darling,' she laughed, 'those awful jeans! Whatever possessed you? You know what Storm will say. But I do like your t-shirt though. What size is it? I might even get one myself…' She searched around for a label. 'Oh, how odd, what's this? Look, your eyes are better than mine.' She held it out for Amelie to see.

Amelie squinted at it, a little scrap of fabric sewn into the seam. Her eyes widened. 'It says: *Please help!*'

'Jeez, that's crazy,' said Isla. 'Look, there's one inside my dress too: *SOS!*' She was now halfway through the door, clutching her phone. ‘Guys, I’m so sorry, can we talk about this later? I promised Tim I’d see him once we were home. I’ll be real quick, I promise…’

‘No worries,’ said Amelie though clearly there were plenty. ‘Mum, there’s another one here attached to my jeans.’ She waited till she heard the door close. ‘Drowned?’ she repeated now she had Lucy to herself. ‘Who were they, Mum? We didn’t notice a thing in town…’

‘It happened further around the bay,’ Lucy explained. ‘Whole families, children lost… Put the television on and see for yourself.’

Chapter Fifty-Two

The Dark Hearts Have Gathered

'Good evening, this is Vanessa Scoop in the studio. While thousands were airlifted to safety during the recent flooding in East Asia, others were obliged to take a more perilous route. It's believed many of the women there were also escaping gender persecution and forced marriage. Three small fishing boats and a dinghy arrived today at the small coastal resort of Littlehaven. Jeremy Loudly reports from there now…'

'Forced marriage!' Amelie recoiled. 'I'd have definitely run away.' She'd read somewhere that girls as young as eleven suffered such horrors. How would Eggy have felt about that, she wondered?

'Not all survived the journey,' Jeremy Loudly began. 'Having travelled miles on foot through the mountains, many then starved or suffocated in overloaded trucks, or finally drowned at sea, as we saw today...' With this his voice began to crack and a stray tear slid down his cheek. Unabashed, he continued: 'Mothers, already sick from the journey, watched helplessly as their own children were wrenched from their arms; toddlers tossed overboard by the swell…

'Oh, no,' said Amelie. 'Poor dear Jeremy, he was so kind to us last year.'

'*Children in Charge*…' Lucy smiled, remembering Amelie's Worldwide Peace March, and how proud she'd been, seeing her on the news. 'What an amazing day that was…'

It seemed that Vanessa Scoop was struggling too. 'Perhaps those who drowned were the fortunate ones, Jeremy. Others will have to live with their loss for the rest of their lives…'

'Indeed, Vanessa.' Jeremy Loudly was standing close to a large *Welcome to Littlehaven* sign where a tall, ashen-faced gentleman had joined him. 'I know the Mayor of Littlehaven has a few thoughts of his own…'

'I have,' the Mayor said bitterly. 'Welcome to Littlehaven, eh! Did you see how those poor destitute souls were met? With jeers and abuse, Jeremy - locals spitting at them while they clambered ashore, travel worn and exhausted, trying to stagger aboard the waiting buses.' He shook his head dismally. 'It makes me ashamed to live here.'

'There's certainly a strong anti-migrant element here in Littlehaven,' Jeremy Loudly agreed.

'Nasty lot,' said the Mayor. 'Makes me worry what might happen to those poor folk once they're found. No one seems to know where they got to.'

With that, Vanessa Scoop cut in. 'I'm sorry, Jeremy, I'll have to interrupt you for a while. We have Bettina Rivas online from the Refugee Council…'

'Quick!' cried Amelie. 'Mum, get Isla, will you? She had two missed calls from her earlier.'

'There's never a good signal in Littlehaven,' said Lucy, rapping on the window. 'Ah, it's okay - they're both coming in now.'

Isla froze when she looked at the screen. 'Oh, Jeez, Tim, I forgot to call her back.'

'What's she saying?' asked Tim, hurling himself at the sofa.

'Busloads of refugees have gone missing!'

Something quite extraordinary had happened that afternoon, it seemed. A horde of refugees had simply vanished into thin air and the buses that met them could no longer be traced. Refugee agencies were now extremely concerned. Their lives could well be in further danger.

'You carry on watching,' said Lucy, 'while I make us some tea…'

Amelie waited until Lucy was out of earshot. 'Isla,' she whispered furtively, 'that bus that overtook us earlier; did you notice where it was heading?'

'Yes, it swerved off to the right, I think,' Isla replied, squeezing in beside Tim.

'What kind of bus was it?' asked Tim. 'It needs reporting.'

'Not an ordinary service bus. Its windows were all blacked out so you couldn't see inside. It almost knocked us off the road.'

Tim frowned. 'Was it near that old industrial estate?'

Industrial estate, blacked-out windows! Amelie's heart raced. 'That's exactly what we saw when Storm flew over that way! Ask him and he'll tell you.'

'No need.' Tim stood up and headed for the door. 'I know that place well. Me and my mates used to go skate-boarding there. That's until we were chased off. It's got bad vibes, I'm telling you.'

'I thought so too,' said Amelie. 'Do you think we should go?'

Isla nodded. 'We'll need our bikes though.'

'I'll just tell Mum we're going for a ride,' said Amelie. 'It won't take more than an hour, will it, Tim?'

'Nowhere near, there's a little cycle track that runs parallel to the road. We'll be back in no time at all.'

Chapter Fifty-Three

Amelie Takes Charge

'Well, this is it...' Tim dismounted and waited for Isla and Amelie to catch up. 'There's an unused path over there. It takes you straight to the estate, well away from the road. Get off your bikes and stash them here behind these trees...'

They did so and followed him along a narrow, stony footpath. 'Just in case there's anyone about these bushes will give us cover.'

They soon came to a large concrete area, potholed and overrun with weeds. Dismal grey buildings rose up before them, old offices and warehouses, by the look of them.

'Not much going on here then,' Isla remarked. 'Not with all those windows smashed.'

'Yeah,' said Tim, 'it's been like this for years.' He gazed around for signs of activity. 'No sign of any buses here though.'

'Well, there were,' Amelie insisted. 'Storm and I saw them.'

'Shush, there's a dog,' Isla whispered, 'over there, chained up. Don't let it see you or it'll start barking.'

'Too late, it already has.' Tim put a finger to his mouth to quiet them.

A squat little man in a black hoodie had appeared. He sat down on a bench and took out a packet of cigarettes.

'Looks like he's taking a break,' said Isla.

Tim nodded and pointed to the nearest warehouse. 'I think that's the building we need to watch. Stay right here and keep hidden - I'll sneak round the back while he's not looking. It's better if only one of us goes.'

He returned almost at once. 'I've found an oubliette.'

Amelie frowned. 'You found a *what*?'

'Like a dungeon where people get chucked in and forgotten about…'

'*Ooblyette…*' It could be a useful new word, Amelie decided, for some future story.

Tim jerked his head towards the man on the bench. 'Great, I think he's taking a nap.'

'Don't forget we've got our Stones of Power if we need them,' said Amelie. 'I mean, this could count as an emergency.' She glanced down at the tattoo-that-wasn't-a-tattoo on her arm. Maybe that too.

'True.' Tim led them to a grid close to the warehouse wall. 'Look down there,' he mouthed and shone his torch into a dingy basement. 'I dare you…'

Amelie gasped. Dozens of terrified eyes stared back at them.

'We must phone Sergeant Buggeley,' Isla whispered.

'I've already tried but there's no signal here.' He began to wrench at the grid. 'Look, if I can just get this bloody cover off I'm going down…'

'If you are then we're coming too,' Amelie said bravely. 'Though I'd like to know how we'll ever get out.'

'We'll worry about that later. There!' Tim sighed. 'It's off!' He peered down into the blackness again. 'I don't think it's too big a drop.' He turned to them both and grinned. 'Wish me luck…'

They watched as he fell, landing nimbly as a cat, and was greeted by a collective gasp. There he stood for a moment, hands on hips, surveying the room. There were dozens huddled there on the cold stone floor, women mostly, children, and a few men too. Something told him he'd never forget the stench; of fear and sickness and months on the run. He knew if he thought too long, he'd throw up.

'What have they done to you all?' he cried and let out a string of Amelie's forbidden words.

But Amelie was quick to forgive. She resolved to put a few pounds in later herself because, seeing what was down there, she wanted to say them too. That's if there ever was a later. Emboldened, she jumped, followed by Isla. 'We'll get you out of here somehow,' she promised, not really expecting anyone to understand. However, one of them did.

'Thank you!' a voice answered. It was a young woman who appeared little older than they were. She began to explain then stopped suddenly and looked around her in terror.

A clatter of chains echoed outside and the iron gates at the far end of the basement swung open. It was the man from outside. He locked the gate behind him and swaggered towards them. Noticing Amelie first, he gripped her wrist and pulled up her sleeve. 'How nice to find this at last,' he cackled, staring at the *Mark of Triandor*.

Amelie's mind raced back to last year when Elias Dankstone had caught her unawares - in Devil's Alley with Tim. But this time it wasn't him. He was imprisoned on Daktron, the furthest planet from the sun…

'Use it, Amelie!' shouted Tim. 'Use it now!'

Nervously, she placed her finger on the Mark of Triandor and fixed her eyes on the man with the most powerful intent she could muster. And it must have worked because suddenly, he began to cower like an old dog awaiting a beating. For a moment, she almost felt sorry for him but there was no time for that. There were too many decent people to save.

Tim and Isla borrowed a spare *hijab*[67] from one of the women and tied the grovelling man's ankles together. Next, they organised the group into a large circle and, with the help of their young interpreter, Amelie began to explain…

Meanwhile, footsteps sounded on the floor above them and Tim put a finger to his lips. 'Don't worry,' he murmured, 'in a moment, it'll seem like we've all disappeared. But we won't have really. Now, watch Amelie and Isla…' He caught their startled expressions as the two girls held up their Stones of Power - and vanished right before their eyes. 'I'm now going to pass my own little crystal around our circle. I want each one of you to hold it a moment and focus, really hard, on becoming invisible too. Once you've done that, it'll look like you've disappeared too. Then pass it on quickly so we can all get out of this dump.'

'But how can we get out?' asked an invisible Isla. 'The gate's locked.' She cast an eye at the man on the floor. 'I don't much fancy searching for his key. You can do that, Tim.'

'We don't need to,' said Amelie, 'and here's why…' Suddenly, she felt extraordinarily grown-up. 'When you hear my command you must run straight at those gates without ever stopping. I'll be right there ahead of you. Trust me…' and she waved her invisible arm. 'We now have enough power to break through anything. *One-two-three-four…*' She stormed across the long basement room towards the iron gates. 'Are you ready? *Charge!*'

'I can't believe it,' gasped Isla, astonished to find herself on the other side of the gates. 'How did you do that?'

'I didn't,' said Amelie, touching the *Mark of Triandor*. 'It was this, *The Power in Me*, and now…' And as she spoke, her feet slowly left the ground. She rose some more, and soon she was gazing down at the old industrial estate, just as she had from Storm's little aircraft. When she turned, she sensed that Tim and Isla had begun to rise too. And a whole flock of sari-clad women and their families behind them. They hovered over rooftops and trees, and were soon soaring invisibly across the evening sky, heading straight for Havenbridge and the fields beyond Hadleigh House. Here, feather-light and ever so gently, they landed, right by Storm's hangar and the entrance to the tunnels.

'Thank you, ladies and gentlemen,' Tim and Isla chanted in unison. They looked at each other, mystified, unsure where the words had come from. 'We hope you've enjoyed your flight with us today.'

Chapter Fifty-Four

O, Child of Luga, you will never be the same again!

'We'll never be quite the same after this, will we?' said Isla.

'No one ever is after using the *Mark of Triandor*, ' replied Amelie, picturing how it had all begun. 'Reginald Sligh almost drowned.'

They wandered into the kitchen where Mrs. Lambe had just laid out their supper. Amelie's face lit up. 'Ooh, hot chocolate with marshmallows. Shall we see if there's anything on the News?'

'Mm, peanut butter and jelly sandwiches too,' laughed Isla. 'I bet she's done those for me.' (Isla always managed to bring out Libby's soft side.)

'Jam,' argued Tim. 'Jelly's for kids' parties. Pass that bowl of crisps, will you?'

'Chips, Tim, remember?'

They squeezed up together on a little sofa in front of the range, warming their hands. The evening had turned quite cool and winter was drawing near.

'Good evening, this is Vanessa Scoop with tonight's latest headlines:

Two men, Maynard Bottomley-Sligh and his accomplice Elias Dankstone, were arrested tonight on suspicion of using immigrants, many of them children, as unpaid labour, and imprisoning them in an underground basement.'

'Might have guessed those two grifters would be behind it,' said Tim. 'But how come Dankstone's involved? He's still on Daktron…'

'They are also suspected of importing stolen cloth from parts of East Asia,' Vanessa Scoop announced. 'Luckily, the terrified asylum seekers are now safe but would never have seen daylight had it not been for young author and activist, Amelie Trott and her team.'

'I wish she hadn't said that,' Amelie groaned, burying her face in her hands. 'It was all of us equally. You're not 'my team'!'

'Oh, but we are, aren't we, Tim?' teased Isla, giving Amelie a deep bow.

'Yeah, only to shut you up,' Tim joked. 'Pass me the remote, will you, Boss? Thanks.' He turned up the volume. 'And just think of the exposure this gives your new book: Dame Eglantyne, famous for her work with refugees.'

'Hey, look who it is,' said Isla, 'Jeremy! I think it's cool he's able to show his emotions. I like that in a guy. See, Tim, that's where we were earlier today.'

Jeremy Loudly was standing by the entrance to *Little Heaven* but how different it looked now with police cordons in place. Close by him, two grim looking officers stood guard. 'Good evening, Vanessa. Yes, it's another victory for Amelie Trott and friends - I shall look forward to interviewing them again.'

They exchanged glances with eyebrows raised and stifled giggles.

'Those poor folk were lured here, Vanessa, given the promise of a safe harbour. Havenbridge has a history of openness to strangers. Unfortunately, they were then taken off course and found themselves stranded several miles to the east, yes, in Littlehaven.'

'It appears the two men have been stealing migrants for some time,' Vanessa Scoop added. 'Intercepting arrivals, and posing as volunteers for the *Refugee Welcome Service*.'

'Oh, man, that's so bad,' whispered Isla. 'Imagine if we hadn't found them!'

Jeremy Loudly indicated the building behind him. 'The two accused also owned this clothing shop.'

'And as you reported earlier, Jeremy, groups of anti-migrant protestors had been gathering on the cliffs, wearing their now familiar black cloaks.'

'That's right,' Jeremy Loudly replied, 'they're known locally as Dark Hearts. Unfortunately there are thousands more like them across the UK. It's fast become a worldwide problem…'

'So, what do you think then?' Amelie asked. 'Could this be our next peaceful protest in Parliament Square?'

Tim nodded. 'Cool, what about next Sunday? I'll let everyone know at school.'

'Awesome,' said Isla. 'I'll do that too. Do you realise, this time we'll all be there together! The only problem is we won't have much time to rally everyone, will we?'

'Haven't you forgotten someone?' said Tim. 'Why don't you ask your mum?'

'Of course!' said Isla. 'She'll have loads of contacts.'

But something had been playing on Amelie's mind for a while. 'It's a very complicated subject though, isn't it? I know a lot of people are afraid of them. Mrs. Lambe is for one.'

'Refugees, you mean?' said Tim.

'Yes, I wish we could get her to understand. I mean, it could easily happen to us one day…'

Tim nodded. 'And it doesn't help that they think they're taking our jobs.'

‘Or getting free accommodation in luxury hotels…’ said Amelie. ‘Libby was going on and on about that the other day. Isla put her straight though, didn’t you, Isla?’

‘Man, she’s so wrong,’ Isla exclaimed. ‘Mom visits those places all the time and says how gross they are; people packed into tiny rooms, riddled with bed bugs.’ She paused for a moment and smiled mysteriously. ‘But saying that brings me to other news…’

‘What news?’

Isla took a deep breath. ‘She now knows about next door.’

‘What?’ Amelie stared at her, aghast. ‘Isla, you didn’t tell her, did you?’

‘I didn’t need to.’

Earlier that day, a SOLD sign had appeared outside The House of Endless Possibilities. The mysterious new owner had apparently heard of Bettina’s work with refugees. She had left a note for her, stating that she would be very happy for the house to be used by “anyone who required asylum.” It was signed a Ms. T. Wilson.

Isla gave a cry of delight. ‘You see, in other words, it’s Tabitha! And that’s the reason Mom called me the first time. Then, almost immediately afterwards she rang to say she was about to be on the News!’

‘Isn’t it wonderful how things work out?’ Amelie murmured. ‘After all the horrors they’ve been through they finally have a safe home!’

Tim looked puzzled. ‘I’m still trying to figure out how Eli Dankstone escaped from Daktron,’ he said. ‘I guess we’ll find out some day.’

Chapter Fifty-Five

Tim Has Something to Say

Thousands of protestors gathered in London that weekend, and made their way to Parliament Square. Nice Mr. Cornthwaite, who loved a good cause, had dragged his unruly tribe with him. Along came most of the school too since they knew there would be no further Maths lessons for weeks, once they kept him talking about Parliament Square. Plus all the sit-ins he'd taken part in as a student, Tim reminded them. As Amelie liked to say, it was in everyone's interest to keep Mr. Cornthwaite happy.

Lucy had travelled up with Storm - by train this time, she insisted, though she had to admit it wasn't half as fun as the microlight. Storm promised he would leave it to Isla in his will and they all shouted at him to stop talking that way. 'You've got years left in you yet, Storm,' Isla insisted. The truth was they couldn't bear to think of a time when he wasn't there.

Dr. Batty wasn't on call that day so he came along too. And so did Bettina with lots of banners announcing: *Refugees Welcome Here.*

'Good to see you again, old chap,' said Storm, spotting Lawrence in the crowd.

'Hello there, Storm, come and meet my soon-to-be-husband Charles,' said Lawrence, and Amelie sighed, seeing how well everyone was getting on.

'Amelie,' Lawrence continued, 'I've left a message for Prof. Trickett

I rather hoped he might come along today. But it's a great turn-out anyway - at least as big as last year.'

'Did you say Trickett?' asked off-duty Sergeant Buggeley who had come along with his wife.

'Yes, Sergeant, do you happen to know him?

'You mean you haven't heard?' began Sergeant Buggeley but his voice was drowned out by a group of African drummers. The crowd had begun to swell as hundreds more protestors arrived and the chanting grew louder:

'Refugees Welcome!'

'Taking all our jobs, you mean!' shouted one solitary objector. He was noisily backed up by a gang of unruly black-hooded youths.

'Who fed you that damned nonsense, Magnus Bottomley-Sligh?' roared Storm, swinging Doris above his head. 'Especially as you've no intention of ever doing a day's work yourself. WE ARE ALL DIVINE BEINGS! Even louts like you lot, hard as that is to believe…'

Many of those gathered around him stopped in their tracks. They felt it, the truth of what Storm had just said; felt it in their hearts and minds and even in their feet as they marched on into Parliament Square.

'I wonder what the Prime Minister will make of all this,' said Amelie as they made their way towards a stage at the far end of the Square. Jeremy Loudly spotted them and waved. 'I'm glad I remembered to bring this,' Amelie said, clutching her little Nepalese bell. 'It's only small but it certainly makes a lot of noise!'

'Rather like someone we know then,' Isla teased and Amelie pretended not to hear.

'Good to see you guys again,' cried Jeremy Loudly, shaking their hands in turn. 'I can't believe it's a year already.' He drew himself up to his full height before saying: 'I won an award for covering that Peace March of yours: dubbed the most sensational reportage on TV.' He looked up at the sky, hoping he'd catch another fly past of UFOs. 'Will they be here today, your Sky Watchers?'

'Earth Watchers,' laughed Tim. 'Sorry, Jeremy, we never know in advance.'

'They'll definitely know we're here though,' said Isla.

'Ah, I remember you - you're Eileen, the girl from New York.'

'It's Isla actually,' Isla giggled, remembering how Storm had once pretended not to know her name. 'And I'm from Washington DC.'

Jeremy Loudly slapped his forehead. 'Thank heavens we're not live. Oh, well, let's get this show on the road then, shall we?' He passed a microphone to Amelie. 'Ready to go?'

But even before she rang her little Nepalese bell, the crowds and the drummers had fallen silent. She was just about to speak when she felt a sudden tap on her arm. She looked up to see Tabitha standing beside her.

'Amelie, there's something I want you to do,' she whispered. 'I'd like you to pass that microphone to your brother.'

'Tim?' She turned and saw that Tim was biting his lip, like he did when he was agitated. In fact, he looked like he was about to explode. 'Is there something you want to say?'

He looked at her in surprise. 'Are you sure you don't mind?'

'No, of course not, we're a team, remember.' She handed him the microphone and noticed that his hand was shaking, not with nerves but anger by the look on his face.

Tim cleared his throat and began to speak as though he'd done this sort of thing all his life: addressing thousands of strangers, right in the heart of London, and knowing that millions more would be watching on TV. In fact, he quite surprised himself. '*I know you've all heard the news this week...*' His eyes roamed the assembled crowds until he found Magnus Bottomley-Sligh, still lurking on the periphery with his gang of black-clad youths. His gaze rested on them - though it was more a glower than a gaze, Amelie noticed. She could hear the fury in his voice. Oh, Tim, no - please don't spoil everything, she thought, don't lose your temper and say something you shouldn't. I'll never forgive you if you do.

But the moment passed and Tim continued: *'A few days ago, some families arrived on our shores, just ordinary people like you and me... except that they'd escaped the most terrifying ordeals any of us can imagine. They were hoping to reach a place of safety at last. But that's not how things worked out. Many died during that journey; they either starved or suffocated. And for those who survived the worst was still to come: children were drowned at sea...'*

It was then that Tim's voice cracked, just as Jeremy Loudly's had the other day on live TV. And a tear threatened to spill.

Amelie and Isla watched him in awe....

'What happened next? Tim looked around him but the crowd was a blur. *'They were greeted with the same cruelty that drove many of them to leave home in the first place. Can you imagine what that feels like - to be an outcast?'*

Go on, Tim. Amelie prompted him silently. *What if it happened to us?*

'*Imagine,*' Tim said. '*Imagine if that happens to you and me one day...*'
He cast around for Lucy and Storm, and then back to Amelie and Isla, looking into their eyes as he spoke. *'I know, like me, you'd all do anything to save your family...'*

At that moment Bettina stepped forward with a little group they recognised from the old warehouse basement. 'May I introduce you to a few of our grateful guests? This is Meena...' She placed an arm around a young woman's shoulder.

She was the group's interpreter, Amelie remembered.

'Meena was one of the lucky ones,' Bettina continued. 'She managed to escape with her twin brothers, Ali and Saju. They now have the chance to begin a new life. Don't you think they all deserve our kindness and support?'

Tim smiled and he didn't seem to care that thousands of people were watching while the tears ran down his cheeks. He wasn't even bothered if anyone called him a cry-baby or a wuss, or worse still, a girl. Because in that one awful and amazing moment he felt what it was to be an outcast. He knew. He glanced at Isla who gave him an approving nod.

'That took some guts…' she whispered, and he wished that moment would never end.

Chapter Fifty-Six

Ben Mc.Kellen Comes to the Rescue

'I think we've finished decorating the tree now, don't you, Storm? Shall I switch on the lights?' Amelie stood back to admire their work. 'Tim and I wrapped all their presents earlier. Everyone in Havenbridge has donated something. I know our guests probably don't celebrate Christmas but that doesn't matter, does it? Anyway, I think they should open them today. Will there be enough, do you think?'

Storm patted her cheek. How fast she was growing up. 'Yes, my dear, more than enough.'

'Good, they'll be here soon.'

It had been Isla's idea to host an impromptu party for the children and their families. The Ballroom was filling up fast.

'An awesome job, babe,' pronounced Isla. 'Mom's called me to say they're all on their way. There'll be stacks of food because everyone's bringing a dish to share. Needless to say, the House of Endless Possibilities smells delicious!

'Just as it did when we found it!' remembered Tim.

'By the way, I've persuaded the Earl of Littlehaven to make a speech,' Amelie said triumphantly. 'He's a distant relative of the Queen, you know, Storm.'

'Hmm, so he says,' grunted Storm. 'Barking mad, like his forbears.'

'Stop it, will you! He's nice.' She glanced at the old clock on the wall and sighed. 'But he's also rather late.'

'I wonder how he'll get here today,' said Isla, remembering Eggy's Community Ball.

'Nothing would surprise me,' muttered Storm.

❀

'What a lovely speech the Earl of Littlehaven gave,' Isla was to comment later. 'It seems like Eggy's been working her magic once again, and I don't just mean his Penny Farthing. Wasn't it amazing seeing him arrive on it though?'

'It was! And you're right, she has,' Amelie whispered. 'Just listen to those two old dears.' She glanced over at Miss Sowerbutts, the Neighbourhood Watch woman and her friend, Mrs. Duff, from the Post Office.

'Breaks my heart,' suspicious Miss Sowerbutts was saying, 'when I think what these poor mites have been through.' She gazed around at the children, playing with their Christmas toys.

Gossipy Mrs. Duff agreed. 'Yes, and all those miles from home Imagine…'

Miss Sowerbutts said she would rather not and brushed a tear from the end of her nose.

'Even mean Mr. Pettifer put a pound in the collection,' Isla confirmed.

'Yes,' agreed Amelie, 'it was the one the vicar dropped. But at least he didn't keep it.'

Tim was beginning to get restless. 'When are we going to have some music?'

Kenny Pratt from the fishing tackle shop had arrived with his microphone and speakers and Amelie told him about the Belgian baby born during the First World War. 'He was called Pratt too.'

'Yes, that was my great grandfather Jean-Louis,' Kenny said

proudly, 'which means I'm part Belgian. Quite a few of them refugees married our girls.' He picked up his microphone. 'One-two, one-two! Oh, blimmin' heck! What's wrong with this speaker?'

Isla cupped her hands and yelled. 'Can any of you guys help, please? We have no sound…'

At once, a tall, gangly youth approached. He had messy brown hair and thick-rimmed glasses. 'Loose connection,' he stated, examining the leads to the speakers. 'Anyone got a screwdriver?'

'I'll find one,' said Tim and Isla gave him a hug.

'Thanks babe. As for you, Ben McKellen, you're an absolute star! This is Amelie, by the way. You saw her photo, remember?'

Amelie frowned, remembering the name, and began to edge away.

'Yeah, I saw her at the Refugees March - and the other one last year…'

Isla grabbed Amelie's arm and dragged her back, just as Tim returned with a screwdriver. He stared at Ben intently. 'Hey, is that your dad over there?'

'Yeah,' replied Ben without looking up.

'Jez McKellen, football coach?'

Ben nodded. 'I'm a bitter disappointment to him, I'm afraid.'

'Why?

'I loathe football.'

Amelie's face brightened and noticing, Ben smiled in return. 'I'm surrounded by football freaks.'

'Me too,' said Amelie. 'What do they see in it?'

'Not a clue.' At that moment Freddie slunk past, stopped to sniff Ben's outstretched hand and nudged it approvingly.

'Nice cat,' said Ben. 'I'm having a houseful when I leave home.'

'Me too,' said Amelie again and stood watching him work.

'Isla tells me you're a writer,' he remarked, intent on joining wires. 'I'm a cereologist, a croppie, but I don't usually tell anyone that because they already think I'm weird.'

'Crop circles!' cried Amelie. 'But that's not weird at all. We've had a huge one this year in the field near us. I'll get Storm to show you next time if you like. That's him talking to Isla…'

'Storm,' Ben repeated. 'Very cool name.'

'He's amazing. You can read about him in my books.'

'Really?'

'Yes, I'll sign some copies for you if you like. To thank you for all this you're doing…'

Ben beamed. 'It's nothing, really.' He tapped the microphone and miraculously everything was working fine again.

And it really was all fine, right up till the end when Tim stood at the window, watching everyone leave. (Isla would be gone very soon too. Why, oh why, did she have to?)

'Mom's job,' Isla reminded them again. 'But we don't do goodbyes, do we, eh?' She spoke cheerfully enough but her eyes said something else. 'Anyway, I'll see you in London on New Year's Eve. We'll make it a night to remember.' She blew them both a kiss and hurried down the stairs.

'Are you all right, Tim?' Amelie asked, seeing his face fall.

He nodded silently and turned away.

She'll be back, you know,' she offered feebly, feeling her own throat tighten.

'Might it help a bit to get back to your trains?' She pictured the heap of rail tracks still cluttering the attic floor. It was all she could think of really, except the Commander's invisible blanket perhaps.

'Yeah, maybe I will,' he said, smiling bravely.

Chapter Fifty-Seven

New Year's Eve 2019

'Well, my dear Bright Hearts,' the Commander began, 'thank you all for joining us tonight. We know you'll want to return to the festivities but we have important news to share before this year quite draws to a close.'

When they entered the House of Endless Possibilities the party at Number Sixty-One was in full swing. They could hear Storm's voice, even louder than usual after a celebratory glass or two of punch, and Lucy trying to teach their *guests* how to sing Auld Lang Syne.

'It's been a good year,' the Commander continued. He bowed deeply, as if to acknowledge their work. 'The Dark Heart Army hates 'aliens' of any kind and will always attempt to eradicate them. They are a selfish lot and want Luga all to themselves. You have once again saved many lives.'

They were happy to see Dorin was there with him.

'We-know-you've-been-wondering-about-your-old-adversary-Elias-Dankstone,' he said suddenly.

'Yes,' said Tim. 'How did he escape from Daktron?'

They sat, agog, while Dorin related the tale. A sudden emergency had arisen on Trankon and those Earth Watchers assigned to police the Dark Planet were briefly diverted.

'This-suited-the-Dark-Hearts-well,' said Dorin. 'For-they-finally-had-an-opportunity-to-invade-Luga-and-steal-the-*Mark-of-Triandor.*'

'Exactly,' said the Commander. 'With our attention briefly elsewhere, Mr. Dankstone was secretly given a new identity and sent on a mission to Luga.'

'As-Professor-Phineas-Trickett,' said Dorin, glancing at Amelie. 'With-his-old-memory-wiped-clear-Dankstone-was-allowed-just-one-item-from-his-previous-life…'

'I can guess!' cried Amelie. 'A packet of cigarettes. When I think of all those clues I had: my sneezing, the cigarettes; his fear of cats. It was just like last year! Remember how he hated Freddie?' Her face suddenly fell. 'I even told him I was about to inscribe the *Mark of Triandor* on my arm.'

'But,' continued the Commander, 'his plans didn't quite materialise, did they?'

Amelie frowned. 'But what about the real Phineas - the one Eggy once knew?'

'The-real-Professor-Trickett?' Dorin hissed like a steam iron. 'He-retired-years-ago-and-lives-in-Bali-with-his-wife!'

They heard clapping next door and a great cheer as someone began to sing.

The Commander smiled broadly and winked. 'And it's well-deserved applause for you all! However, we have a little more to tell you. Are you ready for this, Bright Hearts?'

'Ready?' They looked at each other and nodded. 'But of course.'

'Good. We're now living in the Great Pause that lies between the *Long Gone* and the *Not Quite Yet*. It's a perfect time to lay foundation stones for a New Luga.'

Dorin made to speak and they noticed how his cheerful face had grown solemn. 'A-global-crisis-is-about-to-arise-and-for-this-you-must-be-prepared.'

'How long this will last remains uncertain,' said the Commander. 'However, whatever horrors may come to pass, remember that you were born for this time. You, my friends, are part of a great wave of souls currently sweeping Luga. Exceptional young people already equipped with the necessary qualities not only to survive but to effect real change on your planet.' He rose to his feet and towered above them.

'The *Mark of Triandor* is more powerful than any bomb. However, it can only be detonated by those with a loving heart. It will simply backfire on those who seek personal gain.'

'As-you've-discovered,' said Dorin, 'it-has-the-power-to-literally-raise-you-up.' He glanced at the Commander. 'But-this-is-only-symbolic-of-its-true-power-isn't-it-*Tuló*?'

'Yes, its true power and purpose is to raise the Human Spirit.' The Commander gazed deeply into their eyes. 'Which is why it can only operate through Love. Therefore, depending on how you treat others, you will ultimately experience the blessing or the curse you've inflicted on them. And this is exactly what the *Mark of Triandor* teaches us. It amplifies both the goodness and badness we inflict.' He paused long enough for them to take in his words. 'I want you to think for a moment about Eglantyne's story… We're now a century on from that first ghastly war, and from the global sickness that followed it. Yet what have you Lugans learned?'

'Virtually-nothing,' said Dorin. 'What-more-lessons-will-you-need? Another-pandemic?'

'I'm glad we've got antibiotics now to cure them,' remarked Amelie.

'Not for viruses though,' murmured Tim.

'Dad says pandemics happen roughly every hundred years,' said Isla, 'which means…'

Amelie shuddered. 'Stop it, Isla, don't…'

'Well,' said Tim, 'according to Storm we all need one. *Wipe out most of the population and start again...*'

'What a horrible thing to say. I'll blame Storm if ever it happens. Which it won't, of course,' Amelie added uncertainly.

'It's kind of true though,' said Isla. 'Like Storm says, we've caused enough damage here on Luga. Perhaps if everything just grinds to a halt for a bit the planet might recover.'

The Commander waited for them to settle. His voice sounded distant, as though they had already left.

All I can tell you is this. You're about to enter a war with Nature herself, one that only she can win. Life on Luga will soon change beyond all recognition and the Dark Forces will doubtless use this to their advantage.

Expect deadly plagues and flooding and fires; Lugans running amok on the streets, clamouring for freedom. This is a time of real testing. The next few years will be challenging but you have only to call on us and we shall return. And finally, remember: Together or not, you three are never apart.

'Deadly plagues,' murmured Amelie when they finally stepped out of the lift. 'Flooding and fires...' It sounded very much like the End of the World again. 'Will we never be safe?'

Isla quickly changed the subject. 'I'm wondering how Tabitha's training went with Zolos? Maybe she learned a few things on Trankon things that will help us in the years to come.'

'Like a legacy, you mean?' said Tim.

'Yeah, *The Trankon Legacy*,' laughed Isla. 'Sounds like a book doesn't it, Amelie?'

'Listen,' Amelie said suddenly. 'Can you hear dripping? You haven't left a tap on anywhere, have you?'

'No,' said Tim, 'but I can hear them all singing downstairs.'

It was Auld Lang Syne.

They stopped and listened: '*We'll take a cup of kindness yet...*'

Tim smiled a little sadly. 'It's the end of another decade already. Goodbye, 2019 and Hello, 2020!'

'Shall we just call it *an ending*?' Isla whispered, squeezing his hand. 'It sounds so much less final.'

Amelie nodded happily. 'Yes, endings always lead to new beginnings.'

And silently, they all agreed.

Let's Make the Most of Whatever Time We Have Left

Saturday 4th January 2020

Soon after the festivities ended and the guests had returned to their home next door, there was a flood at Number Sixty-One. A sudden cold spell after Christmas had caused a burst pipe.

'It couldn't have come at a worse time!' wailed Bettina. 'Just as we're packing up to leave…!'

'Amelie said she could hear dripping water,' remembered Isla.

Floorboards were soon ripped up and a small photograph came to light.

'Surprising the things what slip down through gaps,' one of the workmen remarked. 'Anyone know who used to live here?'

'I don't know a lot about them,' answered Bettina. 'But my daughter will. Isla! Isla, you there, honey?'

'Sure…' Isla came running down the stairs. 'What's up?'

'That woman who lived here for a while, wasn't it Dame Eglantyne Trott?'

'Yes, it was. Why?'

Bettina handed her the photograph, an old sepia print, smudged with a boot print and creased a little.

'Oh, my God, Mom…' Tears sprang to Isla's eyes. 'Yes, this is her alright - with Jack, the guy she should have spent her life with. What a cute couple they made.' She peered at it more closely. 'See that on her arm?'

'Looks like a tattoo. Surely girls didn't have them back in the day.'

'No.' Isla smiled. 'It's called the *Mark of Triandor*. Look closely,' she whispered, 'and tell me if you notice anything.'

Bettina shook her head. 'Oh, wait a moment… Jeez, what's happening now? They're moving!'

The figures had begun to stir. First a blink then the twitch of a hand and Jack's mouth opened suddenly as if to speak: *Let's make the most of whatever time we have left…*

Isla looked up and nodded. 'I've a feeling this is a message for us all.'

Author's Note

When I began to write Amelie Trott & The Mark of Triandor, I was unaware of another Eglantyne, a rather famous one as it turned out, who was alive at the very same time. She was Eglantyne Jebb, a social reformer who campaigned to protect the rights of children, having become aware of their desperate plight when millions were starving as a result of the First World War.

I was especially moved while writing those wartime chapters. My own paternal grandfather, a rather stern and forbidding character, survived that war and lived to be ninety-six (just one year less than Eggy herself). He was awarded the Military Cross medal for bravery. There is no doubt that he had risked his life in some remarkable way. One day, therefore, I decided to question him about it. But he refused to answer. Instead, with tears in his eyes, he murmured: 'Soldiers hate war…' It was the only time I ever saw him cry.
By the way, the little stone statue (first mentioned in Chapter Seventeen) is a reference to the birdbath in my grandparents' garden (circa 1912, I believe).

Many other small background details are taken from my own life. As a little girl I was fascinated by the art prints adorning my primary school walls. One in particular took my attention. It was The Blue Riders by Franz Marc. My teacher allowed me to sit on the stairs one day and make a copy of it, just as Eglantyne did in the Munich Art Gallery.

Eglantyne's final visit to Limone was drafted during my own last trip to Italy in 2019. I imagined what it might be like to be a ninety-seven year old, having lived a rich and fulfilling life but knowing that it was now drawing to a close.

Each character has found a special place in my heart (well, apart from the Dark Hearts who should always be kept at a safe distance!). I'd love to know if you have a personal favourite amongst them; a 'book friend' you can identify with as you embark on your own life's adventures.

The Earth Watchers have much to teach us but mostly, their message can be summed up as Kindness. Whenever we're kind to others life rewards us generously.

They would also like to remind us of our own powerful presence on this planet. So, why not stop reading this and place a hand on your heart right now? Then, repeat as loudly as you possibly can: *This is the Power in Me!*

Until we meet again, my friends...

Moyra Irving

2023

N.B. For my younger readers especially: I've included a Glossary (see overleaf) for any unfamiliar words and phrases, especially the foreign ones.

Glossary

1. **Sabbatical** – time-off
2. **Transonometer** – a fictional electronic device with an encyclopaedic memory
3. **Music Hall** – musical entertainment popular in Victorian and Edwardian times
4. **Golden sovereign** – an old British coin
5. **Kaíla** – a trainee Earth Watcher (fictional)
6. **Blotter** – paper used to absorb ink
7. **Suffragette** – a campaigner for women's voting rights
8. **Tuló** – a senior Earth Watcher (fictional)
9. **You're a brick!** - a good person
10. **All dressed up like a dog's dinner** – dressed very smartly
11. **Picture House** – cinema
12. **Haberdashery** – shop selling sewing items
13. **Knickerbockers** – baggy-kneed trousers worn by men in the late 1800s
14. **Enceinte** – pregnant (French)
15. **Mandala** – a symbolic spiritual pattern of Buddhist and Hindu origin
16. **Thangka** – a Tibetan Buddhist painting
17. **Shew** – old-fashioned spelling of show
18. **Sphygmomamometer** – machine used to measure blood pressure
19. **Carte Postale** – postcard (French)
20. **Kaffee und Kuchen** – coffee and cake (German)
21. **Sachertorte** – a special chocolate cake, named after the Hotel Sacher in Vienna
22. **Le belle signorine** – the beautiful ladies (Italian)
23. **The Trevi Fountain in Rome**: the practice of coin tossing was attributed to German archaeologist Wolfgang Helbig who stayed in Rome in the late 1800s/early 1900s. It may also have been a more ancient tradition.
24. **Due gelati, per favore** – two ice-creams, please (Italian)
25. **Webbing** – part of a soldier's uniform
26. **Walloons** – Belgian French language
27. **Flemish** – Belgian Dutch language
28. **Les Belges** – the Belgians (French)
29. **Les Anglais** – the English (French)
30. **Zeppelin** – German airship

31. **Très jolie** – very pretty (French)
32. **Un peu de vacances** – a little holiday (French)
33. **Welkom** – Welcome (Flemish)
34. **Kom met mij mee** – Come with me (Flemish)
35. **The Buffs** – British Royal East Kent Regiment
36. **His Majesty's Pleasure** – prison (slang)
37. **Mannequin** - a fashion model; also a dummy used to display clothes in a shop window
38. **VE Day** – Victory in Europe Day, 8th May 1945
39. **Benvenute!** – Welcome! (Italian)
40. **Trottole** – pasta shaped like spinning tops
41. **Home Service** – BBC radio channel, now called Radio 4.
42. **Global Silent Minute** – a minute of silence and stillness, shared universally at 9pm. GMT; a time when millions can unite in global cooperation, peace and freedom (globalsilentminute.org). It began in WW2 as the Big Ben Silent Minute.
43. **Führer** – leader (German); the title given to Adolf Hitler
44. **Auguri** – Congratulations (Italian)
45. **Lira** (plural: lire) – Italian currency in use before the euro.
46. **Merci, Madame** – Thank you, Madam (French)
47. **Grazie mille, Signora** – Many thanks, Madam (Italian)
48. **Buona notte** – Goodnight (Italian)
49. **Curé** – priest (French)
50. **Cassock** – black garment worn by a priest
51. **Salute!** – Cheers! (Italian)
52. **Nocciola** – hazelnut (Italian)
53. **Tesoro** – darling (Italian)
54. **Certo** – certainly (Italian)
55. **Santo Dio** – Good Lord! (Italian)
56. **Limoncello** – an Italian alcoholic drink made with lemons
57. **Cosa c'è?** – What's up? (Italian)
58. **Biglia** - a marble, as in a game of marbles (Italian)
59. **Hijab** – a head-covering sometimes worn by Muslim women

N.B. In Chapter Three I mention an imaginary watch on Jack's wrist. I've used a little artistic licence here since pocket watches were more commonly used at this time. Soldiers first began to wear them for convenience in World War One, after which they became commonplace in the population at large.

About the Author

Moyra Irving is a writer, storyteller, and Creative Writing teacher who lives in Central England. Her writing career began with a collection of short stories, one of which led to the creation of *The Extra Guest* end-hunger charity which is partnered with Oxfam and SOS Children's Villages.

She has also published two non-fiction guides to retreat: *Take Me to the Mountain* and *Fiery Love*.

However, it wasn't until Amelie Trott came into her life that she discovered the unparalleled joy of writing for young people. Moyra is now committed to supporting the new wave of exceptional young souls currently flooding our planet – those brave change-makers who are forcing us to reconsider how we live.

Moyra also loves cats, starry nights, days by the sea and, more than anything, writing stories for the child in us all.

Amelie Trott & The Mark of Triandor is the second in a planned trilogy. The third, *Amelie Trott & The Trankon Legacy,* is currently in progress.

www.amelietrott.com

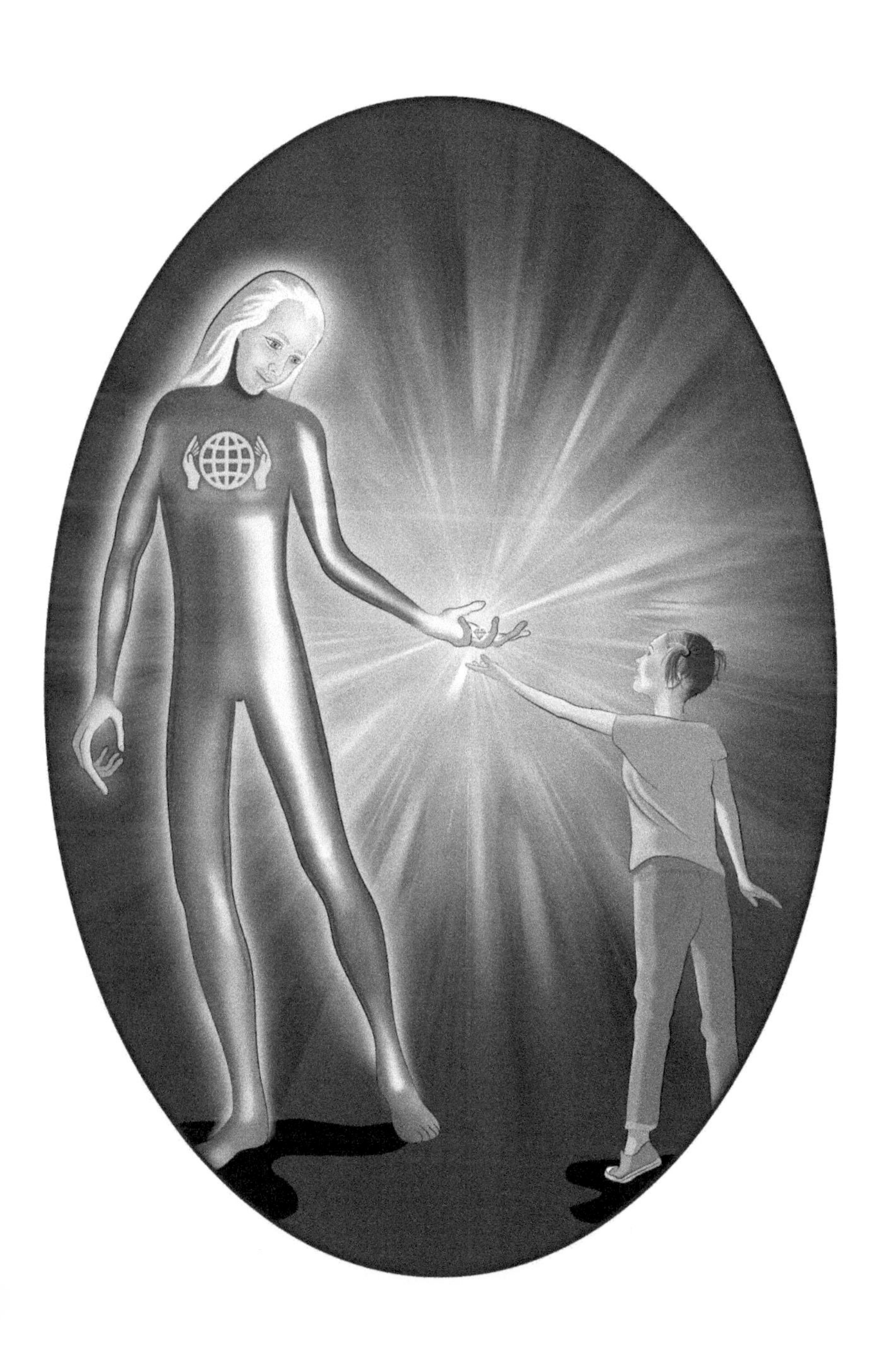

Milton Keynes UK
Ingram Content Group UK Ltd.
UKHW041910211123
433001UK00001B/2